AN EMPTY HELL

AN EMPTY HELL

A JACKSON DONNE NOVEL

DAVE WHITE

Copyright © 2016 by Dave White

Cover and jacket design by Adrijus Guscia
Interior design by E.M. Tippetts Book Designs

ISBN 978-1-940610-66-5
eISBN 978-1-940610-88-7

First trade paperback edition February 2016 by Polis Books, LLC
1201 Hudson Street, #211S
Hoboken, NJ 07030
www.PolisBooks.com

POLIS BOOKS

To
Jason Pinter

"Hell is empty and all the devils are here."
-*William Shakespeare,* The Tempest

PROLOGUE

|||||||||||||||||||||||||||||||||||||||||||||||||||||||||||||||||||||||||||||||||||||||||||||||||||||||||||||||||||||||||||||||||||||||||||

MATT HERRICK TOUCHED the ASP nightstick on his hip and took a deep breath. As he knocked on the door of the log cabin, he thought, *This is one of the dumbest things you've ever done.*

The man inside was in hiding, wanted, and probably armed. Knocking on the door was probably the least safe way to talk to him. Draw him outside, into the open. Give yourself the option to run.

But don't knock.

Herrick rapped his knuckles on the wood and waited. He tried to listen for movement inside, but the late fall Vermont wind howled in his ears. A couple of dried leaves circled around his ankles. The smell of chimney smoke wafted in the air.

A cabin in the middle of the forest. The closest building was a half-mile back along a dirt road, some hotel popular during ski season. If the man inside the cabin opened fire, no one would hear Herrick die.

The doorknob twisted, and Herrick rested his hand on top of the ASP. His muscles tensed, tight as piano wire. The door opened, revealing the man from the pictures he'd seen.

Well, sort of.

The man's face was now covered with a beard, sporting flecks of gray. His face appeared red and tight against his cheekbones, probably windburned. He looked how the townies had described him, and nothing like the papers showed nearly a year and a half ago.

"Jackson Donne?" Herrick said. "I've been looking for you."

Donne's shoulders slumped for an instant. He flared his nostrils.

"So has half of New Jersey. Who are you?" he asked.

Herrick introduced himself. "I'm a high school basketball coach."

Donne tilted his head. He brushed at the left cuff of his shirt. It had a stain on it. He didn't say anything.

"And a private investigator," Herrick said. "Matt Herrick."

"I was one of those once." Donne half-smiled. "I like your last name."

"Can we talk?"

Donne nodded toward Herrick's hip.

"You gonna use that thing?"

"Hope not."

"I'm gonna have a beer," Donne said.

He walked away from the door, but left it open. Herrick followed him, hand still on his ASP. The house smelled like wood, and steak. It was nearly barren. No pictures. No TV. Just two easy chairs, and a coffee table with a paperback on it. He could see Donne through the kitchen door, fridge open. Watched as he grabbed two silver cans of beer.

Donne came back and sat in the chair. He popped open one can and put the other on the coffee table next to the paperback. Heady Topper. The odor of piney hops made its way to his nostrils. One of the best beers in America, they said. Herrick thought about asking Donne for some bourbon.

Nope.

Not while he was working.

Donne took a long pull. Herrick stared at the stain on his cuff. Dark brown, like coffee. Or maybe iced tea.

"Can I save that for later?" Small talk was a good strategy. "It's not for you," Donne said. "Maybe you should tell me why you're here."

Herrick sighed. "I need to bring you back to New Jersey."

Donne laughed. He put the beer can down on the floor next to his chair. His right hand was out of sight for only an instant. Then it came back up full of a gun. A pistol, like the sidearm Herrick had carried in Afghanistan. The one he used to...

"I don't think I'm coming," Donne said. "I like it here."

"Just let me explain..."

Donne continued as if he hadn't heard. "I like my job. I like the weather. I like my beard and even better, I like my beer. Coming back is not in the cards. The second I cross that border, a slew of cops and FBI agents will be looking to round me up."

Herrick shrugged, trying to counteract his hard-thudding heart. "Ex-cops are dying."

"Tell me why I should care." The barrel of the gun didn't waver.

"Because they're ex–New Brunswick PD cops. Ex-Narc cops. Guys you either put away or got fired. Remember?"

Now the gun lowered a bit.

"And people think you did it."

Donne said, "And what do you think?"

"I think it's a lot more complicated than that."

"It certainly is," Donne said.

That was when Herrick realized the stain on Donne's shirt cuff wasn't brown. It was dried and red. Blood red.

PART I

WE TAKE CARE OF OUR OWN

CHAPTER 1

A Week Ago

BY THE TIME the Clifton police officer got to the scene, Route 3 was backed up a full mile. Officer Ron Bleeker pulled to a stop on the shoulder, radioed in his location, and got out of the car. A Honda Pilot was nosed into the shoulder, but its back wheels were still in the right lane. Horns honked as others tried to get to the left and past the jam. Bleeker's car's lights reflected off their hoods.

He walked up to the Honda on the passenger's side and tapped on the window. The driver didn't roll down the window. Bleeker tapped again, a little harder this time.

"Ma'am, can you roll down the window, please?"

She didn't move. Bleeker leaned in to get a closer look and saw she was trembling. Her lips were moving and tears streamed down her face. A shudder ran through Bleeker. He looked over his shoulder at the line of cars, still honking their horns.

"Ma'am? Are you all right?"

No answer.

The call had come from Dispatch that there'd been an

accident, but the person who called it in couldn't see what the Pilot had hit. The caller was driving too fast, and the road went around a curve before merging with Route 46. Bleeker got there as quickly as he could. The ambulance was on its way as well.

Bleeker walked around the front of the car, seeing no damage to the side fender. As he rounded the corner of the car, he saw it. Blood, flesh, and hair crumpled in a way no body should lie. Bleeker couldn't see the face, and was glad. He approached the body and crouched down next to it. The man was wearing jeans and a T-shirt. One arm was twisted underneath his stomach; the other lay flat ahead of him.

Bleeker put two fingers under the wrist. No pulse.

No wonder the driver of the Pilot was shaking. Bleeker listened for ambulance sirens. They were getting louder.

HALF AN HOUR later there were two plainclothes detectives Bleeker didn't know leaning over the body. Another one was sitting in the passenger seat of the Pilot talking to the woman. The ambulance was there too, but he assumed that was just for show at this point. A paramedic took the driver's blood pressure. Maybe they were going to take her away in the ambulance. A police helicopter and two news choppers hovered.

Bleeker approached the two detectives and the body. The heavyset cop with the goatee looked up and nodded his chin at Bleeker.

"You take the notes you needed?"

Bleeker nodded.

"What time do you get off tonight?"

"Ten," Bleeker said.

The cop nodded. "We're going to be here awhile. Go back to the station and write this up so you can go home."

"Who is he?" Bleeker pointed at the body.

The cop shrugged. "No ID."

Bleeker said thanks and was about to head back to his patrol car. The two cops couldn't see it from their angle, but from his he saw a yellow piece of paper peeking out of the guy's right hip pocket.

"What about that?" He took a step closer and gestured.

The detective got up and stepped over the body. With his plastic gloved hand, he reached down and tugged at the paper. It slid free. It was folded like the ones his middle-schooler brought home.

After it was unfolded, Bleeker watched the detective read it. His eyes widened.

"What's it say?" Bleeker asked. The detective's partner looked over his shoulder.

He turned the paper around and held it up for Bleeker to see. Bleeker felt the air go out of his lungs.

"Don't put this in your report," the detective said.

There were three words on the paper, written in magic marker.

FIND JACKSON DONNE.

CHAPTER 2

D REW ISSLER TOUCHED his gun as he looked down at the woman's body, needle hanging from her arm.

This wasn't good.

The sirens blaring outside, and the flicking red light through the blinds, was even worse.

Issler had only shown up here in this run-down Camden apartment to ask Amesha Collins a few questions. It's where this case led him. He didn't expect to find her dead.

He moved to the window and peeked through the blinds. Three cop cars, two cops, each in full-on battle gear. They jogged toward the front door of the building, guns out. Basically, a SWAT team. How did they get here so fast?

Issler ran back to the front door and locked it. He needed time to think. But the footsteps rattling up the stairs weren't going to give him that time. Issler's breath caught in his throat. His hand went to the gun again, and then slipped into his pocket where he felt the piece of paper his client had given him.

Did it have to do with this?

He barely had any leads. His client had given Issler Amesha's name. Issler had done some Internet searches and called a few of her friends and then tracked down this address. He wouldn't even be in the apartment if he hadn't smelled the rotten stink of death. It took him ten minutes to pick the lock. He first heard the sirens during the ninth minute.

The *thunk thunk thunk* of boots grew louder on the stairs. There wasn't any yelling from the police—not yet. That would come in a few minutes. Issler took a deep breath. They weren't after him. Whoever had seen Amesha last must have called them. Maybe someone in the building—this decaying, nearly deserted apartment building.

Shit.

Issler's hand dropped to his gun again. His fingers tingled and sweat formed on his palm. He wiped it away on his jeans and went over to Amesha. He kneeled over to check her pulse again. Still nothing.

Bang! Bang! Bang!

"Police! Open the door!" Now the screaming started.

"My name is Drew Issler. I'm a private investigator. I have a gun. I'm going to open the door."

More shouting came from the police to open the door, the words mixing together into something akin to a flashbang. The shouting was disorienting and Issler stumbled as he took a step forward. He could feel his heart slamming against his chest.

"I've done nothing wrong," he said. "But there is a dead woman in here with me. I came to interview her. I'm trying to find someone."

"OPEN UP!" Someone was pounding against it.

Issler took a step forward and unlocked the door. Before he could turn the knob, the door was kicked in. Issler stumbled backwards and threw his hands in the air.

"PUT YOUR HANDS UP!" Men with semiautomatic weapons streamed into the room.

"I'm working a case," Issler said.

They ignored him. Two men stepped around him and aimed their guns at Amesha Collins' body.

The rest leveled their weapons at him.

Issler struggled to keep his voice even. "I've been hired to find Jackson Donne."

The cops acted as if they never heard him. The words came all at once, mostly blended together—not as commands, but to overwhelm his senses. Issler was only able to pick out a few sentences.

"HE'S GOT A GUN!"

"PUT THE GUN DOWN!"

"GET ON THE FLOOR!"

"HE'S GOING FOR THE GUN!"

The first bullet hit him before he could even lower his arms. The rest tore through him instantly after that, and the world went black.

CHAPTER 3

ALEX ROBINSON STOOD in front of the grave, hands in his pockets, bracing against the wind. Somewhere on the other side of the cemetery, the guard was changing in front of the Unknown Soldier. He looked back at the gravestone and wondered what kind of strings were pulled to get her buried here. Not like his parents would let him in on that information. He was lucky to come to her funeral.

He wiped his mouth, whispered good-bye, and turned around. He jumped back, gasping. A tall, wiry man stood in front of him. Horseshoe bald, with a dark five o'clock shadow, he looked like something out of a Wall Street happy hour.

"It's done," Lucas Mosley said.

Robinson looked at his watch. "You're early."

Mosley sniffled. "I needed to get a map at the tourist spot to find the gravesite. Who knows how many cameras I was on?"

Robinson waved his hand at Mosley. "Don't worry about it. They won't be looking for you here. Did you put the notes on both bodies?"

"I didn't deal with any dead bodies," Mosley said. "My

work was done well before anyone died."

"The notes?"

They started to walk away from the site, up the long hill toward Kennedy. It would take them a while to get to the flame, but that was where they'd head their separate ways.

"You can count on us. What's the next step? I'd like to get paid this millennium."

Mosley walked without effort, while Robinson worked to hide his huffing on the incline.

"The next step is twofold. I want you to track down Jackson Donne."

Mosley didn't even flinch. "I figured you'd say that. My brother is on it. We know some people, and he's halfway to Vermont right now."

"Vermont? Not what I expected," Robinson said. "Christ, Donne, go south."

Mosley didn't respond. He glanced to his right, and Robinson figured he was scanning headstones.

"There's one more person I need you to take out—and I want it to hurt."

Mosley shook his head. "I'm a bounty hunter, not a hit man."

Washington, DC, is the city with the most spies, the most counterintelligence, the most eavesdropping going on in the world, and he said that out loud. But he was worried about being caught on camera. Robinson fought back a grin. The hill crested and they followed the trail left. Some stray leaves blew across their path. Fall was giving way to winter.

"Stop screwing with me."

"Who is this guy?"

Robinson passed a piece of paper to Mosley. After opening it, he said, "Means nothing to me."

"I'm going to do the legwork to get this one started. I'm going to hire him to find Jackson Donne too."

Mosley stopped walking. "You don't trust me?"

Robinson bit his lip. "I trust you and your brother. But this can't come out of nowhere. I want it tied back to Donne."

They stood next to an older couple. The man had his arms around the woman, who was wiping her eyes.

"You're making this too complicated." Mosley started walking again.

"I'm settling all family business."

"You're not as smart as a Corleone."

The flickering flame was visible up ahead. Mosley had specified they finish their conversation by then, and without any words, go their separate ways. Everything needed to be ironed out by then.

"This is my idea, and I'm paying you. We do it my way. Matt Herrick, I want him fucked with. I want it to hurt."

Mosley scratched his nose. "You want me to go full psycho?"

Robinson shrugged. Wind blew hard and leaves and grass rustled.

"And Donne?"

"Bring him back to Jersey, we'll go from there." Robinson coughed. "There's someone I want Jackson to see."

"You got a place for me to stay up there?" Mosley blew air through his nose, as if clearing snot. "Jersey's a hike."

Robinson passed him another paper.

"You've been keeping this place up?" Mosley tore both papers in half. They were maybe thirty yards from Kennedy's grave.

"Got it in a will. It will do. You get the car too. Keys in kitchen cabinet. Take your time, but get it done," Robinson said.

Mosley didn't respond. He stopped to admire the Eternal Flame. Robinson kept walking.

CHAPTER 4

"**M**ATT, I'M IN trouble and I need your help."

"C'mon, Alex. You know I scale back the business this time of year. The season's about to start and my kids aren't near ready. I have a ton of practicing—"

"Forget high school basketball. This is serious."

Matt Herrick leaned back on the barstool and looked over at Alex Robinson. Two New Jersey private investigators just out for a drink. Last thing Herrick expected was to be pitched a job.

"Talk to me," Herrick said.

"Two of my friends, my old colleagues, are dead. Murdered. Drew Issler was shot and Ethan Moore was involved in a hit-and-run."

"I don't do murders, Alex." Matt reached for his drink. Club soda. The ice tinked against the side of the plastic cup. "Talk to the police."

Robinson gulped Coors Light. Then said, "Would you listen to me?"

Herrick nodded once.

"You don't recognize those names?" Robinson asked.

This time, Herrick shook his head. God forbid he interrupted again.

"They're guys I worked with. Got caught up in the same Narc deal I did eight-nine years ago. Got turned in to Internal Affairs. We were lucky. Our boss got put away, we got probation."

Herrick eyed up the pub they were in. No one else was around. No parents drinking away their lunch. No administration. No reason not to have one himself. Except, as always, there were rules. He was working. And it was eleven in the morning. The club soda fizzed under his nose as he sipped.

"Now I'm worried, Matt. Whoever did this is coming for me." Robinson took another gulp of beer and signaled the bartender. "No. Screw that. I know who did this."

Herrick waited.

"And I want you to find him."

"You're not listening to me, Alex. I don't do murders. Basketball season is coming up. Call the cops. You're a PI. Catch him yourself."

Robinson shook his head. "I'm screwed with the cops. Between my"—he made quote marks with his fingers—"'criminal' past and the amount of cops I've busted sleeping with people other than their wives. And I can't do it myself. I go after him, he'll get to me even sooner. I'm not going on the offensive."

Maybe the beer was getting to Robinson.

"You're not making any sense."

"I just want you to find him and bring him to the police."

Herrick shook his head. "You tell the cops to find him if you think your life is in danger."

"*You're not listening to me.* The guy who's doing this … the cops have been looking for him for almost a year now. And they can't find him. Of course, I'm not sure how hard they're looking anymore. But, damn it, they should be."

The bartender brought another Coors Light. After setting it on the bar, she grabbed Herrick's glass and filled it with more ice and club soda. She smiled at him as she dropped a fresh lime wedge in. Herrick thanked her.

"Don't you get what I'm talking about, Matt?" Robinson took another slug of the beer. Some of the white head made a milk mustache on his upper lip. He licked it off. "This is all Bill Martin's fault. He started this, and now here we are. The guy is on a rampage."

"Bill Martin? I'm guessing we're not talking baseball."

"Remember that name? The senator? All over the news last year too."

The pieces started to come together for Herrick. "If the cops can't find him, what makes you think I can?"

"You're good at your job." Robinson wrinkled his nose. "You won't scare him. You're not violent. You don't use a gun. You just—you get the job done."

Herrick drank his club soda in one long swig.

"Define not violent. Because you're getting on my nerves." Herrick smiled as he spoke.

"Find Jackson Donne before he can kill me, Matt. Find him and bring him to the cops." Robinson gave a lazy grin. Two Coors Lights and Robinson was sloshed. "You owe me. You owe my family and you know it."

Herrick put the cup down. His stomach went cold, and he had to force memories out of his head in order to focus again. The flash of sand and burst of gunfire echoed in his brain. He took a deep breath. Memories faded.

Robinson had him by the balls with two sentences.

Herrick took the case.

CHAPTER 5

R OBINSON NEEDED MONEY, and fast.
That was the thing about hiring hit men—no, wait, bounty hunters—you legitimately had to pay them. And the thing about the PI game was this—no one wanted to hire him. Occasionally, some drunk would come in and complain about his wife cheating on him, and he'd make an hourly rate for working an hour. One of the local lawyers liked using him, but that was enough for keeping an office in Kearny, a weekly lunch at Johnny and Hanges, and other necessities.

Not paying off two guys who would settle some old scores. Finally.

Robinson's head swirled a little bit from the beer, but he got into the car anyway. He had someone he needed to talk to, and the courage to do it.

B ETHLEHEM INSTITUTION WAS just off Route 78, near the Pennsylvania border. Robinson parked, his car taking up two parking spaces. He took two deep breaths, looked at himself in the rearview, and then popped a breath mint.

The receptionist saw him and nodded. He didn't sign in. As he passed, the receptionist picked up the phone and said a few words. Just like every other time.

Robinson walked up the hallway—white and tiled like a kitchen—as if he owned the place. An orderly nodded at him. The beer pounded in his head, its power seeping away and leaving only a dull ache. This was a bad idea.

The door on his left was beige, and had one square window in the center. Robinson turned the doorknob and stepped inside. Leo Carver put his crossword puzzle down and said hello.

Robinson didn't return the pleasantry, instead saying, "I'm doing it. Finally."

Carver brushed something off his white scrubs and pulled his legs up onto the bed he sat on.

"Doing what?"

"Taking care of old business. That Donne just let Bill Martin die, it's the last straw."

Carver looked around the room. "Show me your phone," he said.

The dull ache behind Robinson's eyes grew sharper as he pulled his phone from his jacket pocket. He made a mental note to ask the receptionist for Advil before he left.

Carver took the phone, pushed some buttons, then put it next to him on the bed.

"What the hell are you doing?" Carver asked.

Not the response Robinson expected. "I'm going to put Donne down."

"That was so many years ago, Alex. I'm glad you come to see me sometimes, but I've moved on. You should too."

Robinson worked his jaw. "I need money."

Carver looked around the room again. "I'm in a mental institution, Alex. Where am I going to find money for you?"

"You have it," he said.

Outside the door, someone screamed the words to "Living on a Prayer" without any semblance of a tune. Someone else screamed for the singer to shut up.

"What makes you think that?"

"Boss, you should be in a prison. That's where *he* put you. And now he killed your best friend. Put a bullet in his chest. We can stop this. Things were good until he ruined it."

"It was eight years ago, Alex. I'm past it."

"Let me ask you something, boss."

Carver spread his hands.

"Why do you love crossword puzzles?"

Without missing a beat, Carver said, "Complicated perfection."

Robinson scratched his chin. "What does that mean?"

"Think about it, Alex. To solve a crossword puzzle, everything has to go perfectly. One wrong letter can mess up the whole thing. One mistake can build on another and another and another." Carver rubbed his hands together. "But there are tricks too. Shortcuts — solving a crossword puzzle is figuring out a pattern. I love that."

"Reminds me of my dad. From the old days anyway. When we were kids — my sister and I — he used to be really into Rube Goldberg and making those contraptions. We'd come downstairs and have our waffles delivered to us by something I never could understand. Plastic, marbles, and string. We'd have to wait and watch it come our way."

"And now?"

"Not anymore. Because of Matt Herrick."

Robinson rubbed the bridge of his nose. He'd do anything for a glass of ginger ale or Gatorade or something right now. His old boss was so calm, so even. And yet here he was in a mental institution.

"This is the best I'm going to do in my life. What happened to us was a shame, what happened to Bill was even worse — but I'm moved on."

"Because you're not in the state pen anymore you won't help?" Robinson felt heat on the back of his hands. Sweat formed behind his ears. "Donne is not the only thing worth taking care of."

Carver was frozen in the lotus position. His expression

never changed. "Who else?"

"Matt Herrick."

Carver shook his head. "Once a month you come here to visit, and you talk to me. I appreciate it. But this? You know what they say about revenge, Alex."

"This is already in motion. I thought you'd be proud of me." Robinson tugged at his chin. "I went to see her in Arlington yesterday. I miss her so much."

Carver said, "Of all the guys, you're the one I worried about the most."

"The rest of the guys are dead, boss. All of them. This is already in motion." Robinson wanted to punch a wall. "I need money for help."

Carver took a deep breath. "What did you do?"

"It's too late. I'm trying to make everything right."

"You were the lucky one, Alex. You and Drew and Ethan got away."

Robinson said, "Donne killed those two too. This week."

He prayed Carver would believe him. He hated lying to his boss, his mentor, but there was no other way. He needed help.

Carver went pale. "He's back?"

"Or he hired someone to do it."

"You have proof?"

"I need money. I'm going to find him and kill him. I'm going to make you proud."

Carver waved Robinson over to him. Robinson stood up and walked across the room. He leaned in close.

After a moment, Carver whispered, "If you do this, you do it right. And it doesn't come back to me. Never."

Robinson pursed his lips tight, letting the words pass through his frontal lobe. Then he said, "You can count on me."

"I have a trust fund."

The baseball in Robinson's gut dissipated. He put a hand on Carver's shoulder and thanked him. Carver asked for a few days' time.

On the way out, he got his Advil, but was pretty sure he wouldn't need it.

CHAPTER 6

||||||||||||||||||||||||||||||||||||||||||||||||||||||||||||||||||||||||||||||||||||||||||||||||||||||||||||||||||||||||||||||||||||||||||||||

ERRICK GOT TO the State Police Headquarters in Bridgewater in under an hour. The traffic gods must have been looking down upon him and smiling, because Route 287 was nearly empty. He hoped to be able to make at least two stops today before practice, and get his investigation started.

First stop, talk to a State Police detective about the Jackson Donne case. They probably wouldn't tell him much, but Herrick had to do due diligence. The cop in charge of the investigation — Christopher Parsons — was usually stationed in Trenton, but had a meeting in Bridgewater. They put him in touch with Herrick and he agreed to meet on his lunch.

Herrick left his ASP in the car, locked in the console. Last thing he needed was a wandering trooper to spot it. He checked in in the lobby, and the guy behind the desk directed him toward the cafeteria. A laminated pass that said "guest" on it was passed across the desk to him. Herrick pinned it to his shirt.

Parsons waved at him as soon as he stepped into the cafeteria. A few cops in uniform were scattered at different tables, eating off plastic trays, but it was closer to one, and most cops had gone off-shift or back to work. Parsons was the only guy in a suit. And Herrick's jeans, button-down, and guest pass gave him away.

"You want something to eat?" Parsons asked. "On me."

Herrick declined as he pulled the wooden chair out and sat.

Parsons had gray hair, and the suit to match. His skin was tan for this time of year, and the lines digging into his forehead stuck out because of it.

"Looking for Jackson Donne, huh?" Parsons said. "You got a license I can see?"

Herrick nodded and showed it. "Best Cracker Jack prize ever."

"They still make Cracker Jacks?'" Parsons sniffled. "Where were you a cop before this?"

"I wasn't," Herrick said. "I was in the sandbox."

"For five years?"

"I was an MP for five years. Was there for seven."

Parsons took a bite of his sandwich, then wiped his mouth with a napkin. "My son was there for three. Why'd you leave?"

"Wasn't my thing anymore." Herrick felt a pain in the back of his skull, like a memory was trying to poke its way out with a knife.

"I completely understand. My son basically said the same thing." Parsons took a sip of water. "So, Jackson Donne. That case is over a year old. Why now?"

Two troopers took a table one over, but ignored them. The smell of eggs wafted their way.

"Someone hired me to find him. I wanted to see if you had any leads."

Parsons held the sandwich in front of his mouth, but didn't eat. "You think I'm just going to hand them to you?"

Herrick spread his hands. "Worth a shot."

Parsons laughed and took another bite. While chewing, he said, "I like you. You got balls."

"Learned it over there."

"We don't really have any leads. That girl died, Kate Ellison, Donne's fiancée—she was probably the only one who could have helped us. He had some friends at a bar in New Brunswick, but they clammed up when we walked in."

"So New Jersey's most wanted is still in the wind?"

After swallowing, Parsons said, "Well, that's the thing — I'm not sure how 'wanted' he actually is. And he was a cop, so he probably knows this. We only want to question him."

Herrick blinked.

"This is all off the record."

Herrick said, "I don't have a tape recorder anyway."

"Jackson Donne didn't fire the kill shot on the senator. There were powder burns all over Bill Martin's hands."

"Did Donne shoot Martin?" Herrick tried to remember the details of the case. The first day or two were crazy, with wall-to-wall news coverage. As the details started to come out, the news faded away, and people's interests diverged.

Parsons shrugged. "Like I said, he's wanted for questioning. We've even leaked that part to the press, to smoke him out. But forensics doesn't support Donne being the shooter. He's gotta know that."

"But he's still hiding," Herrick said.

"Yeah." Parsons' sandwich was gone. "Wonder why."

"That's why you want him for questioning."

Parsons laughed. He reached across the table and shook Herrick's hand. "You find him, you'll bring him right to us."

Herrick said, "You're gonna use me as cheap labor?"

"With the people in charge in Trenton, I'll take every break I can get."

"I'll be in touch. What was the bar he liked?"

Parsons took out his phone and scrolled through it. "Olde… Queens? No. Olde Towne Tavern. That was it, the one that was on that TV show. Yeah. The owner's name was Artie."

Herrick made a mental note. "That will be my next stop."

"Good luck." Parsons got up and walked away.

The two cops next to Herrick started talking about a hockey game. Herrick didn't stick around to find out if they were discussing the Devils or the Flyers.

At least New Brunswick was on the way back to practice.

CHAPTER 7

|||||||||||||||||||||||||||||||||||||||||||||||||||||||||||||||||||||||||||||||||||||||||||||||||||||||||||||||||||||||||||||||||||||||||||||||||||||||||||||||||||

TWO GUYS SAT at the bar drinking some kind of light beer. The bartender fiddled with one of the taps. Herrick pulled out a stool and took a seat. He eyed the selection of bourbons against the mirrored wall. Decent selection, but he'd probably stick with Bulleit.

Jeez. He needed to stop working cases that put him in bars all day.

The bartender came over to him and asked what he needed. Herrick ordered a ginger ale. Twenty seconds later, he had a full glass.

"You've never been here before," the bartender said.

Herrick looked around at the tiles, the TVs, the Jersey celebrity pictures hanging on the wall. The outside of this place said "dive bar," but the inside had been remodeled and looked like a '50s diner. Chrome, tile, and very New Jersey.

"No. Saw it on TV and thought I'd give it a try."

"You know we don't serve food, right?" The bartender scratched at something on the bar top.

Herrick nodded and took a sip of ginger ale.

"Sure you don't want something stronger?"

"Do you know Jackson Donne?"

The bartender stopped scratching. Herrick passed his ID across to him. The bartender looked it over and put it back.

"I thought you coached high school hoops. I watched your games on NJ 1 last year. Chandler is going to be a player."

"I'm moonlighting. And yeah, he *is* a player. Jackson Donne?"

"I did. You're about a year late."

"Sometimes I get new cases. When was the last time you heard from Donne?"

The bartender looked toward the two guys and their beers. The glasses were still full. His shoulders slumped.

"I don't want to do this again."

"Are you Artie?" Herrick asked.

The bartender nodded. "You do some checking up on me too?"

"Not really. Someone told me your name in relation to Donne."

Artie closed his eyes. "I used to serve him beer. That was it."

One of the two guys gulped down his beer and signaled to Artie. He nodded in return and went to fill up a fresh pint glass. Herrick drank the rest of his ginger ale.

Artie came back after delivering the fresh beer.

"What's it going to take to get you out of here quickly?" he asked.

"I like this place."

"Thanks. But I really don't want to be talking about Jackson anymore." Artie put his hands in his pockets. "When all his crap went down, all sorts of people were in here day and night, and not to drink, just to talk. And, no offense, but you've only ordered a ginger ale."

Herrick nodded. "I'll be quick and get the most important question out of the way. Do you know where he is?"

"You think you're the first to ask that?"

"No, but if I didn't and you did know, how dumb would I look?"

"I can't believe the cops haven't tracked him down." Artie poured himself a Coke from the fountain. Took a sip. "I don't know where he is."

Herrick's turn to nod. He pushed his empty glass to Artie, who refilled it.

"Know anyone who might?"

"His sister? Brother-in-law? Susan Carter is someone to talk to. Do you watch the news?" Artie grinned. "Jackson got involved in a lot of shit the past few years. Not just the senator stuff."

"I don't have a Jackson Donne Google alert set up, if that's what you mean. I was away in the desert. Only got back two years ago. I missed a lot of local stuff. Tell me about Jackson."

Artie said, "A year ago? Man, he had his shit together. He was going to get married. And then—well, you saw the news. But that wasn't him. It couldn't have been. He was a good guy who made a lot of bad decisions. Except he was trying to do the right thing. Just happened that when he did, stuff blew up."

Herrick laughed. Artie didn't.

"Not kidding."

Herrick cleared his throat. "Is there anyone else I could talk to? Anyone else who would know him?"

Artie finished his Coke and checked out the two guys at the end of the bar. They were still nursing their beers.

"This place gets busy at five. These two will sit here and drink maybe four beers until then. As soon as the Happy Hour crowd starts to filter in, they'll leave. That's what Jackson was like. Hated to be here when it got crowded. Always worried about running into someone from his old life. I mean, he'd hang out here late sometimes, but it irked him."

"His old life?"

"The days on the force. He turned in a guy, Leo Carver, and the whole case sent him spiraling."

Herrick jotted Carver's name down in the notes section of his iPhone.

"Where's Carver now?"

Artie shrugged. "Prison? Not my thing, man. I don't know."

Herrick wrote his name and number on a napkin. "If you think of something, call me. Don't call the school. They hate that."

"Good luck this season," Artie said.

"We have a real good shot to win the Tournament of Champions."

Artie shook his head. "Not if you're distracted by my friend you won't."

Herrick dropped a couple of bucks on the bar for the drinks and left.

CHAPTER 8

ERRICK CALLED SARAH Cullen at St. Paul's High School in Jersey City. The parkway was empty, so he probably had time, but it never hurt to check in with Sarah. When she answered, her voice rang through the speakers of his stereo. Herrick loved Bluetooth. He'd rather listen to Sarah's voice than anything on the radio these days.

"I'm might be late to practice. Can you tell the guys?"

Sarah didn't respond right away. Then, "It's the third practice of the year."

"I know. And I'm not canceling it."

"You miss this and our boss is going to be pissed."

Herrick put more pressure on the gas pedal. "When we win state again and keep the doors open, he won't be."

"I hear practice helps."

"I'll be there. I just have a job to take care of first."

He crested a hill and came to a red light. Two kids who should have been in school were arguing on the corner. One was pointing toward the drug store parking lot behind them. Herrick remembered arguing with one of his players on the corner of the street. Pleading with him to go home. And taking him at his word.

Then never seeing him again.

Life on the street.

The light turned green and Herrick passed the kids.

"You have a case?" Sarah asked. It sounded like she bit the words off as she said them.

Herrick said, "Something I can't turn down."

"Can't your assistants tell the boys?"

"They like you."

"I don't make them run suicides every afternoon."

"Good point."

Herrick crossed the Passaic River and started through Nutley. The GPS said he was fifteen minutes away from Montclair. He'd be back in time for practice.

"Don't be late."

"Thanks, Sarah."

She hung up and sports talk radio came back through the car speakers. Herrick should have had a drink at lunch.

A QUICK IPHONE GOOGLE search after leaving the bar sent Herrick to Montclair. Like Artie said, allegedly shooting a state senator wasn't the only ruckus Donne had been involved in. A few years back, he'd worked a case that involved his sister and her restaurant mogul husband. Artie didn't have their address, but Google did.

Herrick parked the car on the curb and looked across the lawn. The "For Sale" sign had a SOLD tag on it. There was one car in the driveway, a Beamer. Its trunk was open and there were two cardboard boxes in it. Herrick waited. On the radio, Mike Francesa yelled at a Yankees fan who wanted to make a trade.

The front door of the house—maybe better described as a brick mansion—opened and a man carrying another cardboard box sauntered out. He stopped, hefted the box again, and made his way to the car. Herrick got out and started across the lawn.

The man looked in Herrick's direction. It was Franklin Carter, whose picture had been prominently featured in the news article Herrick had Googled. He looked a bit older now, flecks of gray in his hair, some wrinkles along his neck. But it was a Long Island kind of old, relaxed and ready to take out the yacht for the weekend.

"Mr. Carter?" Herrick called. "My name's Matt Herrick. Can I ask you a question or two?"

After putting the box in the trunk and slamming it shut, Carter said, "You with the media? I thought this was over with."

Herrick shook his head. "I'm a private investigator."

Carter leaned back against the trunk and crossed his arms. His left eye twitched. "What's the matter? A year goes by and everyone else gives up?"

Herrick shrugged. "I can only do what I'm hired to do."

"I'm just wrapping up packing. I have a long trip ahead of me. There really isn't time for this."

"Where are you going?"

"Apartment in the city to drop this stuff off."

"Is your wife around?"

Carter popped up off the trunk and began to walk to the driver's side door. "She's in Sacramento. Been there for almost a year now. You should really update your records. We opened a new restaurant out there and she's been running it. Ah, you don't care about that."

Herrick shook his head. "Not true at all. I'll listen to you talk all day if you want. Are you two separated?"

Grinning, Carter said, "Aren't you forward? No. Now that the housing market is bouncing back, I was finally able to get rid of this place. I come out here on weekends to check up on the restaurants. Spend most of my time on the coast with her."

"What made you decide to open up a restaurant in California?"

"Untapped market?" Carter spread his hands and exhaled. "That's bullshit. We needed a reason to get out of New Jersey. Get away from all this nonsense. Susan couldn't take it."

The sun ducked behind the trees across the street and the

temperature noticeably cooled. Sunset was still nearly two hours away, but in November that didn't matter. The world was a little darker.

Herrick shrugged against the cold. "You haven't heard from him, have you?"

Now Carter laughed. "Jackson? Do you think he's stupid?"

"Wouldn't have been able to hide for over a year if he was, I guess."

"He didn't do it." Carter zipped up his jacket. "At least Susan doesn't think so. But after all the crap he's been through, I think he just snapped. Bill Martin—Susan used to talk about Bill all the time when she talked about Jackson. Mentor, and then sent him the wrong way. Once Jackson turned everybody in, Martin couldn't let it go. I'm sure he needled Jackson to the point of breaking."

Herrick tightened up. There were more guys Donne worked with? Possibly more targets for him. "Thanks, Mr. Carter. Only one more question."

Carter opened the door of the car. "I don't know where he is, Mr. Herrick. Don't have any idea where he would go. Probably Canada. They have good beer and snow up there. Jackson never liked beaches."

"When Susan talked about Jackson, did she ever mention who his boss was when he was on the force?"

Carter nodded. "Leo Carver. Weird name. She only said it once. I think he's in Rahway."

Herrick relaxed. Tough to kill a guy in prison. Maybe even tougher to get in to talk to him, though.

CHAPTER 9

‖‖

PAYDAY.

For the past year, Monday was Joe Tennant's favorite day. It was payday. After Mario went through his profits for the previous week and then inventoried the work Tennant did, he counted out bills and passed them across the counter. Tennant never counted it, not in front of Mario. But he always shook Mario's hand before he left.

The fact that Tennant was able to find a reliable cash-only job was a miracle in itself. But Mario — a New York native — must have taken pity on Tennant's Jersey accent and offered cash only. A gentle soul. Tennant didn't ask if Mario paid the other employees of the Vermont Scenic Motel in cash. He did his job, took his money, paid for rent, groceries, and Heady Topper. And maybe a paperback novel, if there was any left over.

After a weekend of chopping wood for the stove Mario's restaurant used to cook pizzas, not to mention fixing two leaky sinks, a shower, and the heat in room 105, Tennant expected a decent payout. Maybe two novels this week. Or a second case of Heady? No way he'd be that lucky.

Tennant pushed open the door to the office where the front desk was. Mario looked up and rubbed his bald head.

"You're just in time, Joe."

Tennant nodded, and reached into his pocket to retrieve the piece of paper he used to keep track of his work. Mario reached across the desk, took it, and looked it over.

Nodding, he said, "Productive week."

"Well, your place is falling apart." Tennant gave a short laugh.

"Twenty-five years and eight months. Still here. Still packed every winter."

"Busy season coming soon." Tennant looked over Mario's shoulder and examined the two framed pictures of a woman posing at the top of a mountain. In one she wore a snowsuit and held ski poles. The other was taken from behind, with the woman halfway down the hill.

Tennant looked at the pictures each week. He never asked about the woman. Mario never offered either, though he must have noticed the staring.

"You going to get a cell phone come December, Joe?" Mario had begun counting cash on the desk, lining the bills up like he was going to play Solitaire with cards. Tennant tried not to count.

"No. Not my style."

"Be worth it for you," Mario said. "Any time something goes wrong, I could give you a call. Throw a little extra work your way. What else are you doing with your life?"

"Reading. Drinking some Heady." *Trying not to focus on the past. Move forward.*

Mario pushed a stack of bills across the counter. Tennant picked it up, folded it in half, and pocketed it.

Tennant looked at the picture of the skier one more time. He would ask one day.

"Got any work for me today?" Tennant asked, returning his gaze to Mario.

Mario wasn't looking at him, however. His mouth had gone

slack and he was looking over Tennant's shoulder, unblinking.

"Not today," Mario said. His voice was far away somehow. "Maybe you need to walk away right now. Go out the back."

Tennant turned back toward the front door, and didn't understand A black car had pulled into the lot. A tall, thin man in a black suit and long topcoat got out.

"Walk away, Joe. Don't run." Mario's voice was somewhere in the haze.

"I don't know what you're talking about." Tennant's insides were screaming at him to run. Something about Mario's tone of voice. It caught him deep in the gut and set off the fight-or-flight instinct.

"He's not here for you, Joe."

Tennant looked back at Mario to see him still staring out the window, standing nearly at attention. His palms were flat on the counter.

"I've made a lot of mistakes," he said. "I knew this would happen one day. But once I got up here, I just didn't care."

"Come on, Mario. I can help." He jammed his hands in his pockets.

"You have your own problems. Go." Mario's face was ashen.

"Thank you." Tennant didn't have any other words.

"Remember. They never stop looking for you."

Tennant turned and walked past Mario, the echo of the words ringing in his brain. He cut through the back room. Another picture of the woman hung on the wall. Tennant ignored it and pushed the door open. Cold air slapped him in the face.

He headed for the hill.

As the ground inclined, Tennant took wider steps, still fighting the urge to run. None of them called after him. No one asked him to stop and wait. Most importantly, no one called him by his real name. The name he tried desperately to force out of his head.

No one wanted Jackson Donne.

Not today, anyway.

The wind cut through Tennant like an icy knife. The trees rattled, and as the forest grew thicker along his walk, some of the branches gave up their final leaves. He had been hiding here in this cabin for a year now, confident no one would track him down.

So confident, in fact, he was no longer armed.

He'd gotten stupid. Complacent.

What had Mario done that someone had tracked him down after all this time?

Or worse, Tennant thought, when would they come for him?

He'd followed his own case here and there, but never believed what was in the press. They needed to talk to him. One day they'd find him, but until then, all he could do was climb the hill.

CHAPTER 10

A FTER ADDING CARTER'S contact information to his phone,
Herrick left a message with Rahway State Penitentiary —
which wasn't called that anymore, but most New Jerseyans
weren't quick to change. He told them who he was, who he was
looking for, and that he hoped to set up a meeting. As he pulled
into St. Paul's school parking lot near the gym, he still hadn't
heard back.

He was a full three minutes early for practice.

The bounce of basketballs off a parquet floor, along with a
few "Hey, Coach" shouts, greeted him. Herrick told them to be
ready in five minutes, after he got changed. Sarah Cullen gave
him a short wave from the bleachers.

Five minutes later, he emerged from the locker room clad
in black shorts, a gray St. Paul's T-shirt, and a whistle around
his neck. Sarah leaned against the door, arms crossed, flashing
a crooked smile. She filled her red blouse and black pencil skirt
well. Her brown hair hung at her shoulders.

"You're on time." She looked at her watch. "Basically."

"And you doubted me. Tsk, tsk."

She rolled her eyes. "Grow up."

"Drink later?"

"Can't. I have a date."

A wave rolled through Herrick's chest. "On a Monday?"

"You wanted to drink on a Monday."

Touché. "Have fun." He hoped the words didn't sound hollow.

The reverberation of dribbling petered out. They were watching Sarah and Herrick talk. Herrick blew his whistle and called out for suicides.

That elicited groans all around.

"You should have listened to me," Herrick said. "And kept shooting around."

"Hey," Sarah said. "Are you going to have a good year? Lots of people rely on this team."

Herrick shook his head. "If I'm allowed to push them the way I need to, we'll be fine."

Sarah nodded. "We'll get that drink later this week." She tapped him in the chest. "Pal."

Herrick watched her leave. When he turned around, the team hadn't started their suicides yet. Instead, they hit him with a chorus of "oohs" and playful "damns."

They ran extra suicides.

Two HOURS LATER, Herrick dismissed the team. As the players packed up—some calling for a ride on their cell phones, others checking the bus schedule—Herrick checked his own messages. There was one from the prison. Herrick listened to it.

"Mr. Herrick, thank you for your interest in our population. Unfortunately, I cannot facilitate a meeting between you and Mr. Carver, as he is no longer a prisoner here. He has been moved to Bethlehem Institution."

The speaker left a phone number.

Herrick put the phone down and rubbed his chin. Leo Carver was in the nut house. That was unexpected.

"Coach, you got a minute?"

The sweat that glistened on Horace Chandler's shaved head reminded Herrick he had to call the boosters and try to raise money to add showers to the locker room. Along with filling the scholarship pot. Herrick had a good track record of getting kids full rides to some big-time colleges, but not every kid made it. And not every kid could afford not to make it.

Not Horace Chandler, though. He had Duke written all over him—literally. Duke had sent him about three pairs of warm-ups and ten T-shirts. If Coach K wasn't going to land him, he was at least going to make him a walking billboard.

"What's up?" Herrick asked, tossing him a towel.

Chandler wiped the top of his head, then sniffled. "We gonna be good this year?"

Jesus. Everyone is worried about this.

"You're kidding, right?" Herrick smiled. "What have I always told you guys?"

Chandler shook his head. "Not what I meant, Coach. I mean after—" He paused and looked at his shoe. "Last year, what you told us about Afghanistan. Are we gonna be good? Do we gotta worry about you?"

Herrick took a deep breath and then sat down on one of the bleachers. Chandler didn't sit until Herrick patted the seat next to him. Chandler threw the towel down and sat on it. Herrick hoped the kid didn't see the slight tremor in his eye.

"What happened in Afghanistan happened a long time ago. I did it to save my friends and to save myself. It doesn't affect how I deal with everyday life. Before I told you, would you have known?"

"Nah."

"Meanwhile, I'm just the coach. You're my leader. My best player. I have to count on you."

Chandler looked up.

"You and Corey are my seniors. It's your job to get everyone through practice, keep their chins up and keep them focused on the team and the games."

Across the court, Dan Faber was shooting threes. A freshman point guard who was pushing for a much bigger role than Herrick had planned on when he put this team together.

"I don't know if we can do that, Coach. The guys are—"

Herrick held up a hand. "That's fine. Maybe this is a lost year. I thought my Afghanistan story would motivate you. Guess not. It's no problem. I'll be here next year and the year after that. You have the world in front of you, Horace. You've seen the coaches sniffing around. Offering you scholarships. And you want to wait until May to sign. That means if you— and the team—have a big year you can go anywhere you want. But you've got to focus."

Chandler nodded.

"I know, Coach. I know."

"You have a problem with something I do, talk to Corey. Talk to me," Herrick said, and then tilted his head across the court. "But don't let someone like him see it. Dan's got to learn. So does the rest of the team. And they'll learn from you."

Herrick held out his hand and Chandler clasped it. After the handshake, Horace Chandler left. And Herrick had some visiting hours to check on. He stood up and gathered his belongings.

"Come on, Dan. Time to pack up," he yelled. "I got work to do."

CHAPTER 11

ERRICK WAS BACK on the road the next morning at 9 a.m. He'd spent the previous evening not out drinking — as he'd suggested to Sarah — but instead, researching. The Private Investigator's best friend was always Google. And some other databases the average Joe didn't know about.

Bethlehem Institution was out Route 78 near the Pennsylvania border. Before making any more moves, he wanted to talk to Carver and get a feel for Donne when he was still on the force. If Donne had lost it and started murdering his old colleagues, maybe something from his past would lead to his hiding spot.

It was a long shot, but info on Donne was hard to come by. The evidence from the senator's shooting was still under lock and key. Most of those involved were dead. No, Herrick was going to have to dig deeper and look further back into the past.

The lobby of Bethlehem Institution reminded Herrick of an old folks' home. There were couches which were a bit worn, and tables with day-old flowers in vases on them. The scent of bleach and Pledge hung in the air. People sitting on the couches ignored making eye contact with everyone else, instead focusing on their phones, or—in the case of one older gentleman—a Robert Crais novel. There was a reception desk to the left and a long hallway ahead of him. Herrick could hear mumbled conversations, some beeping machines, and the echo of someone screaming. No wonder no one wanted to make eye contact with anyone else.

A woman with dyed red hair, too much mascara, and a cigarette voice helmed the waiting desk at Bethlehem. She asked him who he wanted to see and Herrick informed her. The woman frowned.

"Do you have an appointment?"

Herrick looked at his watch, making a show of it. "It's visiting hours."

The receptionist rested her chin on her fist. "Uh-huh."

Herrick took out his wallet, and then his private investigator's license and handed it to her. She glanced over it, then handed it back.

"Oh. Okay. Let me get you in to see the former prisoner lickity-split. Not a problem, sir." She turned and went back to her computer.

It shouldn't have, but it took Herrick a second. Then he sighed. "What do you need me to do?"

Without turning, she said, "If you need or would like to see Mr. Carver, you need to be a family member with a photo ID. Otherwise, I need written permission from a law officer."

"So you're the school nurse now?"

The woman didn't chuckle or glare back at him. She just kept her eyes on the screen. Herrick's skin felt warm.

He pulled his iPhone and dialed. Working as a private investigator out of Hoboken, New Jersey—a city one square mile in size—and the head coach of a top high school basketball team, you get to know a lot of the cops in the area. From beat cops to the homicide guys, they all check in for one reason or another. Most of them to figure out if their alma mater is going to land their favorite local player. Herrick would feed them nuggets of information here or there when he could.

Now it was time to call in a favor.

Homicide cops in the area were county cops; they didn't only work for a city. A letter with a county header on it might get a little more respect than a Hoboken one.

"Tell me good news," Wally Sandor said when he picked up. "Tell me Conrad is going to 'Cuse."

Conrad Jenkins, a junior small forward who been watched by Jim Boeheim's minions from the day he set foot on St. Paul's campus. Rutgers had been watching him too, hoping to get an early commitment. The Rutgers coaches didn't know Jenkins' favorite color was orange. They actually thought they had a shot.

"He hasn't decided yet. Coaches have been around, though. I'll let you know."

"He better not freaking go to Rutgers," Sandor said. "I mean come on. Rutgers? They haven't done anything in— How long has it been since they did something?"

Herrick took a short breath, making sure Sandor was done. "I don't know, Wally. Kid hasn't made a choice yet."

"It's those goddamn AAU guys."

"Yeah. That's the problem." Before Sandor could respond to the sarcasm, Herrick said, "I need a favor. Can you write Bethlehem Institution a letter which would allow me to speak with Leo Carver?"

"Who is Leo Carver?"

Herrick didn't know how honestly he should answer that question. If he gave away too much information, Wally Sandor was the kind of guy who'd pass that along to some cops who'd give him trouble. If he gave Sandor nothing, he wasn't getting the letter.

"A con who's been moved out of the penitentiary. Has to do with a case I'm working on."

There was silence for a beat. Then, "What case?"

"Conrad is taking an official to 'Cuse next weekend. I'd bet he likes it up there. Keep it under your hat. Rutgers has no shot."

Sandor laughed. "That is great news. When do you need the

letter by?"

"Can you fax it to this number?" Herrick read it off a business card at the desk as the receptionist stared at him. "In the next ten minutes?"

Sandor agreed and Herrick hung up.

"I can get stuff done. Once that letter comes through, I expect to be talking to Mr. Carver." He sounded so damned smug. Act like you've been there before, he reminded himself.

Always coaching.

The receptionist huffed and turned back to her computer again. She was playing FarmVille.

Herrick waited.

Nine minutes and thirty-eight seconds later, Herrick heard a phone ringing behind the desk. The receptionist looked up, and then turned her head to the fax machine. She huffed and then caught Herrick's eye. He grinned. The machine rattled, hummed, and buzzed as it spit out paper. She caught the printing and read it over. She shook her head and Herrick's smile widened.

"I'll call the doctor," she said. "You can speak with her, and she'll take you to see Mr. Carver."

CHAPTER 12

THE DOCTOR—A WOMAN with glasses, white coat, and ponytail—told Herrick all the rules. Do not give anything to the patient. Do not agitate the patient. If the patient gets upset back off and press the red button on the wall. The doctor will be right outside the door if you need help.

"He's very easygoing, Mr. Herrick," she said as she turned the door handle. "We've had no trouble. I'd prefer you didn't start any."

Herrick grinned. "You can trust me. I don't like upsetting anyone."

"I'm sure." She blinked. "Does Ms. Pentag at the front desk know that?"

The doctor opened the door before Herrick could answer. He stepped through. It clicked shut behind him.

A man sat on his perfectly made bed. The top of his head was full of matted silver hair. Herrick couldn't see his face, as it was hidden behind a newspaper folded in quarters. Herrick could hear a scratching sound and the paper shook slightly. The man wore pink scrubs with Nike sneakers. His knees bounced, and as they did the bed creaked.

Herrick cleared his throat. The man didn't move.

"Mr. Carver?" Herrick asked.

Still nothing.

Maybe he was catatonic. Other than whatever he was doing to the newspaper. All that work for someone who couldn't speak.

Herrick put his hands in his pockets and leaned against the wall. The room was bare, tan-painted walls, an empty bookcase, a small coffee table, and a red throw carpet covering tiles.

Soon, the scratching stopped. Carver looked up from the paper, showing eyes younger than his hair gave away. No wrinkles, smooth skin, and sharp gray eyes.

"Five letter word. *Sesame Street* dweller. Any idea?"

Herrick didn't hesitate. "Oscar?"

Carver went back to the paper, licked his lips, and wrote in the word. When he was done, he put the paper flat on the bed. He ran a hand over it, smoothing it out, then laid his pen on top.

"I should have known that." Carver crossed his arms. "It's been too long. My kids are in their late twenties and early thirties. No grandkids. I don't get to watch PBS here anyway. I'm sorry for ignoring you, but I need to finish these things when I start them."

"That was the last clue?"

Carver shook his head. "Just the across." He looked down at the newspaper, then back up again. "How can I help you?"

"Jackson Donne," Herrick said.

Carver didn't react, didn't even flinch at the name. "That's a name from a long time ago."

"My name is Matt Herrick. I'm a private investigator and I've been hired to find him. Track him down."

"He's missing?"

"You don't get the news in here? You have a newspaper."

Carver patted the paper again. "Only the crossword. It's all they let me have in here. They're very uncivilized."

"You're missing some great snarky headlines these days."

Herrick filled Carver in on the state senator stuff. That Bill

Martin was dead and Jackson Donne was on the run. Herrick thought Carver might have flinched at the Bill Martin part. He couldn't confirm it, though.

"That is a shame," Carver said. "But it is not a reason for you to be here."

Herrick nodded. "That's true. I'm kind of going a roundabout way through my story. But I've been told not to upset you."

Holding up a hand, Carver said, "I'm a grown man."

"The real reason I'm here is people are dying. Two of your former men when you ran the Narc Division in New Brunswick were murdered. My client is worried. Alex Robinson. Do you remember Alex?"

Carver said, "Yes."

Herrick hadn't realized he was pacing. Back and forth, the throw carpet soft under his shoes, and the tiles slippery.

"Alex thinks it's Mr. Donne who is coming after them. A final act of revenge now that Martin is gone."

Carver chewed his lip. "And why are you telling me this?"

"Two reasons," Herrick said. He stopped pacing. "One: I think you should be concerned. You probably should ask for some added security. Don't tell them why, but—"

"Don't tell them why? They already think I'm insane." Carver leaned back on the bed, holding himself up by his elbows. He stared at the ceiling. "I'm sure I'll be fine. It's not easy to get in here. Especially not with a weapon."

"Next," Herrick said, pushing forward, "I was curious if you had any idea where he'd go to hide out."

The back and forth was easygoing, and Carver didn't appear flustered. In fact, Herrick thought, he was cooler than he'd imagined. When the doctor took him to this room, there were at least three meltdowns going on in the hallway. One patient was screaming for no reason. Another had her fingers jammed in her mouth, biting hard on her knuckles as tears streamed down her cheeks. A third was rocking back and forth, mumbling over and over. But Carver seemed to be in complete control, other than the occasional quick glances at the newspaper, as if making sure the unanswered parts of the puzzle were still blank.

"How long has Mr. Donne been on the run?" A smirk appeared at the corner of his mouth.

"Over a year."

Carver nodded. "I've not thought about Mr. Donne in quite some time, but the fact that the police force hasn't caught up with him yet tells me they don't truly care to find him. And after the assassination of a state senator, that seems somewhat odd, don't you think?"

Herrick didn't give an answer. "Anything you can help with would be great."

"What did you say your name was again?"

"Matt Herrick."

"Matt, Jackson Donne means nothing to me. If he's going to make an attempt on my life, let him come. He won't get through. An attempt on my life doesn't make any sense, though. Not really. He's the one who put me away. Isn't that enough?"

"Alex Robinson thinks he snapped."

Carver shook his head. "People don't just snap like that."

Herrick avoided an easy joke. "What do you think is going on, then?"

"I have to get back to my crossword puzzle. I'm sorry I couldn't be of more help. I appreciate the warning, though."

Carver stood up and walked past Herrick to the door. As he passed, Herrick could see the long scar against the width of his neck. Carver knocked on the door. The doctor opened it.

Carver turned back to Herrick.

"We're done here, Matt. But I appreciate the visit."

CHAPTER 13

||||||||||||||||||||||||||||||||||||||||||||||||||||||||||||||||||||||||||||||||||||||||||||||||||||||||||||||||||||||||||||||||||||||||||||||||||||||||||||||||||||||||||||||||||

ERRICK AND THE doctor—her name was Rettig, according to her tag—walked back toward the waiting room.

"So," Herrick said. "Why is he here?"

Rettig stopped and checked a patient's chart. The patient was lying on a bed with wheels. It was pushed against the wall. The patient appeared to be sleeping. She put the chart back and faced Herrick.

"I don't mean diagnosis or anything like that," Herrick said. "I mean, he was in prison and then he was moved here."

"Diagnosis would be why he'd be moved here." Rettig adjusted her glasses and then scratched her nose.

Herrick shrugged. "Usually."

She took a deep breath. "He didn't tell you?"

"No."

"Hmph. He tells everyone." They started walking again. "It's not really public knowledge, I never saw a news story on it, but a lot of the cops that come in here—they heard it."

Herrick waited, running some guesses through his brain. None of them passed the smell test.

"Hurricane Sandy," Rettig said.

That didn't even come up in Herrick's thoughts. He nodded for her to go on.

"The story goes like this," she said. "The night of Hurricane Sandy, half the state lost electricity, didn't they? Two years ago, I lived in western Pennsylvania, so I can only go on what he says."

Herrick nodded. "Pretty much what Restore the Shore was all about, yeah. Electricity was the least of our problems."

That wasn't exactly true, but it sounded good in Herrick's head.

"Well, our friend in there says the electricity went out in his prison, and the generators were flooded by all the rain. And according to him, when that happens, all the cells open. They're run on timers, so he said it all got frazzled and all the doors popped."

"Sounds like an urban legend."

Rettig shrugged.

They were in the lobby now. It wasn't as crowded. Only two people playing on their iPhones. The Crais fan was gone.

"Anyway, the doors pop and ninety percent of the inmates storm the guards. They riot. But the other ten percent, they track down Mr. Carver. They knew he was a cop and put a bunch of people away. So they beat him to within an inch of his life. He ends up in intensive care and his lawyer starts playing up an insanity card. Gets him moved here after a year and a half of arguing. Either he was crazy and it never happened — which is the prison's official story — or his life was in jeopardy and he couldn't be in that prison anymore."

"So, he's not crazy?"

Rettig shrugged. "That would be getting into his diagnosis, wouldn't it? I do know the higher-ups in the penitentiary swear this never happened."

Herrick stuck out his hand. She shook it. "If I have any questions," Herrick said.

"You can call, but I might not be able to tell you anything."

"I think you already told me plenty."

Doctor Rettig took a business card out of her pocket and handed it over. Herrick took it and noted her first name was Natalie. He put the card in his wallet.

"I'll call," he said.

Rettig smiled. "Have a nice day."

Herrick nodded and checked his watch. Almost time for practice. He had to stop cutting it so close. He jogged to his Camry.

CHAPTER 14

||||||||||||||||||||||||||||||||||||||||||||||||||||||||||||||||||||||||||||||||||||||||||||||||||||||||||||||||||||||||||||||||||||||||||||||||||||||||||||||

MARIO NEVER PICKED up the phone. Tennant spent the evening calling and then even walked down to the motel, but it was dark. His gut was knotted, but calling the police wasn't an option for him. Not last night. Hopefully, not ever.

The following morning, Joe Tennant made his way back down the hill. The wind came up at him, cutting through the skin on his face. The air smelled of snow, and the sky was a pale gray. It was only November. The pebbles on the road crunched beneath his feet with each step.

The motel parking lot was empty. Some police caution tape flapped off the handle of the door, snapping against the stone wall next to it. The rooms were dark. The place didn't feel like it was ready to open up in a week, it felt abandoned. Then again, it pretty much *was* abandoned. But maybe Mario left something behind that could be important.

The remnants of last night's two Heady Toppers rattled around Tennant's brain, trying to force the pressure out through his eyeballs. Two beers and he had a hangover. He was getting old. Ignoring the pain, he crossed the parking lot and headed right toward the caution tape. He held his jacket closed tight against the wind.

When he got to the front door and put his hand on the knob, he heard a voice.

"Joe?"

Tennant turned around at the sound of the woman's voice. It was Doris Terwilliger, an older woman who brought Mario coffee every morning. She had two cups in her hand at that moment.

"What's wrong?" she asked. "Why isn't Mario here yet?"

Tennant walked over to her. The wind was blowing her hair hard to the left, but she barely seemed to notice. Wind like this was nothing to the natives. The other thing that was nothing to the natives was current events. It was perfect when Tennant settled here. They rarely spoke about the past, and they worried more about local issues rather than national ones.

And, a lot of times, they actually even missed the local ones. Too worried about bringing in skiers in the winter and hikers in the summer.

Beyond that? Everything else was small potatoes.

"A man came to talk to him," Tennant said. "Mario got worried and told me to leave through the back door. Said life was catching up to him. Or something to that effect."

For an instant, it looked like Doris was going to drop the coffee cups. She took a step back and her hand lowered a few inches. She sputtered some words that Tennant couldn't make out, and then steadied herself. After glancing at the now safe coffee, she handed one cup to Tennant. He took it.

"Sorry," she said.

"What's going on?" he asked.

Doris looked down at her coffee cup. "Why didn't you say anything?"

"To who?" Tennant took a sip of the coffee. No sugar. He tried not to scowl. "I didn't want to come running into town panicking in the middle of the night."

The trees rattled in the wind. Beyond that Tennant could hear the bustle of four or five cars making their way into the business district of town. People were hitting the small convenience store for food, or grabbing a late breakfast. Most people left town and headed to Burlington or Montpelier for work. But around this time of day, there was usually a bit of action downtown.

Tennant almost always stayed away.

"Me," Doris said. "You know he means something to me."

"You don't seem shocked." Tennant took a breath. The steam from his mouth shot out and then dissipated. "You seem scared."

Doris drank some coffee.

"I am," she finally said.

"What is this all about?"

"Mario was a good man."

"There are a lot of good men out there, Doris." Tennant finished his coffee. The liquid warmed his cheeks and chest. "They don't disappear." The words stung as soon as they came from his mouth.

"Whatever he did, it was a long time ago. He never told me. He just told me it was over. That I shouldn't worry about it."

"But you did."

Doris shook her head. Steam rose out of the hole in the lid on her cup. "I always worried. He told me that wasn't him anymore. You know he was originally from New York?"

Tennant shook his head, but the warmth in his cheeks and chest faded fast.

"Something he did there, it hung over him. Made him run. I never pushed. It wasn't any of my business. He was just such a nice man. We'd both lost people. Me? I lost my Herbert. And Mario—"

"The picture. The woman skiing?"

Doris nodded.

"What do they have to gain by coming for him now? Whatever he did, he made up for it. In spades. He was so good to people, Jackson. He hired you when you needed help."

At first, Tennant didn't even catch it. Images of Mario were flashing through his head, the day he got hired. The times Mario would watch him chop wood during lunch break. And when he gave the advice of the easiest place to find Heady Topper. Mario looked out for him.

But Doris's words cut through his reverie.

"What did you call me?"

Doris said it again. The name he kept trying to forget. "Mario told me. He liked you. Whatever you did, he said, you probably did it for the right reasons."

Tennant dropped his cup. "Jesus Christ."

"Don't worry. Your secret is safe with me," Doris said. "That's how Mario wanted it. No one else knows." She took another sip of coffee.

"Maybe," he said. He backpedaled. Gravel kicked up beneath him.

Doris must have seen something in his face. "Don't worry," she said again. "People like you here. They'll protect you. You're the only person in town who can get a case of that stupid beer every single week. Do you know how rare that is?"

Tennant just shook his head.

"But you did stuff like this for people when you were in New Jersey, didn't you?"

"What stuff?"

"Solve problems?"

"Not in a long time."

Doris shook her head. "I think it's time to start again. Maybe you can help me. Help me help Mario. Find him. Bring him back."

He didn't answer.

Not immediately.

Joe Tennant wanted to run back to his cabin and lock the doors.

Jackson Donne wouldn't let him.

CHAPTER 15

||||||||||||||||||||||||||||||||||||||||||||||||||||||||||||||||||||||||||||||||||||||||||||||||||||||||||||||||||||||||||||||||||||||||||

DAN FABER GOT on the bus after practice. Herrick gave him a wave and said a silent prayer. He always did when the last kid left, hoping they'd get home safely. In this neighborhood, even the kids coming in from out of town could be in trouble if they looked at someone the wrong way. He put his right hand on the hood of his Toyota Camry, wishing he could get in the car and drive home now. Instead, he had to change and collect his stuff.

Long day.

He shrugged his shoulders against the cool air, the remaining sweat from practice sticking to his neck and sending a shiver down his spine. Turning back toward the double door that led to the gym, Herrick exhaled and saw his breath for the first time since last winter. Meant the season was about to begin. He smiled.

And then the door slammed shut in front of him, and something hard smacked off his shoulder. Herrick tried to spin further out of the way, but lost his balance. He fell back first onto the pavement. A tall, scrawny man wielding an aluminum baseball bat stood above him. For an instant, the bat was over his head, then it wasn't—the glare of the streetlights gleaming off it as it arced in his direction.

Herrick rolled left, into the wheel of his car. The bat clanked off the ground next to him. He rolled back and kicked his leg out. His assailant groaned as Herrick's foot crunched into anklebone. But the attacker didn't go down. He took another swing with this bat, this one like a golf swing. It breezed an inch over Herrick's chest and thunked into the metal of the Camry. Before the attacker yanked it out again, Herrick kicked his foot out again and connected. There was a snap, and the assailant went down to one knee. He screamed. The bat clattered away.

Using only his abs, Herrick sat up and swung a right cross, connecting with the guy's temple. The guy fell back and Herrick got to his feet. The attacker scrambled to his knees and started to crawl away. There was no way he was going to escape this easily. Herrick bounded forward about to reach for his jacket, when he heard a familiar click.

It was impossible for Herrick to switch his momentum quickly enough. The attacker whirled, and stabbed. The switchblade tore through his T-shirt, and there was fire against his ribs. The attacker tried to make another stab at Herrick, but his ankle gave again. He fell forward, the blade digging itself into the front tire of the car.

Herrick ignored the pain in his side and reached for the bat. He grabbed it by the handle and got to his feet. His shirt was wet, warm, and sticky, and his left arm didn't want to help lift. That wasn't good.

Back in Afghanistan, a sergeant standing next to him once caught two pieces of shrapnel from errant grenade debris. They didn't embed themselves in Sarge, instead slicing through his skin and getting stuck in the jeep behind them. The sergeant bled out in something like twenty minutes.

Basically, Herrick felt like he needed to end the fight now. He hefted the bat in his right hand and whipped it at the attacker. The guy ducked and the bat clanged off the brick school wall.

The attacker stared at Herrick. They were both frozen,

wondering who'd make the first move. The eyes in the ski mask made their way down Herrick's side. Instinctively, Herrick reached across his body to cover the wound. His hand was immediately slickened. The attacker tested his ankle, holding the knife out in front him like he was Errol Flynn.

The ankle would not hold. As Herrick's vision blurred a bit, he caught the attacker losing his balance.

"Stalemate?" Herrick tried.

The attacker didn't answer.

"I can give you money if that's what you need." Herrick grinned. "But drugs aren't the answer."

A puff of steam from the attacker's mouth.

"Yeah. I didn't think that's what you wanted."

The attacker didn't make a sound. He turned and limped away. Herrick tried to pursue, but it wasn't happening. Fire burned up his left side, and his breathing was shallow. He reached in his pocket, found the master key, and pulled the door to the gym open. He walked the sideline, using the bleachers to hold himself upright. He went into the locker room and stood in front of the mirror. His SPHS shirt was torn nearly in half. It was stained a deep red. A red so deep it was almost brown.

Grunting, he pulled the shirt over his head. Stars appeared before his eyes and he looked down, waiting for it to pass. When it did, he looked back up; he could see the wound, gaping. It wasn't as bad as it felt, but he definitely needed to stop the bleeding, and get stitches. He was so exhausted from the brawl and blood loss, there wasn't any way he could drive.

He made his way through the locker room to his locker and found his cell phone. He couldn't call for an ambulance. Even if they got here, they didn't have a key, and Herrick didn't trust himself to stay awake waiting for them.

Sarah Cullen picked up on the second ring.

"I know you turned me down for a drink the other night," he spit out. "How about spending the night in the emergency room with me?"

"Matt? What the hell happened?"

"I'm in the gym locker room. I'm bleeding, so you might

want to put a towel down on your front seat."

"What—?"

Herrick took a deep breath, despite the protest from his ribs. It wasn't a peaceful protest. The cops would have fired tear gas. "I'll tell you later. Just get here." Herrick chuckled. "It'll be a treat. You can see the men's locker room."

"Shut up and don't die," she said. Then disconnected.

Herrick stumbled over to the sink and grabbed a handful of paper towels. He pressed them against his wound. Certainly not sanitary.

The wooden bench was comfortable. He lay on it, pressed the towels hard against his ribs, and closed his eyes.

Sarah'd better hurry.

CHAPTER 16

||||||||||||||||||||||||||||||||||||||||||||||||||||||||||||||||||||||||||||||||||||||||||||||||||||||||||||||||||||||||||||||||||||||||||||||||||||||||||

DONNE STEPPED UNDER the caution tape, kicked the door in, and walked to the front desk. He pulled the handkerchief he'd brought with him from his pocket and opened the first drawer.

Emptied.

He opened another.

The same.

The check-in book, which always rested on top of the counter—even when closed for the season—was gone as well. The cops had cleared this place out well. Donne wondered if they were even going to bother to come back. They probably came in, cleaned the place out, took photos, and left. Who the hell wanted to be in Vermont that long anyway?

But then again, maybe they missed something. The pictures of the woman skiing were still hanging on the wall. Donne took them down and felt along the frame. Nothing was hidden there, or, if there had been, it was gone as well. There were four numbers written on the frame of the skiing picture—2978. Could be a date. Could be nothing. Donne put the pictures back up on the wall, straightening them out. They were important to Mario, so they deserved respect.

Next Donne went into the back office. Here's where the police sped up. Papers littered the floor, pictures had been knocked over. A computer monitor rested perilously on the edge of Mario's desk. The hard drive was gone. Donne got to his knees and started sorting through the papers.

They were receipts, some more than ten years old. Handwritten on carbon paper, other than the dates, they were meaningless numbers. No names. No phone numbers. Donne wondered how Mario was able to even do business. If Jon Taffer or Robert Irvine had gotten ahold of these, there'd be a lot of screaming going on.

Donne kept digging, kept sifting. Nothing caught his eye. If it didn't catch his eye, it certainly didn't catch the cops' eyes. He went over to the desk. The drawers hadn't been replaced, still half hanging out of their sheaths and balancing on the floor. Most were empty. The ones that weren't had more receipts. Donne looked at a few more, took a deep breath, and gave up.

There wasn't anything here that could help him.

He left the office and went back into the lobby. His chest felt heavy and his cheeks burned. Donne leaned against the wall and tried to settle himself down. How long had he been looking through those different receipts? His eyes weren't focusing right, and he blinked a few times to clear them. In his peripheral vision, he caught it. A blinking red light.

Donne walked past the desk over to the corner window. It was Mario's office phone, the exact same kind he had in each hotel room. The blinking red light indicated there was a message. Donne lifted the receiver and pressed the red button under the light.

"Please enter the passcode," a robotic voice said.

Donne stared at the keypad and thought, *It couldn't be that easy.* He typed in 2978 and waited.

"There is one new message in your mailbox. Press one to listen to that message."

Donne obliged.

"First message."

Donne steeled himself, expecting it to be someone asking when they opened up for the season.

It wasn't.

Mario's voice rang over. "Joe, I'm pretty sure you're going to find this."

Donne exhaled.

"You're a good guy, but I've always known that about you. Maybe most people in this town do. But they just mind their own business. They're treating me pretty well, but they also think I'm dumb. I'm not in a prison, this isn't a jail." A pause. Some mumbling. "Shut up. I'm not an idiot."

Donne smiled despite the snake slithering through his intestines.

"I made a mistake a long time ago, Joe. And this is how I'm paying for it. Do not come looking for me. Do not try to help. This guy—he wants to find Jackson Donne. They don't know what he looks like, seems they only have old pictures. Tell Jackson to run. Get away. Can you do that for me, Joe? Please."

There was a pause. Then a gargle. Donne gripped the phone so tight, the skin on his palm pinched together. Something on the other end clattered.

Followed by a voice.

"Tell Jackson Donne we're looking for him. And if we don't find him soon, this guy—this Mario is dead. He's a sinner anyway. He deserves it. So does Jackson Donne. Okay, Joe? Or whoever gets this message? Get us Donne. It'll be worth your while."

Click.

"To repeat this message press one. To erase it press—"

Donne listened to the message again. The warmth in his cheeks had migrated and turned to sweat at his brow. His teeth were gritted together like a '90s comic book character.

When the message ended this time he deleted it. He walked out of the room into the cold air. The sweat on his face cooled and steam rose off his head. His beard, the scars, and age on his face had hidden him yesterday. The only thing that saved him.

But now — did he want to be saved?

And if the cops weren't after him, who was?

Doris was gone and the parking lot was empty again. Donne stood there for a few moments, almost expecting the cars that rushed the lot would show up again, kicking gravel and squealing brakes. It'd all be over.

And he would probably welcome it.

But that wasn't fair to Mario, or Doris. There was still work to be finished. And if the cops weren't after him, whoever was would have to pay anyway.

CHAPTER 17

S ARAH GOT TO Herrick before he could pass out, and drove
him to the hospital. She did make him sit on a towel, and
gave him the silent treatment the entire way. Except for this:
"You know, if you'd called nine-one-one, an ambulance
would probably get you quicker treatment in the emergency
room. Also, a police report."

Herrick grunted. The fire in his side hadn't subsided. "How
was your date last night?"

Back to complete quiet.

A Jersey City emergency room after dark is never empty.
From drug overdoses to people living under the property line
getting their kids checked out, there's always a wait. But when
Sarah dragged Herrick through the automatic doors, a trail of
blood dripping behind him, the nurses didn't waste any time.
They got Herrick on a stretcher and brought him right in.

They cut off his shirt and washed the excess blood away.
The doctor came in, this one an Asian man who looked like he
hadn't slept in three weeks. He took a look at the wound, shook
his head, and then said, "You're lucky."

Herrick tried to adjust himself to get a better look at the wound, but stabbing pain kept him down.

He said, "Yeah, seems like a good day to play the lottery."

The doctor ignored him. "The cut is not that deep, but you did bleed a lot. We're going to clean it out, stitch it up, and then discharge you. I'll write a script for an antibiotic to take in case of infection."

"Is it the kind of antibiotic you're allowed to drink beer with?"

The doctor didn't answer verbally. Instead, he pressed a soapy wet sponge into the wound. Herrick hissed to keep from screaming. The stitching went by a lot easier—so he guessed they used some sort of numbing agent. When the doctor was done, he told Herrick that it would be sore in the morning and to take it easy for a day or two.

Herrick asked if he could lie there and rest for a few minutes. The doctor told him he had at least fifteen minutes before they would get him his release papers. He told the nurse about Sarah, and the nurse said she'd try to find her and send her back. Herrick exhaled when they left.

And then his phone rang.

Herrick reached into his pocket and retrieved it. Checking the caller ID, he saw a blocked number. Rule number one of being a private eye, always answer blocked numbers. You can hang up mid-conversation if you need to.

"Matt Herrick." To describe the voice would be like describing grass growing. Nondescript. Emotionless.

Herrick said that it was. Somehow, he knew this wasn't a telemarketer. He glanced around the room to see if anyone was eavesdropping. It didn't appear that way, too many people concerned with their own illnesses and injuries. He saw Sarah come through the double doors and head in his direction.

"Were you a fan of my visit today? Have you stopped the bleeding?" The voice on the phone asked.

"Only ten stitches, he said. But they had to cut my shirt off. I liked that shirt."

Sarah approached his bed, but Herrick held up a hand.

Noticing the phone in his hand, she nodded and turned her back. It still felt like a rude gesture, even if she understood.

"Let me ask you a question, Mr. Herrick. That boy who got on the bus before we met. Is he a student of yours? Do you care about him?"

The pain in Herrick's side turned to ice and spread throughout his body.

"This has nothing to do with him."

A small chuckle. "But what if it did? What if I made it so?"

"You're asking for a world of hurt," Herrick said.

Sarah flinched, but didn't turn around.

"I've been doing my research on you," the voice said. "I've only known about you for a few hours—a day maybe? But you're easy to find on the Internet and you've got a lot of demons."

Call his bluff. "No more than anyone else."

"Hmmm." The tapping of keys. "Matthew Benjamin Herrick. Afghanistan, shot a child suspected of being a suicide bomber. That must keep you up at night. It was the boy or your battalion, right? Must have been. But to kill a child, you must work hard to chase that one away."

Herrick didn't respond. Whatever words came out of his mouth would only give this guy more information than he needed.

"And then, only years later, your team, your precious team, lost a valuable member last year, didn't they? You're a private eye. Could you have stopped it?"

Yes.

"Your dreams must battle each other. Which nightmare will take top billing that night."

"How's the ankle?"

"Better than your psyche, I assure you." The man exhaled. "Let me explain to you why I'm calling. This is your one and only warning. We are not going to let you continue on this case you're working. We have methods. This is step one. If you continue on the path you're traveling, you will suffer."

Sarah now turned back around. She shrugged in his

direction. Mouthed *Who are you talking to?*

Herrick shook his head back at her. *Don't worry about it.*

"You don't scare me. You went down pretty easily. Bring it."

"You think I was trying to kill you today? That is not how we work. No, we will take everything from you. We take things from everyone. You'll think of me every time you leave that gym. Every time one of your players leaves. Maybe I'll be there. Maybe I won't."

"Don't you dare."

Another chuckle. "One afternoon. That's all it took. You are not a complicated man, Mr. Herrick. Not one bit. I know what you care about. You care about your team. Oh, and tell Ms. Cullen I said hello."

Before Herrick could respond, the line disconnected. Suddenly the burning sensation in his side wasn't the worst pain he felt.

Sarah approached the bed, but Herrick wouldn't speak. He was too busy focusing his breathing.

Controlling it.

Because that was all he could do at this moment.

CHAPTER 18

||||||||||||||||||||||||||||||||||||||||||||||||||||||||||||||||||||||||||||||||||||||||||||||||||||||||||||||||||||||||||||||||||||||

A LEX ROBINSON PULLED up to his parents' house in Lyndhurst. He was lucky to find a parking spot on the narrow street. Driveways were at a premium and cars overpopulated the town, filled up the curbs. But Robinson had a stroke of luck and was able to park just outside.

The house was dark save for the flickering TV in the living room and the glow of a light from the bedroom. Probably his mother's lamp on the bed table. He got out of the car and went inside without knocking.

"Dad?" he called out in the dark.

The grumble back came from the living room. Beyond that was the hum of a crowd and the *thunk* of bodies flung into the boards—his dad was watching a hockey game on TV. Bernie Robinson loved hockey.

He found his dad exactly how he expected to find him. Sitting in the recliner, bottle of Jim Beam and empty glass on the end table next to him. The bottle was open, and the glass had a film on it. Robinson wondered how much he'd had, and expected he'd be able to guess by the time their conversation was over.

"What are you doing here?" The words were said slowly, as if his dad was focusing on them. The past two years had shown Robinson he was focusing on not slurring.

"How's Mom?"

"Upstairs. Hasn't said a word in three days."

"Is she eating?"

"Here and there."

"Are you eating?"

His dad waved a hand at him. Then he poured a drink. "Want some?"

Another beer would be great, but that would wait until he got home. Not in front of his dad.

"No."

"Go say hi to your mother."

"In a minute. I want to talk to you."

The silence hung in the air after his dad hit the mute button. He drank, and Robinson watched.

When his dad put the glass down, Robinson said, "I'm going to make you proud of me, Dad."

His dad licked his lips and then said, "There's a first time for everything."

Fire ran through Robinson's skin, and it felt like something was tugging at his brain, pushing it into his sinuses. He wanted to scream, and was glad he turned down the drink. He counted to ten.

"All our problems would be solved," Robinson said.

"How are you going to do that? You're going to bring Angie back from the dead?" Spittle dripped from his dad's cheek as he spoke. "That would make me proud of you, son."

"She died fighting for us, Dad. All of us."

"You can't even say her name." Bernie wiped his mouth. "She made me proud. You? You were a terrible cop. You're lucky not to be in jail. And now you're a private eye, right? How can you even hold an apartment?"

Robinson counted to ten again.

"Just—I'm not going to see you for a while. I wanted to give you a head's-up."

His dad poured another drink and downed it. Three fingers and it went down like a shot.

"Go see your mother. Then leave. When it's time for me to be proud of you, give me a call."

Robinson stood up, hovering over his dad. He wanted to give him a hug. Something to show him it was all going to be all right.

Instead, he turned and climbed the stairs to his mother's room. The light was on like he suspected and Esther Robinson was under the covers. There was a TV on their dresser, but it wasn't on. There was a book on the table next to her, but it was closed. His mom's eyes were open, however. She stared at the wall in front of her.

"Mom?"

She didn't flinch.

"Mom. I just wanted to tell you that I love you. I'm going to try and fix things."

He leaned over and gave her a kiss on the cheek. His mom blinked. The only acknowledgment he'd gotten from her in the past two years was a blink. Ever since the funeral, she wouldn't talk to him.

Robinson descended the stairs and yelled goodbye to his dad. No answer. He left the house and went back to his own apartment, dreaming about the case of Bud Light he'd splurged on.

Before he started driving, he checked his phone. There was a text that read: *It's started.*

CHAPTER 19

THE NEXT MORNING, Herrick called the Jersey City police station and got in touch with Patrick McKinny. He requested they send a cop down to hang around outside the school during practice time. When McKinny said they couldn't spare a cop, he promised he would try to get some recruiting dirt from the football team. McKinny, a die-hard Notre Dame fan even though he went to Saint Peter's — found some extra overtime pay in his budget.

After the phone call, Herrick got back to work, despite the aching side. Clearly, someone had been tracking his movements because of this Jackson Donne thing. He'd only spoken to two people. Franklin Carter didn't answer his phone, so Herrick left a message asking for a return call.

The institution transferred Herrick's call to Dr. Rettig and she answered on the fourth ring.

After he identified himself, he said, "I'm going to try and do this right way, so please don't lie to me."

"I'm not sure you need to take that tone, Mr. Herrick."

He wanted to shout that he was nearly killed last night, and he would take whatever damn tone he wanted, but, after a deep breath, decided that would be a bad idea.

Outside his window, a Hoboken bakery truck dropped off fresh hamburger and sub rolls at the nearby bars. People rushed toward the PATH train to get to their Manhattan office jobs. It was cold out, and those pedestrians clutched their jackets and steaming coffees tight. A handful of people milled around, checking cell phones or eating breakfast. Herrick wondered why they didn't find shelter.

"Can Carver make or receive phone calls?"

"You're wasting my time with this? Can't you OPRA the court report?" She coughed.

"Asking you is quicker than the government."

"He's not in solitary confinement, but no. His lawyer can come speak to him, and you saw what he has to go through to have other visitors. Otherwise, he can't talk to anyone. It was the compromise they made in court."

Another phone call beeped through on his cell. Taking his phone away from his ear, he saw it was another blocked call. An icicle formed in his stomach, but he let it go to voice mail. It was more important to talk to Rettig.

"Did anyone come to see Carver yesterday?"

"You. That's it." Rettig cleared her throat. "Mr. Herrick, I'm not really that happy to answer your questions, and I am really busy here."

"One more," Herrick said. "After I spoke to him, did Carver act any differently? Agitated? Angry? Happy?"

"Mr. Herrick—come on now. In the past twenty-four hours, I've given you way more information than I should have. I really can't be discussing patients with you. Everything I've told you is public record. But I feel like I'm even toeing the line on that front. Have a nice day."

Click.

Herrick ran a hand through his hair and took a deep breath. His wound didn't hurt that much when he breathed, which had to be a good sign. The prescribed painkillers bottle stayed on the kitchen counter, untouched. So many of his buddies had seen worse in the sand and gone without it. He could too.

He checked the voice mail via speakerphone, and the voice from the previous night hovered in the room.

"Hello, Matt. I wanted to check in with you this morning. Make sure you were okay. And, well, apologize. It was rather clumsy of me to come at you with a knife, wasn't it? I'm better than that. And you. You've been in that sort of situation before, haven't you? I do hope you're okay, because our game is just beginning."

Herrick set the phone down and went to the refrigerator. As the voice kept going, Herrick gulped some orange juice.

"Anyway, I have a question for you. One I thought about all night. What was it like that day in Afghanistan? Leveling your gun at a boy, just a boy. Was he screaming? Were you? Did you look him in the eye? There had to be something else you could do. They hug suicide bombers, don't they? Wrap their arms tight around the attackers' arms to keep them from pressing that fateful button. You were close enough. I'm sure you were.

"Why didn't you just hug the child?"

There was a long pause. The orange juice had gone sour. He put the carton down and rested his hands on the counter, staring at the phone. The timer on the voice mail showed there were still thirty seconds of message left.

"Could you imagine that image if a news reporter had gotten a hold of it? The headline: MARINE JUST WANTS PEACE. With you holding that kid tight. People would see it as a sign of peace. You just praying the kid didn't blow up. Oh, it could have been a watershed moment."

Herrick's breathing was ragged. He could see the small boy in front of him. Standing there, praising God. People running, while Herrick's hand went to his holster.

"But that's not how it worked for you. Or for the kid. That's gotta be why you don't carry a gun anymore. Yeah, I found that out too. There are a lot of stories about you out there. *Time*— that inverview about the kid. How you just wished you could talk to his family."

Herrick squeezed the trigger and the boy fell, hands at his

side. Blood splattering the corporal standing behind the kid, three steps away. The screaming echoing in his head.

"And all your cases covered by the *Star Ledger*. And all those big wins too. Those boys, do they look up to you?" He heard traffic in the background. The squealing of a bus.

Herrick's eyes burned.

"Well, this message has gone on long enough. We'll talk soon. Unless you stop what you're doing." A deep sigh. "We both know you won't stop. Until next time..."

The voice mail cut off.

Herrick was sweating. He slammed his palms down on the counter and let the pain reverberate up through his wrists into his shoulders. The phone's screen faded into black while he stood there.

The images burned into his frontal lobe didn't.

CHAPTER 20

JACKSON DONNE'S MORNING was different. The wet, showered beard, the defined lines on his face, and the overly bitter coffee were the same, but the morning was different.

There was no place to go. No wood to cut. No repairs to do. Just silence in his cabin. He sipped the coffee and thought. His next move would be key. Mario could be dead already, the voice mail essentially signing his death certificate. But if he wasn't, and this wasn't ever about Mario, finding and saving the man rested on Donne's shoulders.

And he would have to do that without being caught.

The one thing Donne had stayed away from was the Internet. In the year he'd been here, he'd only checked once, and the pain still rested in his shoulders. She was still dead, and checking a web browser wouldn't change that.

But knowing Mario better would help. The Internet was a tool, not a trigger. Donne put the coffee down. He wondered how long he'd get at the café. Would the men be tracking every IP address in the area? The possibility seemed remote, too overwhelming.

Especially if it was only one man.

Donne promised himself he would be quick. Google Mario, get as much information as he could, and get out.

He wouldn't look up *her*. Wouldn't find pictures, wouldn't read the obituary. He wouldn't Google Jeanne either. He already knew there'd be nothing to find on that end.

She was better than he was at hiding.

Donne rinsed out his coffee mug, pushed his hair back, put on a wool cap and jacket, and left the house.

THE CAFÉ SMELLED the same as it did a year ago. Roasted beans and sugary baked goods needled their way into his brain. Images of Kate flooded back to him, and for an instant he squeezed his eyes shut, fighting back the pain. He'd been through this before, settling into years of darkness.

He wouldn't let it happen again. Life was worth too much. She'd have wanted him to go on. She'd saved him.

Donne walked to the counter and ordered another coffee and a corn muffin. The barista—or whatever this place called him—wrote "Joe" on the cup without asking and told him to have a seat, it'd be a minute or two. Takes a long time to pour a cup, apparently.

Finding an open computer, Donne sat down and logged onto the Internet. Google came up. Donne ignored the doodle of the day and typed in the name of Mario's motel. The website loaded and Donne scrolled through it. Start simple; see if anything catches your eye.

If someone were watching for Donne, he'd have found him already.

Nothing stood out on the motel website. The barista put his coffee down on a coaster next to him. The corn muffin too. Donne took a bite, and the butter added some salt to the sweet. He typed Mario's name into the Google search this time.

Nothing but the motel site again.

Donne smiled before taking a sip of coffee. Mario was just as good at hiding himself as Jeanne was. Low profile, no Internet footprint. Maybe Mario wasn't his real name.

Which meant, besides the coffee and the muffin, the risk of the Internet café was not worth the reward. He logged off, ate quickly, and left. Donne took the coffee with him.

Doris Terwilliger would have more information.

THE HOUSE Doris lived in was on the corner, about three blocks away from the center of town. Her property was lined with trees which had already shed their leaves, and grass that had turned brown. A tattered American flag swayed from a pole near the driveway. Her old Nissan was parked in the driveway itself.

He rang the doorbell and waited. He'd finished his coffee on the walk over, using it to warm himself against the weather. Clouds had formed overhead, and it was likely one of the first snowfalls of the season was imminent.

No answer.

He rang the doorbell again and heard no movement. No rustling.

A tremor went through him, a familiar sensation—almost a sixth sense. He'd been here before, too many times. Ringing a doorbell, looking to talk to someone about a case only find *they'd* gotten to that person first.

The smell of death was always strong, cutting through wood and aluminum siding. But Donne didn't find that now, didn't sense it. But something was wrong, had to be.

He took a step back, ready to land a crushing kick into the deadbolt. Preparing himself for the inevitability of a dead body on the floor, knife sticking from her gut, or a sucking chest wound.

His muscles tensed. He took a deep breath.

And the door opened. Doris Terwilliger gave him a smile.

"Did you find him?" she asked.

The air went out of Donne, replaced by fire through his blood.

"No," he said. "I don't know where to even start looking."

A hand went to Doris's mouth, and her eyes glistened.

"Is he dead?" She staggered and Donne reached forward, catching her before she fell.

"No. No," he said. "I don't think so. Let's go inside. Let's talk. I need your help."

Doris rested her head against his chest for a minute, her small hands gripping his arms tightly. Donne could feel the strength return to her as she pushed off him.

"I need you to help me, Doris," he said.

"How?"

"Tell me everything you know about Mario. Tell me why they're after him." He almost said "after me."

"I promised him…"

"The more I know, the more I can use to track him down."

Doris shook her head. "There's just … there's just so much blood on his hands."

They went inside.

CHAPTER 21

D ONNE TOOK THE wool cap off and tossed it on top of the chair his jacket rested on. Doris was in the kitchen, been there for too long, doing who knew what. The room was overcrowded with pictures of cats, family, plastic flowers, and Christmas ornaments. The furniture was plaid and the carpet was dark brown. The room smelled of Pine-Sol.

"Mario — I don't even know his real name," Doris called. "It took me forever to get him to talk to me."

Donne sat on the couch and stared at his jacket. There were dust and dirt stains on the elbows, artifacts of the work he did for Mario. Cleaning a jacket was a luxury for the money he made, but now he wished he'd gotten rid of the stains.

"He was like you," she said, as she emerged from the kitchen. She didn't carry anything, food, coffee, water. Her hands were wet. "He showed up and started working. Doing odd jobs for people, saving money, finally bought the motel. I think that's why he liked you."

Doris shook her hands and a small spray of water caught the light. Leaning against the only part of the wall without a picture or a decoration on it, she kept talking.

"He never came downtown, except to buy groceries. That's where I saw him. Every week, on Tuesday, at nine fifteen, he'd stroll down the street, grab a cart, and go into the Stew's. He started with produce. Is that what you do, Jackson?"

Donne shook his head. "I start with the beer."

Shaking her head, Doris said, "That stuff ruined our state."

Donne disagreed.

She waved a hand at him. "Anyway, that's how Mario and I got to talking. We talked about strawberries and then pears, and then our favorite coffee. Then I started asking him about the motel and business. He was quiet. Didn't like to talk, gave me one-word answers. I think it took a whole year before we actually had a conversation about more than just produce."

She picked up one of the ornaments, a snow globe, and shook it. For a moment she watched the snow fall.

"But eventually we got to talking about business. How much it picked up once the snow started falling. He was from New York City, and he *hated* the snow. How it would turn all gray and black with the exhaust fumes and people's dirty shoes. But here, he said he loved it. It was pristine. He and Emma used to come up and ski, he said. Emma was his wife.

"I didn't ask him about Emma. Not for a long time. Even though I stared at those pictures behind the desk. I wanted to ask, but I couldn't bring myself to. You know the feeling?"

Donne shifted his weight on the chair. "Very much so."

"You want to know why he was on the run?"

Donne nodded.

Doris put a hand to her mouth and still stared at the snow globe. "The mob killed her. Emma. And then Mario killed one of them."

Donne felt his cheeks flush.

"He owed them money. He didn't call them mobsters." She laughed. "He called them colleagues. He ran numbers and wasn't hitting his quota—I don't even know if that's the right term. He couldn't pay when they asked. They broke his wrist. He still couldn't pay. So they killed her."

Doris put the snow globe down, then wiped her eye.

"He didn't tell me how he killed the one that killed her. Whether it was that night or if he tracked the guy down. He never said. But he killed that man. And then he ran."

The house creaked against the wind outside. Somewhere, chimes tinkled. Doris crossed the room and sat next to Donne. She put a hand on his knee.

"You came. Mario knew immediately who you were. He told me."

Donne took a deep breath. "I didn't do it," he said. "I was framed."

"Then why did you run?"

"It's complicated," he said. "I'm sure they know I didn't do it. Forensices don't lie. But I like it here. I like hiding."

"You don't follow your case?" Doris said. She paused and looked at the ceiling.

Donne rolled his shoulders.

"You have to save him," Doris said.

"I was there when the guy came in. I could have."

"You were all over the news for a while. You look much different now. Older, grayer." She reached toward his beard, but stopped. "I know things have been hard for you. They were hard for Mario too. But you're right. You could have."

"Was Mario worried about the cops?"

"Of course." Doris shook her head. "There was a man who worked the case, but he moved on. He wasn't a member of the NY police force anymore. He went to New Jersey. That's when Mario finally felt safe."

Hair on Donne's neck prickled, so he asked, "Who?"

"His name was—" She snapped her fingers, trying to remember. "It was an odd name. Leo—"

Donne's stomach went cold. Waited a beat. It couldn't be.

"Leo—"

Donne spit it out. "Carver?"

She pointed at Donne. "Yes!"

Carver's image flashed through Donne's brain. Snorting coke at a party after the latest bust, morphing into Carver passing out the remains of the drug money they confiscated. He was the New Brunswick Narc Division ringleader. The city's biggest scandal in years. The one that pushed Donne out of the force.

"It can't be him. It's too big a coincidence."

"Why not?"

"I put him in prison years ago. He was a bad, bad man."

Donne got up. His mind was static, his hand jittery. He tried to swallow, but his tongue went dry. He grabbed his jacket and his hat. He left without saying goodbye.

If there was one thing he'd always hated, it was a coincidence. And this one was too big.

He thought he'd gotten away from it all. Instead, he brought the past right back to him.

CHAPTER 22

||||||||||||||||||||||||||||||||||||||||||||||||||||||||||||||||||||||||||||||||||||||||||||||||||||||||||||||||||||||||||||||||||||||||||

MATT HERRICK FOUGHT through the pain. It wasn't much, he told himself. Just a flesh wound. He wasn't going to sit around and mope over a voice mail either. There was work to be done.

And so, at lunchtime, he found Alex Robinson at his favorite Fairlawn haunt: Johnny and Hanges. It wasn't a pub or a bar or a famous New Jersey diner. Johnny and Hanges was one of New Jersey's unsung restaurants. The hot dog joint. Johnny and Hanges was known for their Texas Weiners, also known as a chili dog with raw chopped onions and mustard.

When Herrick spotted Robinson, he'd just sat down at a booth and bitten into his first dog. Herrick got two dogs of his own and joined him at the table. Robinson nearly choked.

"You can't sit with me," he said.

Herrick tilted his head. "You're my client."

"I don't want anyone to see us together."

"You're kidding, right? The last time we met in a bar."

"Yeah, a Jersey City dive bar with one wino sitting in the corner. I'd be stunned if he even remembered us. People love this place, you never know who can walk in."

Herrick shook his head and then took a bite of his hot dog. He wiped chili from the corner of his lip after swallowing, then said, "You shouldn't have such a predictable schedule then."

Robinson pointed at his hot dog. "How could I resist?"

"Weekly?"

Robinson spread his hands. "What do you want?"

"Wait, back up a second. Why are you so nervous about people seeing me with you?"

"You got mugged last night?"

Herrick's hand went to his side. Each swallow of his meal exacerbated the dull ache.

"Yeah," Robinson said. "That wasn't a mugging. That was someone trying to take a shot at you. Because of Donne. They know you're looking for him."

"Alex, how do people know?"

Robinson ate a fry draped in cheese and brown gravy. "It's New Jersey, man. This state is the equivalent of high school, you know that. Everybody knows everybody and everything. That's why we shouldn't be seen together."

"And..." Herrick waved his hand, trying to get Robinson to speed up the pace.

"People know what you're doing."

"They also probably know you hired me."

Robinson shook his head. "That's on my end. I'm taking care of it."

Behind them, the servers yelled out orders. Soda machines whirred, trays rattled, and a couple of people made polite conversation about the New Jersey Devils. Another normal day. No one knew what Herrick was talking about. Herrick found Robinson's paranoia both curious and annoying. It was tough to decide which feeling held more weight.

Herrick finished off his hot dog and said, "Who came after me last night, Alex?"

Robinson said, "Whoever is trying to kill me?"

Herrick slapped his hand down on the tabletop. The plastic tray rattled and the cacophony of background noise momentarily silenced. The vibration from the slap went directly into the knife wound, and Herrick's breath caught in the back of his throat.

When air came back to him, and the pain settled, Herrick said, "Then why are you having me try to find Donne? You said Donne was trying to kill you."

Robinson shook his head. "Are you stupid?"

Herrick was beginning to wonder the same thing about Alex Robinson.

"You think Jackson Donne is just waltzing into people's homes and shooting them? Or running them over with cars? Is that what you think? He's hired people. Sounds like it's two guys. Two famous guys."

Robinson coughed into his hand and grabbed another fry. Herrick thought he could actually see the chili congealing on the hot dog Robinson hadn't touched yet. Over his shoulder, out the window, two minivans pulled into the lot. They parked and the drivers — one male, one female — got out and let out their minions. Kids, a ton of kids. It was about to get very loud in here.

"The Mosley brothers," Robinson said. He sat back, eyes wide.

Herrick waited. Ate his hot dog. Robinson stared at him.

Finally, he sighed and said, "I wonder if you even grew up in this state."

Herrick hadn't. Not all of his childhood, anyway. His parents were a sore subject, so still he waited for Robinson to continue. Not a topic he was going to bring up today. If he could help it, he wouldn't bring it up any day.

"Most of the bounty hunters in this state are meatheads. Failed linebackers who couldn't get through the Monmouth College offensive line and found a career beating the shit out of husbands who ran out on their wives."

The — by Herrick's count — nine kids amped the volume of the restaurant up to ten. He leaned in to make sure Robinson could hear him as he spoke.

"This guy was thin, man. Not a linebacker."

Robinson held up his hand. "Wouldn't be. Not these two. They're smart. They mess with the guys they're after. A couple of psychos. Lucas, man, he gets into your head, figures out what you're scared of. And Steve? He just has a way with words."

Herrick guessed which one he'd been talking to.

"Rumor has it, Donne hired them." Robinson popped another soggy fry.

"And he's on to me that quickly?"

Robinson shrugged. "Who'd you talk to yesterday?"

"Your old boss and—" Herrick froze. "Donne's brother-in-law."

"You think the family doesn't know where he is? They've been running the state cops and the Feds off the scent for months. They've been waiting for this."

Robinson finally picked up the second hot dog and devoured it.

"You couldn't have told me this the other day," Herrick said.

"I'm just trying to save my own ass."

"You need me to accomplish that." Herrick finished his meal. "So maybe next time, if someone is going to come and try and take a swing at me, you can keep it in mind. Let me know in advance."

"Find Donne," Robinson said. "You do that, this is all over quick."

"I'm trying." Herrick pushed away from the table and left Robinson with the rest of his meal.

CHAPTER 23

HERRICK PEELED OUT of Fairlawn, directing his car back toward Montclair. Odds were Franklin was long gone, but Herrick needed to know. Traffic was light, most people back in their cubicles post-lunch. The chili dogs gurgled in Herrick's stomach as he accelerated.

Twenty minutes later, he pulled back into the Montclair mansion's driveway. It was empty. Herrick got out and walked up to the front door. It was fashioned with a Realtor lockbox, one of those that were impossible to break. Without the matching computer chip, the lockbox wouldn't open and reveal the key. However, that didn't mean Herrick couldn't break the door down.

Of course, that would attract attention anywhere, especially this area of Montclair. After Donne had the area shot up a few years back, the town amped up its police presence. A cruiser could pass any minute.

Herrick made his way back around the house. The backyard was pristine, trimmed and edged. There was a stone patio with an area for a permanent gas grill. The Carters must have taken theirs with them. Herrick made his way to the back window, one that stood at waist height. He peeked into the kitchen and saw no one.

Herrick pulled out his ASP nightstick, flicked his wrist, and extended it. Cops better not find him now. ASPs were illegal in New Jersey. With a quick swing, he shattered the glass. Waited. No one yelled. Nothing moved. No sirens.

He climbed inside.

The kitchen smelled musty. Small motes floated in front of him. Some of the cabinets were still open. Herrick inspected a few, finding them — unsurprisingly — empty. He left the kitchen, going through the house room by room.

There wasn't a sign of anything, no hints of the former residents, no signs of Jackson Donne. Herrick didn't know what he expected, but the house wasn't giving off any vibes. No clues. The Carters hadn't made a mistake, didn't leave behind any evidence of Donne's whereabouts. They didn't leave anything behind at all.

The house hadn't been sold yet, but it was certainly move-in ready, needing only a sweeping. In what must have been one of the bedrooms, Herrick tried the floor panels, looking for secret compartments. He checked the house from head to toe, and came up with nothing but clothes covered in dust.

The ding-a-ding from his cell phone signaled a text message. He took a quick look out the second floor window to the street to make sure the house wasn't surrounded by a SWAT team before grabbing his phone. The street was empty. The text, however, was chilling.

Unknown Number.

Didn't matter. The words were all he needed.

Shouldn't you be practicing right now? Doesn't your team need you?

Herrick sprinted for his car.

E GOT TO St. Paul's early, before the school had dismissed. He did a lap of the school and saw nothing out of the ordinary. No one stood out. No one limped. The cop that would patrol during practice hadn't even gotten there yet. He signed in in the office and went to see Sarah.

He leaned against the wall in the hall outside her office, waiting for her to finish with a student. Five minutes later, the girl wiped her cheeks as she left. She gave Herrick a quick glance and then turned the other way down the hall.

He waited a beat, then knocked on Sarah's door.

"How's the kid?" he asked, nodded toward the hallway.

"How's the cut?" she asked back.

"Aches, but not too bad. Flesh wound and all that."

"You probably should have taken the day off. Couldn't Charlie run practice?"

Charlie Noonan was Herrick's assistant coach. He would need to fill Charlie in on some of the police stuff. But first, Sarah.

"Listen," he said. "Last night freaked me out."

She nodded. "With good reason."

"I called one of my police pals. They're going to send a patrol car around for practice."

Sarah nodded. "Clear that with Mitch?"

The St. Paul principal.

"I'd have more luck talking to the nuns. I just wanted you to know."

"Thanks," she said. "I have some paperwork to finish here."

"Happy hour?"

Sarah shook her head. He felt his cheeks flush.

Without saying bye, Herrick went to practice. He ran the kids hard. They responded. The first game was a week away, and they were chomping at the bit. They played so hard, they didn't even notice how many times Herrick reached for his ribs.

CHAPTER 24

ERRICK STOOD AT the door for the second night in a row and watched every one of his players leave practice. Only this time, he did it with ASP in hand. The cop car circled twice, the driver tipping his hat when he saw Herrick.

The street was empty and quiet, the only noise the distant rumble of a highway. Herrick paced as each of his kids left. A few came over for a fist bump. One asked about the ASP. Herrick didn't give them an answer for that. Just told them to get home safe. It was his usual goodbye, so the kids thought nothing of that.

Once everyone was gone, Herrick waited, listening. The cop came around one more time and Herrick sent him home. He leaned his back against the bricks and exhaled. The crisp air settled on his skin and sent a chill through him.

And then he heard the whistle. It sounded like an Irish shanty, bouncy and fast. Something someone coming home from a pub would whistle. There were missed notes and a ragged tempo. Herrick stood straight.

St. Paul's gym sat on the end of a T. There used to be a fence that blocked the parking lot from the outside world, but it was so old and decrepit, the school decided it would be cheaper to just tear it down. They never replaced it. The street that abutted the T was where Herrick saw him. A thin man, hands in his pockets, ambling forward. Maybe not ambling. Limping.

This man's right leg was injured. Herrick popped off the wall, body tensing. He snapped his wrist and the ASP extended. Which leg did he injure last night? Herrick couldn't remember. The man kept limping toward him. The shanty grew louder. Herrick waited.

The man reached the corner and stopped. He stared at Herrick. A shadow covered his face. Herrick counted.

One, two, three, four, five…

The man turned left and kept limping down the block. Herrick was about to follow when more movement caught his peripheral vision. He turned and saw another gaunt man. Another limp. This man came out from behind the school, but was across the road. He wasn't whistling. The muscles in Herrick wrists were taut.

This man limped to the corner and turned right, heading away from the school. Herrick watched him limp away into the darkness.

What the hell?

Now two more limpers came his way, one stepping around the man he just saw. One coming in the direction the whistler went. They both wore hoodies pulled up over their head. They passed each other. Neither looked at Herrick. A car drove past and honked the horn. Herrick jumped. The limpers just kept walking.

And then his phone rang. Herrick didn't even have to look to know who it was.

"Did you see my friends?" the voice said.

"Which Mosley are you? My guess is Lucas."

Silence.

"I mean, if you're trying to get in my head, you're not doing the best job. Tonight's work was a little silly, wasn't it?"

"I saw you. You were worried. That little stick of yours.

It's amazing what fifty bucks can get you. Four guys. Or was it three? Maybe I was one of them. Just limp down the road."

"You're not going to stop me, Lucas."

Laughter. Not a guffaw. More a chuckle than anything else.

"You've been doing some homework on me?"

"Just a little."

"I'm glad. The longer you worry about me, the less time you'll have to find him."

Herrick said, "Why do you care?"

"I do what I'm paid to."

"You expense that fifty dollars tonight?"

Another chuckle.

"And where's your brother in all this?"

"Wouldn't you like to know?"

"That's why I asked."

The road was empty now. The limpers were long gone and the streets were empty. A streetlight flickered and went out. Herrick turned and went into the gym, pulling the door shut behind him. The smell of sweat, hot and acidic, caught him hard.

"My brother is working a different case. You'll never meet him. You'll be dead long before you came back."

"I don't think so. I've got your number."

"No you don't. And you're my last target. I get to put all my effort in on you now."

"Who else were you chasing?"

"My last one — oh, he was fun — I don't think he's even been found yet. Still warm as they say. You knew him."

Herrick's stomach went rock hard. He tried to breathe, but it felt like the humidity in the gym was choking him. He prayed. Please don't say a player's name. He couldn't take that. Not again.

"Who?" Herrick spit the question out of his mouth like chaw.

"You two had lunch today."

Herrick exhaled. All the air that was in him. He muscles relaxed and his eyes felt wet.

Not the name he was expecting.

Not the physical reaction either.

Herrick pulled the phone away from his ear. As he fumbled for the END CALL button, he heard more words.

"You're next."

His finger missed the button.

"But not before I have some more fun."

Herrick found the button and slumped to the ground. He let the room come back into focus. Deep breaths filled his lungs and his heart slowed. Before he completely caught his breath, Herrick was rushing to his car.

He got behind the wheel, started the engine, and waited for the Bluetooth to connect. He was already two blocks away from St. Paul's before it did. Herrick called Alex Robinson.

The phone rang.

Herrick came to a stop sign and barely paused. He turned right.

It kept ringing.

Herrick pressed the gas hard. He waited for voice mail.

There was a clicking sound.

Herrick hit the Turnpike entrance and took the ramp as fast as he could.

"Hello?" The voice was gruff and familiar.

Herrick tapped the brakes. His hands, wrapped around the steering wheel, were soaked with sweat.

"Alex?" Herrick asked.

The answer came back loud and clear. "Yeah. What's up?"

CHAPTER 25

HERRICK SLAMMED ON the brakes, jammed the car into reverse, and backed down the on-ramp. He prayed no one needed to get on the highway at that moment. He needed twenty seconds, God, just give him twenty seconds to get down the road.

Praying rarely worked for Herrick, but it did that time.

Aiming the car back toward St. Paul's, Herrick floored it.

"Matt? Matt, what's up?" The voice reverberated through the car speakers.

Herrick ran a red light. Somewhere nearby a horn blared.

"What is it? Why are you calling me?" Robinson was shouting.

"Lucas Mosley said you were dead. He said he killed you."

"Jesus."

"You're clearly not dead."

This time of night, cops were at dinner or changing shifts. It was a good time to speed down Grove Street. Or rob a bank. Herrick kept his foot to the floor. But he had to slam on the brakes when a woman pushing a baby carriage tried to cross the street in front of him. The woman cursed at him the entire time she was in the crosswalk.

"Why did he say — is he coming for me?" Robinson asked.

After some rattling, Herrick clearly heard a magazine pushed into a gun.

"I don't think he's worried about you at this moment. Seems like he's found a new plaything. Me."

Herrick hung a right and could see St. Paul's at the corner of the T. He looked for more limping guests. No one was around. Meant nothing. Though it was nearly six, there were some lights still on in the building. Probably custodians. Maybe a go-get-em teacher working way too late.

"That doesn't make any sense. Why is he after you?"

"Hell if I know," Herrick said. "I gotta go."

He hung up the phone before Robinson could respond. Rubber burned as he pulled into the parking lot. He rammed the car into park, got out, and snapped the ASP into attack mode. Head on a swivel, he headed toward the building. No one was around, not even a bum. The gym door was open. Rarely a good sign, but Herrick couldn't remember if he locked it in the first place.

The lights were still on. Herrick's heart was pounding, and there was sweat on the back of his neck. He focused on his breathing. That's what they taught him in Afghanistan.

Mosley's taunt had to be a distraction. Get Herrick away from the school so Mosley could come and do something. But what? Herrick's stomach twisted like a bread tie. His sneakers squeaked on the court floor with each step. Straining his ears, he still heard nothing. Give him something — a creak, a crash, or even a cough.

But nothing came.

Herrick moved toward the locker room, lightly tapping the ASP against his thigh. It'd been nearly a year since he used it, beating the hell out of someone who he thought would learn a lesson. It wasn't a gun, though.

Never again.

Herrick pushed the locker room door open. Lights were still

on there as well. He took a deep breath and stopped just inside the doorway. Listening. Looking. He raised the ASP, fully expecting to bring it down on some thin guy's head. But the locker room was empty. It appeared that nothing had moved. Nothing had changed.

Herrick exhaled.

What was the phone call all about?

Heart rate returning to normal, he realized he still hadn't changed out of his practice clothes. He went to his locker, popped the lock, and swung it open. He pulled his clothes out. Then he returned the ASP to its safe position and put it down on the bench.

Herrick took his shirt off and pulled his polo over his head. The fabric brushed against his knife wound, sending a bolt of electricity down his side. He caught his breath and changed into his jeans. He sat on the bench to put his shoes back on.

After placing his gym shorts back into his duffel bag, he put his car keys into his pocket. A piece of paper tickled his index finger. Another jolt of electricity, and Herrick's heart rate rose again. He pulled the paper. It wasn't his. It wasn't a surprise twenty-dollar bill or forgotten coupon. It was a small piece of loose leaf. It had a note on it, written in black ink and precise handwriting.

"You are an interesting soul, Mr. Herrick. I'm going to need more time with you. Thanks for making a run for it. You love to run and hide. That gave me a few moments to look through your things. I found out more about you. There's so much I don't know."

Herrick read the note in the voice of the man on the phone. Lucas Mosley.

"You are going to be worth every penny. My employer is going to want this done faster than I want to do it. No, I want to get to know you. Get in your head. I'm going to make it hurt, Mr. Herrick. I'm going to make you scream. Did he scream? The boy? Did he have time?

"Believe me, you will have time to scream. Tonight was fun. Talk soon."

Herrick crumpled the paper in his hand. His breath was ragged and he focused on it, trying to bring it back to normal levels. He closed his eyes.

Herrick was pretty sure the moment he brought cops in without clearing it with the principal, he was out on his ass. He couldn't do that to the guys. He owed them.

The door behind him creaked open. Herrick grabbed the ASP and extended it as he whirled around.

Sarah Cullen stood in the doorway.

"Jesus. I was knocking. For a while. Hoping you were decent."

"You scared the hell out of me."

Sarah leaned against the door jamb and crossed her arms.

"I was thinking about it," she said. "I'm bored tonight. Let's do happy hour."

Herrick's heart sped up again. This time for a different reason.

CHAPTER 26

THEY MET AT the Iron Monkey, a craft beer bistro downtown. In the summer, the Monkey had a rooftop bar, but this time of year — on a Tuesday, no less — it was closed. They took a high-top table at the downstairs bar. A few guys who'd come back from their day on Wall Street were finishing up their beers. A couple sat on a first date, fumbling through conversation.

Herrick ordered a Hudson Valley bourbon. Sarah ordered a mojito. Who cared if it was a craft beer bar? After placing the order, she flipped through the food menu. Herrick tapped his fingers on the table. He watched the bartender pour two fingers. She rested the glass on the bar after it was full and then started muddling mint.

"Why are you so jumpy tonight?" Sarah asked.

"Work stress."

"The team's going to be fine."

"Not that kind of work."

Sarah tilted her head. "It was a joke."

"How'd your date go last night?"

"Terrible. He was a jerk."

"Sorry." Not sorry.

The bartender brought the drinks around and placed them on the table. She asked if they wanted to order off the menu and Sarah told her not yet. Herrick took a long pull of the drink, letting the burn rest on his tongue for a moment before swallowing. Lots of vanilla. Sarah stirred her mojito.

"You don't have to be," she finally said. "Part of the deal with dating, right? Weed out the terrible ones?"

Herrick nodded. The last time he dated, a friend tried to set him up on a blind date six months ago. The woman was nice, but asked too much about the war.

"You want to tell me why he was a jerk?" The words felt wrong as soon as he said them. His cheeks felt hot. Quickly, he took another sip of bourbon.

"No." Sarah shot him a grin. "I want you to tell me what you're doing that's causing so much stress. Something's wrong."

"It's a high-profile case."

"No, it's not. I've been looking in the paper."

Herrick shrugged. "It's also top secret."

Sarah said, "Tell me." And then took a sip of her mojito.

Herrick leaned in over the table. Sarah giggled and leaned forward too. Her wrist bumped the drink she'd just placed down and it rattled, but didn't spill. Her bangs fell in front of her eyes. Herrick tried to focus.

"Do you remember Jackson Donne?" Herrick whispered.

Sarah nodded.

"I've been hired to find him."

Sarah leaned back and bushed her bangs back into place. "Jeez," she said. "That is big. The cops gave up looking?"

"They told me that at this point, after looking at all the evidence, they just want to talk to him. Take him in for questioning. He's not a true suspect. They don't like that he ran, though."

Herrick finished his bourbon and signaled for another. A short alarm bell went off in the back of his head warning him to watch it. But Sarah finished her mojito and signaled as well.

"Two on a Tuesday. Work is going to be fun tomorrow."

She shook her head. "So where is he? Where is Donne hiding?"

Herrick shrugged. "That's the problem. I don't really know. I don't even have a lead."

"Come on, you're better than that."

"I talked to his favorite bartender, the cops, his brother-in-law, and boss from way back. Neither of them gave me anything."

"Except a knife wound in your side."

"That was a mugger."

"Sure it was."

The bartender brought the next round and Sarah ordered nachos. They were topped with pulled pork. Herrick was surprised when she said, "We'll have..."

"What do you know about Jackson Donne? I mean really know."

"Not much," he said.

"When I was a kid ..."

"No, you don't do that to me."

When Sarah talked to some of the students, and they were bonding, that was how she connected with them. How she gave advice. She always started with "When I was a kid" and then concocted a story out of thin air. The kids knew most of it was a bunch of bullshit, but they loved it anyway.

"This is real," Sarah said.

"No, it isn't."

She laughed. "Would you let me finish?"

Herrick sat back.

"When I was a kid." She stifled a giggle. "When I was a kid, my mom's sister ran away. My aunt. She had some stuff going on at home, things didn't go well with her then-husband. I don't know exactly what, I was little."

She stopped and sipped her mojito. When she finished, she licked her lips.

"So my aunt runs away and my mom is crying and my dad calls the cops. They can't help, she's too old. She can take care of herself. But my mom is insisting something's wrong, and that we have to find her. No cell phones, no apps. Nothing."

The bartender brought the nachos over. Sarah pulled a chip and popped it in her mouth. Herrick looked for the perfect mix of cheese, meat, and jalapeños before choosing his chip. It nearly buckled under the condiment weight before he got it in his mouth.

"So my dad starts asking my mom about Carol—my aunt. He knew her well, but he figured my mom knew her better. And they started talking about when Carol and Mom were kids and how they used to spend the last week of August in Ocean City, Maryland. My mom hadn't been there in years. Never talked about it. They stayed in this ratty hotel. And my dad called the hotel. The next thing I knew we were packed in the car and going on vacation. And, surprise, surprise, we met up with Aunt Carol. She just needed a few days away."

"That was family." Herrick's bourbon was nearly empty. He waved for one more.

"Okay. I knew you weren't going to get a Bud Light. How's that?"

Herrick shrugged.

"Do I really have to tell you how to do your job? The more you get to know Donne inside and out, the easier it'll be to guess where he's gone. Does he have family?"

"His brother-in-law bailed town. His sister was gone before that. Donne doesn't seem to have much. Just a lot of loss. And a lot of violence. You've seen the news stories."

Susan shook her head. "There's more. He's gotta know people around here."

Herrick shrugged again. "Why did you really ask me out tonight? You said no earlier."

Sarah took another sip of mojito. A short one. "I'm impressed with you."

"How so?"

"Two of your players came in to talk to me, about how great practice is. About how much they believe in you. No one ever does that with me about teachers."

"Did you tell them about the time you played basketball for the Harlem Globetrotters?"

"When I was a kid?" She swirled her glass. "Of course."

"Will they run through a wall for me?"

"You're a good man, Matt." Sarah pushed hair over her ear. "I know what you're doing is important, but these kids, they need you too. Don't forget about them."

Herrick thought about the unmarked phone calls. The fact that he had a cop car circling the school all afternoon.

"I won't," he said. "They're much more important to me than Jackson Donne."

Now if only everyone else cared about other cases, he would be in the clear.

Sarah knocked back the rest of her drink. "All right. Enough of this serious shit. Let's talk sports or something."

"Works for me," Herrick said. And for the first time in two days, he laughed, and the tension rolled out of his shoulders.

CHAPTER 27

D ONNE FOUND HIMSELF outside the motel again. It was just as empty, caution tape still flapping in the wind.

After crunching across the gravel parking lot, Donne went back into the lobby. He wanted a phone, but not a cell phone. Being tracked was easy these days, GPS, triangulating cell phone signals, Facebook. He'd given up cell phones back when he'd moved up here. He had a landline under Tennant's name. He never used it.

With the call he was about to make, he didn't even want to slip up there. Never give anyone a reason to track you, if you can help it.

Donne found the phone and smiled. Did star 69 even work anymore? He tried it and the phone rang. This was a shot in the dark. A hell of a shot in the dark. But leave nothing unturned. Sometimes overlooking the simplest thing could lead to the biggest slip-ups.

He counted five rings, then someone picked up. Donne nearly crushed the plastic receiver in his hand.

"Hello?" A female voice.

"Hi. I got a call from this number and I'm returning it."

"Who is this?"

He almost said his name. But he forced himself to pause a beat, then said the name of Mario's motel.

"Oh! Yes, yes. Thanks for calling me back. Do you have any vacancies for the weekend of February eighteenth?"

Donne said, "I'm sorry, ma'am. We're closed that weekend."

"But the website says—"

"Family event." He hung up.

Donne took a breath and put his palms flat on the counter. He stared out into the parking lot, as if trying to will another car to appear. None did. But the phone rang. The shrill tone made Donne jump and he nearly knocked the receiver to the ground. He caught it instead and answered.

"Yes?" An odd response to his greeting.

Donne took a deep breath and then said, "I'm looking for Mario. He needs to come home safely."

"He doesn't matter to me."

Donne didn't say thing, trying to figure out what that sentence meant.

"I've been waiting for you."

What Mario had said on that answering machine message must have been true.

"I want to talk to Mario."

"Your best bet is to turn yourself in."

"I need to know Mario is alive."

There was a small chuckle. "Yeah. Okay. He doesn't matter to me, except that he matters to you. He's not dead."

"Prove it."

"Uh-huh." Pause. "I don't think so. I think you're going to do what I say."

"I'm really not."

Donne gripped the phone so hard that the skin on his knuckles was taut like a trip wire.

"You don't understand." The voice turned almost to a growl. "Everyone does what I say."

"Let me talk to Mario."

"I wasn't the guy who came into the hotel yesterday. When you ran. That wasn't me."

Donne didn't say anything.

"Nah. I was waiting down the hill. Knew you were around, but my brother and me, we like to have fun."

"I don't understand."

"That phone cordless?"

"Yeah."

Donne looked at the picture of the woman again. It *was* crooked. And he had straightened it yesterday. He remembered doing it, when he looked at the number on the back.

"Take the phone and go to room 107."

Donne didn't bother to respond with a negative. It wasn't worth arguing anymore.

"I'm going," he said.

He took the phone and was back on the gravel. The wind dug into his cheeks and ears, to the point where the cold burned him. He found room 107 and approached the door. That's when the wind caught the smell and took it to him.

"No," Donne said.

"I didn't hear you open the door yet. You don't know what you're going to find."

"I know."

"You sure?"

Donne turned the doorknob with his free hand and pushed the door open. He barely had to take a step inside. The acidic smell burned his nose and brought tears to his eyes, as if he was cutting an onion.

On the ground, with one bullet wound in his chest, was a man in a black suit. One of the men Donne saw yesterday.

"I can tell by your breathing you see him. That is a cop, Detective Arlen Cricket. From down the road. His colleagues are going to be pissed. Told you it was smarter to turn yourself in. And wait until they find out it was you."

Donne wanted to throw the phone away.

"Or you can turn yourself in to me."

Donne took a breath and nearly choked on the smell. He really didn't have any choice at all.

"Come get me," he said. "I'm yours."

CHAPTER 28

DONNE HEARD THE car before he saw it. His thigh muscles tensed and he was ready to run if he had to. The Feds weren't going to be the ones to take him down. Not with Leo Carver's name still floating out there.

He had to talk to Mario, and if getting caught by the lunatic on the phone was the way to do it, so be it.

A black Cadillac rolled into the lot as Donne watched. It came to a stop near room 107. Donne checked the parking lot entrance. No other cars. The Cadillac idled. Donne counted to ten. The Cadillac still idled.

After two deep breaths, Donne stepped out of the room. The smell was still palpable, but at least the air felt fresher. The driver's door opened and a man got out. Tall, dark hair, James Bond–like. He even wore a black suit. He came around the front of the car, his finger trailing along the hood. Donne felt air catch in his throat.

The man stopped about three feet from Donne. He stuck out his right hand. Donne ignored the gesture.

"Hello. My name is Steve Mosley. I'm the man who's going

to kill you," he said. "Just not yet."

Donne rubbed his beard.

"Mario," he said. "I want to see him."

"You look different," Steve said. "From the pictures we have, anyway. Must have been how I missed you. I mean, you were thirty feet away from me. That's never happened before."

"I asked to see Mario."

Steve shook his head. "Actually you demanded."

"Then you ought to listen."

Donne tensed the moment Steve put his hands in his pockets. But he only leaned against the car. Nothing else.

"You're not scared of me," Steve said.

"You should be scared of me." Donne sniffled, trying to clear the odor of death out of his nostrils. "You know what I've done."

Steve laughed. Outright guffawed. "Done? Please, Jackson. I've killed men far tougher than you. You're an ant without a hill. I'm going to step on you."

"I'm still waiting to see Mario."

Sighing, Steve said, "Oh, you're no fun."

He came out of his pockets with the car keys and pressed a button. The tinted back window rolled down halfway. Donne peered inside. Mario sat there, face bloodied, hands behind his back, staring at his knees. His eyes were closed, but his chest rose and fell in regular rhythm.

"You didn't have to beat him up," Donne said.

"You're right." He shrugged and pressed another button on the car keys. Donne heard the lock pop. "Get in."

The wind whipped past them. It was Donne's first whiff of clean air in the last ten minutes. He breathed it in, savored it. Steve tapped his foot, it gravel bouncing each time he did so. Donne nodded and opened the back door.

He slid into the seat next to Mario and pulled the door shut. The sound of it jarred Mario. He blinked and lifted his head up, catching Donne's eye.

"Oh, you idiot," he said.

"Thanks," Donne said. "We have to talk."

"No." Mario blinked several times. "Did you get my goddamn voice mail?"

"I did."

"And you're still here." He chewed his lower lip, as if he was actually sucking blood from one of his cuts. "You really are an idiot."

"You said that already. How bad are you hurt?"

Mario nodded to the front seat. "Slick up there isn't exactly a doctor. Me neither. But everything hurts pretty bad."

Steve got into the car and started the engine. He didn't say a word, just accelerated out of the parking lot.

"How long's the ride?" Donne asked Mario.

"You got some time," Steve said from the front seat. "Feel free to catch up, because after this ride, the fun ends for you."

They hit a bump and Donne bounced off the seat. He grabbed the headrest of the front seat to steady himself, then sat back and fastened his seat belt. Mario still chewed on his lip.

"I talked to Doris," Donne said.

"Oh, Christ. What did she tell you?"

"About your girl."

Mario shook his head. "I like you, Jackson. Why are you digging?"

"Because Doris was worried about you. She asked me to help. She was scared. So here I am, in the back of the car, apparently on my way to my death."

Steve laughed from the front seat. "You can edit out the 'apparently.'"

Donne ignored him again.

"You don't have to know about my past," Mario said. "You don't have to know about me. I'm not important."

"You are to Doris. And—something she said—you are to me."

The car took a hard left and Donne looked out his window. He tried to gauge where they were and where they were going, but it was just a mass of trees and a stream far off through them. It all blended together. It was Vermont and that was all he knew.

"What did she say?" Mario asked. His chin was stained

with blood now.

"What is your connection to Leo Carver?" Donne noted Steve turned his head a quarter turn before turning back to the road.

"Jesus Christ," Mario said.

"Talk to me, Mario."

"What did Doris tell you?"

"He was my boss and then I put him in prison. I haven't heard his name in years. And now, hundreds of miles away from where that happened—from where I'm from—his name comes up. It's too coincidental."

Mario's face twisted and he started shaking. His nostrils flared and then he started screaming.

But not at Donne.

"You son of a bitch! What did you do? What did you say to her? You were supposed to leave her out of this! You promised! I could have gotten him here. How dare you!"

Steve pulled the car over and put it in park. It all happened so quickly, Donne didn't have time to react. Steve turned around, brandishing a Glock. He aimed it at Mario and pulled the trigger. Mario's body jolted forward and all the air went out of him. Blood splattered against Donne's face, against the front seat, and against Steve. Steve turned back and put the car back in drive.

"God damn it," he said. "Now I have to clean this thing."

CHAPTER 29

THE WARM BLOOD on Donne's face did not match the white-hot fire burning up his insides. He leaned forward toward Steve, grabbing the back of the passenger seat. Steve put the barrel of the gun against Donne's nose. It burned his skin. Donne jolted back.

"Stay there," Steve said.

Donne's nerve endings jangled and his intestines twisted into knots so complicated, Boy Scouts would be impressed. He wanted to scream, but held it in.

"What?" Steve accelerated away from the curb. "That's what I do with a gun. It's not a toy."

Mario's skin had begun to turn gray, and a smell filled the backseat of the car. Not the same smell as the one in the hotel room, this was more acidic and sour. The combined smell of cordite and rotten egg. He gurgled, a death rattle clicking from deep within his chest. Meanwhile, the wound stopped spurting blood. Donne's face and hands were sticky.

"Why are you doing this?"

"My job."

"You said you were going to kill me." Donne fought the urge to return his gaze to Mario. Instead he stared forward, trying to see out the windshield.

"When we get back."

"Back where?"

"New Jersey. There are a lot of people who want your head back there. Don't you watch the news?" Steve's matter-of-fact tone scratched Donne's ears like a cheese grater.

"Who are you?"

"I told you." Steve hung a left with enough force that Donne almost fell into Mario's body. The smell was intensifying.

"You're a killer." Two days ago he was having a conversation about hops and barley. But now he was talking about trained killers.

This is your life, a voice in his brain said. It always comes back to this. What was it his father used to say? Violence begets violence. Once it begins, the cycle never ends. He always thought his dad was talking about abuse in a relationship. Now he doubted it.

"No. I'm a legitimate businessman. I track down criminals. Which reminds me, I could go for some bacon."

Donne had no idea what the guy was talking about.

He sat back and wiped at his face with his sleeve. He looked down at his cuffs to find a smear of red. It was hard to see into the rearview mirror, which was tilted away from him, but if Mario's body was any indication, Donne was in bad shape.

He turned toward Mario, actually had to force himself. The body's head hung forward on his chest, a stream of blood dripping from his lip like drool. His eyes were wide open, staring into some horrifying abyss.

He pictured Doris sitting on the couch waiting for news, some shred of hope that Donne had found Mario and was bringing him back alive. But good news would never come.

Violence begets violence.

"I'm surprised you haven't heard of me. Of us. The Mosleys. We're quite popular in the circles you travel."

"You're acting like you're a band."

"We have fans." Steve laughed. "And even a message board, come to think of it. It's weird."

"Sounds psychotic."

Steve shrugged and then hung a hard right. Donne bumped into the door. He thought about pulling the handle and tucking and rolling. He reached up and grabbed it.

"It's child locked, dude. I'm not an idiot," Steve said. "And at this speed? You'll be a pizza. And where will you go anyway? There's a dead cop back at Mario's and your fingerprints are probably everywhere."

"Why don't you just kill me now? You killed Mario. Why am I still alive?"

Steve slowed down to make another turn. Donne tried to get a sense of how long they'd been in the car, but the gunshot threw off his sense of timing. His brain was scrambled right now, and he was fighting just to keep his composure. Banter and conversation with this nut job was all that was holding it together for him.

"There are certain rules I have to abide by to get paid."

"Are you taking me back into Jersey right now?"

Steve laughed again. It was like he was a studio audience member, and this was just a good old sitcom. If only it could be wrapped up in twenty-two minutes. Donne started to shake. He tensed his muscles to fight it, but it was no use.

"We have a car to clean. A body to dump. I hear you're good at that."

"Like I'm going to help you."

Steve nodded. "You're going to do anything I say."

"You're just going to kill me."

"I have a way with people. You think all those stories you heard from Doris today were true? You think Mario didn't know this was coming? I've been planning this for a while."

Steve pulled up to a large building. What looked like a ski lodge built with logs. There weren't any other cars in sight.

"This is how I work. People do what I say. Mario and Doris? I used them to set you up."

CHAPTER 30

ERRICK LEFT HIS car in the parking lot across from the bar and walked to the Light Rail. Sarah had assured him she was okay to drive back to Nutley, gave him a quick peck on the cheek, and was gone. She'd only had the two over their three-hour conversation. Herrick felt the warmth from the booze in his cheeks, and thought the train would be smarter.

Sometimes he made the right move.

He sat on the Light Rail train, waiting for it to depart from the station. The lights of Manhattan reflected off the window — a wonderful view — but Herrick vetoed it, instead picturing Sarah scratching her chin while she thought of a clever answer to his question. He smiled to himself. Must have been the bourbon. The woman across from him peeked over the Kindle she was reading and rolled her eyes.

Herrick's phone buzzed, and he jumped in his seat. He pulled his phone and saw Alex Robinson's number pop up. The woman across from him rolled her eyes again and turned in her seat, showing Herrick her back. He took the call.

"Where the hell are you?" Robinson was shouting.

"On the Light Rail, heading home."

"You can't fucking cut off a call like that, Matt. You were worried if I was alive and then you hung up. It's not like you were in some forest covered in snow and away from any good cell phone reception. You were legitimately worried I was dead."

"You're fine."

Shut up, booze, Herrick thought.

"You don't understand this guy. He gets in your head. He messes with you. I think he's messing with me. I'm on fucking pins and needles here. Locked my door, loaded my gun. He could be coming for me."

"I'm on the Light Rail going home. If you're that worried, call the cops."

"Yup, those guys love me. I'm sure they'll help. Get your ass over here."

"It's been a long night, Alex. We'll talk tomorrow."

Robinson said, "You can get here."

A chill went down Herrick's neck, but he wasn't sure why. Like a primal instinct.

"Not driving tonight."

"Are you drunk? My life is on the line. Donne could be coming for me at any minute. Or sending those two psychopaths."

Herrick couldn't process what Robinson was trying to get past him, and figured he'd hit the bottle as well.

"Alex, you're fine. Put the bottle down, stay sharp, and I'll talk to you in the morning."

"You got me freaked, Matt."

"Sorry. It was a ploy to get me away from school. To scare me. Not you. I shouldn't have called you."

"You're *my* client. Yes, you should have. You also should be coming over here."

"Get some sleep."

"Fuck you too, Matt."

The phone call ended and Herrick stared out at the Empire State Building. It was lit orange for Thanksgiving.

The conductor announced the next stop. Herrick wished it was the end of the line.

CHAPTER 31

LEX ROBINSON GOT up, grabbed a Starbucks, and went to the office. He spent twenty minutes going through mail. Bills, bills, and bills. The money was not rolling in, and he wasn't sure how much longer he could ignore said bills.

It was time to talk to Leo Carver again.

The room smelled like tea, Earl Grey. It was the kind his mother made when he was a kid, steeping it for five or even ten minutes to make sure it was strong enough. She'd talk on the phone to the neighbor down the street about the latest Lyndhurst gossip—usually something to do with the schools. Robinson could picture her hand going up and down as fast as her lips did.

Carver, however, just let the paper cup sit on his desk, tea bag string hanging limply at its side. The crossword was already completed—in pen—next to the cup. Robinson wondered how Carver would handle a crossword puzzle app if they'd let him use a phone. He probably wouldn't speak.

But now Carver sat on the bed, again cross-legged, waiting. He was so far away. Why wouldn't he sit closer? They *needed* to talk.

"Jackson is coming back," he said.

Carver bit his lower lip.

"Did you hear me?" Robinson asked.

Carver shifted on the bed, his eyes glazed over.

Robinson stood up and walked across the room, and leaned in close. He could smell aftershave.

"Back away," Carver said.

"You're not listening to me."

"I don't even want you here."

Robinson's insides went hollow. A dull warmth radiated from his ears and his cheeks.

"You promised me money." The words flew from him like angry bees from a hive.

Carver blinked.

"You told me you had a trust fund."

"This is not supposed to come back to me."

Robinson tapped his foot twice. He stepped back from Carver. Outside, the gentle hum of the hospital workers reverberated.

"It won't."

"Then why are you here? If you keep coming here, they might follow you."

Robinson hadn't thought that through. He slumped his shoulders.

"You idiot," Carver said. "You didn't think of that."

"No one followed me."

"You don't know that. I've already had a visitor. Your friend Matt Herrick came to see me. I don't know what your plan is, but it shouldn't involve me."

Fire raged behind Robinson's eyes. He couldn't do anything right. Nothing was good enough for anyone.

"I'm just trying to make things right."

Carver said, "It is what it is. Maybe there are some things you can't make right. But stop trying to make things worse."

"My sister is dead. Bill Martin is dead. My parents hate me."

"Too bad. You're an adult. Deal with it."

Robinson turned around and kicked over the chair he'd been sitting in.

"I said *be an adult.*"

"Haven't I ever done anything right? Anything well?"

Carver dug his teeth deeper into his lip. Robinson expected to see blood.

Then he said, "It's time to go. This does not come back to me, Alex. It doesn't."

Robinson turned and stormed out of the room. He shuffled to his car, his eyes scanning the surroundings.

Nothing out of the ordinary.

Carver didn't know what he was talking about.

CHAPTER 32

ERRICK COULDN'T SHAKE the conversation with Alex Robinson from the night before. At first, Herrick had thought maybe Robinson had hit the bottle a little hard that night, but his tone of voice stuck out. It wasn't slurred or drowsy, it was bright and sharp—like a trumpet during a Sousa march. Robinson was aware.

Like he promised, Herrick was going to visit Robinson. Robinson just wasn't going to know about it.

After grabbing his car from the parking lot at the butt crack of dawn, he was outside Robinson's office in Kearny just twenty minutes later. Early morning traffic in New Jersey is fine, as long as you're not headed toward the city or a school. Herrick sat back and played with his phone while he waited. He wished he'd grabbed a coffee, but wasn't sure his bladder would be able to handle it. He sipped water from a Poland Spring bottle instead.

At nearly nine, Robinson pulled up, his bright blue Pontiac convertible standing out amongst the rest of the sedans and SUVs on the road. Robinson sipped from a Starbucks cup as he entered his office, making the caffeine craving in Herrick's stomach beg for mercy. Herrick made a note of the time and went back to the Google app on his iPhone.

Herrick had searched Jackson Donne for what felt like the umpteenth time, this time trying to find something more than news articles and old private investigator Craigslist ads. Facebook, Twitter, LinkedIn. Something. The pickings were slim. Donne was a ghost.

Except for one name that popped up in both Twitter and Facebook. It was two accounts that hadn't been used in over a year. There were a couple of Donne mentions in both accounts, news articles she'd shared. Except she'd added hearts next to the name Jackson — almost like a middle-schooler with a crush. One of the Facebook comments on the link confirmed it, and said, "Girl, you're head over heels." She'd responded with a smiley face and "He'll never see." That comment had been liked a ton.

The woman's name was Kate Ellison — the woman Parsons had mentioned. Herrick scrolled some more and his stomach turned when the friend comments piled up. Most were filled with sad faces, RIPs, and "We'll miss you"s. Herrick put his phone down and sipped more water.

Twenty minutes later, Robinson left his office. As he approached the Pontiac, Herrick made another note of the time. He started his own car and gave Robinson a five count before following.

It wasn't long before they were on the parkway south. By the time they reached Route 78 west, Herrick knew where they had to be going. Herrick took a calculated risk, jammed down the gas pedal, sped by Robinson, and tried his best to get to Bethlehem Institution before Robinson. He did, finding a parking space in the corner, an eye on the entrance. Herrick waited, guessing he had a five-minute lead on Robinson. If he was right, that was.

Robinson pulled in four minutes later. He hurried out of his car, brushing his slacks as his went, like he was wiping off his hands. He had a skip in his step. Herrick made another note of the time, and wondered if this was a regular thing.

Dark clouds hung in the air, threatening to rain the last of the dead leaves off the trees. Herrick listened to talk radio, callers wondering whom the Yankees would sign next and if the Mets would sign anyone. He didn't care about the callers or either team. It was background noise. The soft din of conversation helped him concentrate. Complete silence always made him edgy. The feeling started in Afghanistan, as he imagined the enemy approaching their tents as they slept, planning an ambush. Herrick even slept with the TV on now.

He went back to the phone, thankful for his car charger. Now he was on to Kate Ellison's pictures. There were two of her graduating from college—cap and gown, diploma in hand. Another of her at some bar in the city toasting someone he didn't recognize. And then he found it, a selfie: her and Donne mugging for the camera, tongues out and eyes crossed. It didn't fit the image the media had built of Donne, that's for sure. This made him seem like a real person to Herrick, not some crazed Bringer of Death.

Herrick watched the time. Robinson had been inside for nearly half an hour. The clouds opened, a steady stream of rain machine-gunning off the hood of his car. A few leaves stuck to his windshield, but didn't obstruct his view. Herrick scrolled around some more, but didn't find anything.

He put his phone down and leaned back in the driver's seat.

Robinson came out nearly an hour later, stalking to his car as if he was actually trying to dodge raindrops. Herrick watched him drive out of the parking lot, but didn't follow. Instead, he stretched, the wound in his side protesting as he did so. Once he was finished and the pain subsided, he turned off his car engine and got out. He let a few of the drops slam into his shoulders. After being in the sandbox for so long, the rain was always enjoyable.

He went inside, and the receptionist saw him. She nodded his direction and said, "No visitors right now."

"I have police permission. You have it on file."

"He's not to be disturbed right now."

Herrick opened and closed his fists.

Before he could say anything else, the receptionist said, "Don't make me call security."

He didn't have time for an argument. He'd have to ask Alex Robinson what he and Carver talked about instead.

CHAPTER 33

THE SUN PEEKED through the window. Donne watched the sliver of light widen minute after minute. His hands were tied behind his back with a plastic strip cops use during riots and kids' toy packagers use to annoy the piss out of parents. His eyelids felt like beanbags were tied to them, and the muscles at the corners of his shoulders had tightened somewhere around 3 a.m.

He hadn't slept, instead watching the darkness shift with the wind and waiting for Steve to come back and end things. He listened for creaks of wood or footsteps or the racking of a shotgun. Some clue the end was near. But it never came.

Now the sun came up, but Donne didn't feel any better. He'd been in these spots before, and he'd gotten out of them. He would again. But the question remained, why hadn't Steve just attempted to kill him last night? Donne had never believed a "Bond"-type villain existed in the real world — one who'd come up with that elaborate plan. People were just shot, stabbed, or poisoned.

This felt different, somehow.

The creak of wood came, and Donne stiffened. He waited for the gun click or something showing impending death. He looked around the bare room for the umpteenth time, finding nothing to use as a weapon. He got to his knees and then to his feet, grunting as his muscles worked overtime. His breath came in and out in short bursts. He worked to try and control it.

The doorknob turned.

Donne braced himself, trying to decide on a strategy.

Steve Mosley stepped through the door holding a shovel. He stopped and grinned at Donne, looking him over from feet to eye level.

"You look exhausted." Steve shook his head and tapped the shovel on the ground.

He went to Donne and grabbed him by the elbow. After uttering a command to follow, he tugged. Donne stood his ground.

Steve sighed and said, "We have a busy day ahead. Let's not waste daylight."

"You're going to kill me."

Nodding, Steve said, "Not right now. Come with me."

He gave Donne's elbow another tug. Donne went. They walked through the cabin, empty room followed by empty room. His heart was pounding so hard, he could feel it in his temples.

They went out into the sunlight, into the cold air. Steve kept pulling and Donne kept following, past the car through the brush into a grass clearing. Mario was on the ground, soft and gray. Steve threw the shovel on the ground and went to Donne's back. At the click of the switchblade, Donne jolted upright, but suddenly his hands were free.

Steve said, "You've got to dig."

"I'm not digging my own grave."

Steve shook his head. "You're digging for Mario. We're getting rid of him, and then we're moving on."

"Right. You can do it yourself." Donne plopped down on the ground, the grass cold on his rear end.

Steve pulled the switchblade out of his pocket again and

released the blade. He threw it at Donne. Donne rolled out of the way and said, "Jesus Christ." It embedded into the dirt an inch to his left. The only reason the knife missed was because he guessed right, like a soccer goalie on a penalty kick.

He wasn't quick enough anymore. Chopping wood, fixing sinks, carrying toilets, they'd rebuilt his muscles, but not his reflexes.

"Here's the thing, Jackson. I have specific orders. My client wants you to hurt, and he wants to see it happen. I'm not supposed to kill you yet."

Donne raised his hands and waved toward himself. *Come on.*

"Don't you want to know why this is happening?"

A spider crawled around Donne's intestines. "What do you mean?"

"There is crazy stuff going on. You're a wanted man. There are *two* people after you. Think I'm crazy? The other guy's a real lunatic. A former Afghanistan soldier. He killed a kid he thought was a suicide bomber. Doesn't use a gun anymore, but my guess is he can still rip your head off."

"Uh-huh." Donne was full of spectacular comebacks.

"I can kill you now. I will still get paid, though probably not as much. My job will be done and I can go on to the next one. But if you dig, and then I take you home, you'll find out who's behind this and you'll find out why before you expire. You know that's what you want. So come on, let's dig, bury Mario, and head back to Jersey. This clean air is hurting my lungs."

Steve had waded closer to Donne, just like Donne had hoped. He counted to three and made a lunge for the knife. But his speed was gone; the reflexes a hair slow — like an aging baseball player unable to catch up to a fastball. Steve caught him in the ribs with a swift kick.

Donne landed on his back and gasped for air. His ribs felt like ground meat.

"Last chance," Steve said. He knelt down next to Donne. "The answers are six hours' travel time from here. You'll get them."

The spider inside him, crawling around every time Steve mentioned answers, was a million times worse than the kick. Donne couldn't help it. He thought he'd found peace here in Vermont. But now, he only felt like he was missing something.

He sat up and took the shovel. He got to his feet, gave Steve a look, and then drove the head of the shovel into the dirt. The waft of Mario's body was getting stronger in the cold air.

"See?" Steve said. "I told you I could make people do whatever I wanted."

CHAPTER 34

T HE DIGGING CAME easy at first.

The ground had begun to harden because of the cold temperatures the past week, but once Donne got through the top layer of soil, he was able to find a rhythm, much like the rhythm he needed to split wood.

Steve sat next to the body, taking occasional glances toward it, as Donne dug. He'd put away the switchblade, but held the gun he'd used to shoot Mario loosely in his hand. It wasn't aimed at anyone, but Donne knew Steve could easily snap it back into position, at the ready.

Donne stayed focused on the work. He jammed the blade into ground with a crunch, scoop, and toss. Though the air was cold, sweat formed on the back of his neck and dripped under the collar of his shirt and down his back. His triceps tightened with each movement. He tried to keep his breath steady, but the cold didn't help his lungs and inhalation became ragged. He kept digging.

Steve didn't talk much, which surprised Donne. Donne figured he'd know the whole plan by now, and answers would be coming left, right, and center. But Steve sat silent, watching. Except for the occasional *tsk tsk* when Donne would take more than a seven-second break, the only sounds were the wind and the crackling of tree leaves against it.

Donne asked how much more he should dig, but Steve didn't speak again. He just rolled his hand at his wrist. *Keep going.*

More digging. The sun crested the top of the trees and brought some warmth down on them. Donne's sweat intensified, soaking through his shirt. Rough, burning blisters started to form between his thumbs and index fingers. Blade in, lift, toss. He was shin deep now. At this rate, it was going to take all day.

Steve reached over and tapped Mario's body, rolling it on to its back with a dull thud. The body was stiff, rigor mortis setting in. Donne's stomach turned, and he choked bile down.

What felt like an hour later, with Donne now thigh deep, Steve finally spoke.

"You're really taking your time there."

Donne gasped for air before responding. "Why don't you give me the gun and take a turn with the shovel."

Steve laughed then nodded at the body. "Didn't he pay you to do this kind of work?"

"Not exactly."

"I'm getting hungry."

Donne didn't respond. The sourness after the bile incident kept his appetite down, but he would have forced a protein bar down just to keep his energy up. Steve stood up and walked to the car. Donne eyed him, trying to gauge distance and speed. He decided against making a move.

Steve came back with two plastic bottles of water. He tossed one to Donne. It was cold, no doubt a result of sitting in the car for several hours. Donne downed it in two long gulps. He wiped his mouth with the back of his hand and then went back to digging.

Another hour later and he was waist deep. His muscles screamed in agony, the back ones just as tight as his triceps and forearms. The muscles in his neck were as taut as a tightrope. He leaned against the shovel.

"I think this is deep enough," he said.

Steve stood up and walked to the edge and peered over. It wasn't a perfect square, not a professional job, but Donne had gone deep and wide enough. He tried to catch his breath while Steve inspected.

"All right, fine." Steve stuck his hand out.

Donne took it and got out of the hole. He brought the shovel with him, eyeing Steve's gun.

"Tell me one thing," Donne said. "What Doris told me ... was Mario's story true or was it all part of your bullshit?"

Steve turned. "Let's get the body into the hole."

"Tell me first."

"All true."

"Even the Leo Carver stuff?"

Steve smiled, and the gun lowered for an instant. "No, that was all me. Thought that would catch your eye."

Donne nodded and then swung the shovel like a baseball bat, right into Steve's temple. He crumpled to the ground and the gun fell away.

Three more shots to Steve's head, and Donne completed the job.

CHAPTER 35

STEVE'S BODY ROLLED with ease, dropping into the makeshift grave with a dusty thump. Donne looked away before Steve's bloody, open eyes could sear themselves into his brain. He blinked several times, letting the image dissipate. He took a few deep breaths.

He then kneeled next to Mario. The maggots had shown up, crawling over the grayed skin. Donne choked down some more bile, leaned back and put his feet to Mario's back, and pushed. The effect wasn't the body rolling. Instead, it slid against the dirt, inches at a time. The maggots scattered as he pushed.

It was akin to using a leg lift at the highest resistance. The body didn't have much give, the skin hardened. Donne kept pushing. His breath steamed from his mouth, but sweat dripped from his forehead. The wind blew, leaves fell, and still he pushed. Donne could see the edge of the grave getting closer. He tightened his muscles and pushed even harder. Mario's skin made scratching sounds as it moved.

The body reached the edge and gravity took hold. It flipped over the edge and the thump it made was more like a slap.

Made sense. Skin against skin.

Donne caught his breath and waited for the last of the maggots to escape. His chest heaved and settled, and as much as he wanted to scream, he kept it inside. Finally, he stood, picked up the shovel, and started to replace the dirt. If what Steve had said was true — there was another one on his trail — he didn't have much time.

An hour later, he was finished. He had taken the keys off Steve's body earlier, one of the smartest moves he'd made the past few days. Now, he pressed the button and popped the trunk. He dropped the shovel inside, and then inspected the extra gun that was on the trunk floor. Clean, in good working order, and two extra clips. That would work just fine.

He replaced the gun and got in the driver's seat. He headed back to town. According to Steve's GPS, the ride would take forty-three minutes. Donne stepped on the gas, hoping to peel some of those minutes off the time.

D ORIS'S HOUSE.

Donne parked the car around the block and out of sight of the main road. He got out of the car and stretched his back. His muscles had tightened so much during the drive, the last few turns were torturous. It was as if he'd spent the entire day playing basketball at top speed; his legs ached, his arms screamed, and his back felt like it had a sharp needle stuck right in the sciatic nerve.

Doris answered the door on the second doorbell ring. Donne didn't have to say a word for her to know. She eyed his face and covered her mouth. She turned away from him with shaking shoulders and walked into the house. She didn't close the door, so Donne followed her.

He found her in the kitchen sitting at the table, a half-empty cup of tea in front of her. Doris's eyes glistened, but the tears weren't pouring. She'd controlled the sob as well.

"Tell me," she said.

He did. Doris listened, and buried her face again when he

told her about the car. The car that—it occurred to Donne—Steve must have cleaned overnight. The bloodstains were gone.

When Donne finished the story, he waited for Doris to regain control. He didn't comfort her or say anything. He leaned back against the kitchen counter and kept his mouth shut. Doris drank the rest of her tea. The cup rattled when she put it down.

He counted to ten and then said, "Your turn."

She looked up at him, steel in her eyes. The tears were gone, and her face was rock.

"He came to us two weeks ago. Found us in the coffee shop. He bought us both scones. He was so nice. Said he knew who you were and where you were. Wanted us to drag you out."

Doris put her hands flat on the coffee table, and then tapped a little beat.

"We refused. Yes. We knew who you were, but you weren't causing any problems here. The police had never come for you. The beard, the flecks of gray, it's nice, but it's not exactly the best disguise for someone who's been all over TV news.

"We told him there had to be something more going on here. We're not stupid."

Donne rubbed his beard and noted the flecks of blood still on his sleeves. He snapped his hand down to his side.

"They're still looking for me. They may not think I'm the killer, but I'm sure they still want to talk with me."

Doris nodded. "I asked you the other day, but you didn't answer. You don't read the news?"

He thought of the last time he searched the newspapers. He thought of seeing Kate's name. His stomach sank.

"Try not to. Too many memories. Maybe it's easier for me to believe they're still after me. I don't want to go back."

"The world moves on, Jackson. You're a person of interest, a suspect. You're right. They just want to ask you questions. Mario told me. He follows the news from back home, but said you seemed comfortable here. We didn't want to be a bother. But now this Steve comes into our lives. We told him we weren't interested, and he starts going into it with Mario, telling him everything about Mario's past. About Emma. I still don't know how he knew."

"He's good at his job," Donne said. *"Was* good at his job."

"He told us if we didn't do what he said, he would arrest Mario. That's when he told us what he wanted to do. That he was going to have the cops here, and he was going to take Mario into custody. All I had to do was get you interested. And mention Leo Carver."

"I'm sorry about Mario."

Doris nodded.

"But you're safe now."

Doris nodded again.

"The cops are combing this city, Jackson. There was a body in Mario's hotel."

Donne stood up off the counter and stalked across the kitchen.

"It wasn't me," he said. "It was Steve."

"Well, this is going to bring the investigation -- the spotlight back on you."

"I know." Donne rubbed his beard again. "Why didn't he just come and get me? If he knew where I was — why you?"

Doris said, "I don't know. We were scared, Jackson. You have to believe that."

"I have to go."

"Good luck, Joe," she said. "That's how I'm going to think of you. Joe Tennant. I don't like what happens when Jackson Donne is around."

Donne didn't respond.

CHAPTER 36

"I DON'T CARE ABOUT this game anymore."

Lucas Mosley stood in the middle of the apartment—the one Robinson had arranged for him—fists balled and red-faced. Robinson sat in the chair, palms sweaty, watching Mosley's stillness.

"We have to play it."

"My brother hasn't answered his phone in three hours. He hasn't checked in with me since last night. There is something wrong. I'm going to kill Jackson Donne. I'm going to go get him."

"Wait. Wait. Let's find out what happened first."

Mosley took a long breath in through his nostrils. They flared, the only movement of his body. Meanwhile, Robinson couldn't stop bouncing his knees, or wiping his hand on his pants.

"I know what happened. I've been doing this a long time. Steve and I had a system."

The smells in the room were so familiar. Musk and old coffee. He remembered the pats on the back from his colleagues after a big raid. Carver would always brew a pot before they broke out the beers and the coke. He needed to get a buzz before the buzz. Robinson wondered how much partying he actually partook in.

"I'm sure he's just busy. We can't give up now."

Robinson blinked and Mosley was on him, left hand tight around his throat, squeezing the air out. He grabbed Mosley's wrist with two hands and tried to push it away, but couldn't. His mouth was open, and eyes were bulging, but air wouldn't come.

"This is not a game anymore," Mosley said. "I don't care what you're paying me. My brother is dead."

Robinson tried to say *you don't know that* but the words wouldn't come out. Blackness crept in at the corners of his eyes. Robinson shot his legs out underneath him, but couldn't catch Mosley.

Suddenly, air was back in a huge gasp. Mosley let go. Robinson coughed, his lungs filled, and the blackness faded away.

"I know you're frustrated," he said. "I understand it, but think of it this way."

Mosley punched the wall, but didn't break through.

"Listen to me!" Robinson coughed more.

Mosley stopped, was completely still again. He stared down Robinson, and Robinson worked to stare back.

"I know what it's like," he said. "To lose a sibling. To want revenge. I know."

A tremor ran through Mosley, and then he was still once more.

"But think of it this way. Don't you want those responsible to suffer? To feel the pain that you're going to be living with for the rest of your life? Don't make it quick. Make it hurt."

Mosley said, "Fine. Then I am going to tell Herrick where Donne is."

"Why?"

"I will make it hurt. I will make both of them hurt, but Donne needs to be back here. I can't work out of two locations.

You wanted Donne back here anyway."

Robinson rubbed his throat.

"So Herrick will succeed in his job—not that you really wanted him to. You just wanted him busy and distracted, am I right?"

Robinson nodded.

"I'm going up there." The words sounded like broken glass. "I will bring them back. And then I will crush them both. They will feel pain. I promise you that."

Before Robinson could say anything more, Mosley was gone.

CHAPTER 37

"**F**OURTEEN HOURS."

Herrick inadvertently hit the brakes as the voice he'd started becoming familiar with came through his Bluetooth. A car behind him hit the horn and then swerved into the center lane to pass. Out of the corner of his eye, Herrick caught the driver flipping him the bird.

Rain slicked the highway, and Herrick needed to pay more attention on the road.

"You have fourteen hours to go get Jackson Donne and bring him back here to me."

"I don't know where he is."

"That's okay, because I do." There was a knife edge to the voice that hadn't been there before.

Herrick forced himself to breathe, checked his blind spot, and then pulled over into the shoulder and stopped the car. His heart was thudding hard and sweat began to form on the back of his neck.

The icy cool to the voice was back now. Calm, but Herrick thought he detected a slight strain. Something minor, but he could feel it reverberate through the speakers. "If you do not go get Jackson Donne and then get back here in the next fourteen hours, I will kill everyone. Your team. Your family—oh wait, what family? Where is your father? Yes. I know about him. How about the friend you drank with last night? You think I don't know what I'm talking about? You've lost enough in life, Matt Herrick. Don't make the wrong decision now."

Herrick looked at the clock. Nearly noon. If the truth was being told, Donne couldn't be too far away.

"I thought you wanted me dead."

Herrick watched the raindrops explode off his windshield. He turned his wipers off and the drops turned into a clear sheet of water. He wiped the sweat away from the back of his neck, and then turned the temperature of the car down.

"How well do you know Vermont?"

"Killington?"

"We're going to go with a bit of a deeper track."

"If you know where he is, why don't you just go and get him yourself?" He bit the end of the question off.

"You don't need to know that. You don't need to know anything more about me."

Herrick chose his next words carefully. He kept thinking of this man as just a voice on the phone, but he needed to personify him. Make him more real than he was.

"Did I hurt you, Lucas?" The name was hard to say when it wasn't a challenge. Making Lucas real caused his chest to tighten, as if a python was squeezing the air out of his lungs.

Lucas answered with a hiss, like he'd let steam escape through his nose.

"How's your ankle, Lucas? Is that why you're not going to get Donne yourself? Maybe you can't. Maybe that's why you have to send decoys to try and frighten me. Because you're physically unable."

"I'm going to kill you for free. I'm going to finish the job that little Afghan boy couldn't."

Herrick closed his eyes. The sound of traffic slicing through the rain and past him was the only noise for a moment. Lucas had done this before, clearly. He knew the exact words to cut deep into the soul.

"So come and do it now," Herrick said.

"I need you. Isn't that clear? I will kill you. Yes, I will, but not before you do what I want. And you will, if you want the least amount of chaos to come back on you. Write this down."

Herrick scrambled for a pen and Post-it he kept in the console. Lucas rattled off an address of a town in Vermont he'd never heard of.

"Google Maps says you should be able to get there in about five and a half hours. At the time of night when you head back, it'll be a little less," Lucas said. "I'm being fair. That will give you just about two hours to do what you need to do."

"Is Donne putting you up to this?"

Now Lucas laughed, a deep belly laugh that washed over the interior of Herrick's car like a tidal wave.

"You have no idea what's going on, do you, Matt?"

"No, Lucas. I guess don't." Herrick typed the address into his GPS as he spoke. The little box gave him an arrival time of just over five and a half hours. "I just want to do my job and keep my friends safe."

"I know what you've been hired for. I know everything," Lucas said. "Maybe I'm helping you get paid."

"By threatening to kill my friends?"

"I had a teacher once, you know what she used to say when she would get me in trouble?" Thinking of Lucas as a child sitting in a middle school classroom wasn't computing. "She used to say 'It's not a threat, it's a promise.' You have fourteen hours."

"I need to find someone to cover my practice. Give me more time."

"You can figure that out on your own. Thirteen hours, fifty-nine minutes, and forty-six seconds."

The line went dead. An instant later, classic rock came pouring back through the speakers. Herrick allowed himself thirty seconds to get his nerves back. It was an old trick he taught himself in the desert, because if you stayed still for too long, they might just find you.

Fourteen hours.

Fourteen hours to find Jackson Donne, bring him back here, and figure out what the hell was going on.

Herrick pulled back on to the highway.

CHAPTER 38

DONNE LEFT THE car where it was and walked back to his cabin. The walk took an hour, and Donne used that time to clear his head — to try and chase the images of Mario and Steve away. He hoped the blood on his shirt and pants wasn't visible.

His chest and back felt tight and heavy, as if an anvil had been tied to his muscles. They pulled and tried to unwind, but never really did, no matter how much Donne stretched and twisted his torso as he walked. He had to look like a lunatic.

He opened the door and scanned the room. Nothing looked out of place. Nothing had been moved. If Steve was telling the truth, there was someone else coming. Donne could pack his stuff and hit the road. He'd already done it, but he wasn't ready to leave. No, his best bet was to stand his ground and wait for the new assailant. Once that person was dispatched with, Donne could figure out his next step.

With two bodies on his ledger, staying here didn't seem like a good idea. Donne went to the fridge, grabbed a Heady, and then went to the shower. The sweet hops and hot water eased his muscles. He stayed in the shower until the beer was gone, then toweled off and put the same clothes back on. If someone was going to find him tonight, he might as well wear the same stuff he'd already stained.

Donne went into his bedroom and found his gun. He cleaned it, loaded it, and went back into his living room and sat in the chair. He picked up the paperback he'd been reading and struggled with it for a while. His mind was still going too fast to focus on the words, and the muscles in his back ratcheted back into place again. He put his head back on the headrest and stared at the ceiling, controlling his breathing.

Around 6 p.m., there came a knock at the door. Donne took the gun and went to answer it.

NOTHING INTERESTING HAPPENED on road trips, Herrick thought. At first, he called his assistant to cover practice. He also called his buddies on the force to make sure there was a police cruiser outside for the entire practice, and then another hour beyond that. They reluctantly agreed after Herrick promised to take them all out for drinks during the Final Four.

Then he called Sarah. He expected her not to answer, after she hadn't responded to his text. Maybe he'd said something wrong the night before, the alcohol garbling his mind, but nothing stuck out to him, and he certainly wasn't blackout drunk. She hadn't said anything either, nothing that he found offensive.

The phone rang three times. She could be in a meeting, or in her office. The rules were so strict on cell phone usage during school hours that he figured she could just be ignoring him. Hadn't been that way in the past, but it seemed this would be the way it was. What had changed between them?

Sarah didn't answer.

"I'm going to be away this afternoon," he said.

He paused. What would Sarah want to hear in a message like this? Herrick took a deep breath, and tried to force the adrenaline in his bloodstream out of his voice.

"The players are gonna be okay." He filled her in on the

covered practice. He didn't say anything about the fact that a psychopath had threatened her and the team.

She hated when he did this. Any time he caught a case and had to run off and leave the practices in the hands of someone else, she let him hear it. The kids needed him.

"It's part of the job. It can't be helped. Hopefully, when I get back, this will all be over."

The GPS prompted him to merge left and he did. He watched twenty minutes quickly tick off the ETA of his trip. He must have avoided traffic somewhere.

"I just want to say I had a great time last night," Herrick said.

Pregnant pauses were the worst part of phone calls. If only he could see her face, and try to read her body language when she listened to the message.. He wished she was on the other end of this call, talking to him. He passed a car on the left.

"Maybe we could do another happy hour." He tried to put a smile in his voice, and as he said the words, he worried he'd pushed too far.

"I'll call you when I get back."

The line went dead, and Herrick stuck with satellite radio and the drone of the GPS voice for the next five hours.

DONNE POINTED THE gun in the man's face. The man—what did he say his name was? Herrick?—was spouting something about going back to New Jersey. Meanwhile, he had an ASP nightstick on his hip. Donne wasn't stupid, and he wasn't going to let this guy beat him to death.

Something about Herrick seemed legit. He was calm, no sweat, no nerves. Not the kind of tremor that signaled an assault anyway. Donne watched his eyes and saw that they didn't waver. They didn't look for an opening. He stayed calm, even with a gun aimed at him.

Then he said it.

And Donne agreed.

Things were incredibly complicated.

"I don't think you're a bad man, Jackson." Herrick had his hands jammed in his pockets. "I've talked to a lot of people about you. Your brother-in-law. Artie. Leo Carver, and they say—"

Donne felt the air go out of the room and his throat go cold.

"You talked to Leo Carver?"

Herrick nodded and licked his lips. "Yes. His name came up so I tracked him down."

"Where is he?"

"Come back with me to New Jersey, and let's sort this out."

Donne said, "Like hell. I hadn't heard Carver's name in years, and now it's come up twice in twenty-four hours."

He held the gun tight. If this guy twitched funny, all Donne had to do was squeeze.

PART II

GLORY DAYS

CHAPTER 39

THE MOMENT HE couldn't take it anymore.

It was three in the morning, and he wanted to firebomb something. His brain was buzzing with ideas of what to do next. Who to go after. Jesus Sanchez was always an easy target. They could make a run over there, bust him up some, and take his stash.

Bill Martin was all for it, his eyes red rimmed and his nose running. It must have been a special night. Usually, Martin was in check, keeping everyone in line.

Leo Carver sat back, arms crossed.

"Let's see what Alex brings back," he said.

"Alex sucks at this, he's going to bring back—downers probably." Donne rubbed his chin. He bounced his knees. His cell phone buzzed for the fourth time that night.

"Don't mess with Alex," Martin said. "He's a good egg."

Someone laughed, but to Donne it sounded like it came from far away in an echo chamber.

His cell phone buzzed again.

"Come on, Jesus is always good for more coke. And he's

probably got a case of Smirnoff Ice in the fridge. We're all off tomorrow," Donne said.

"Be cool," Carver said again. "Take it easy. We push too hard, we blow it. And we're having too much fun with blow to blow it."

Another laugh. Donne looked to his left but couldn't find the source. The room tilted and then righted itself. Like he was on a goddamn boat. His cell phone buzzed again. Maybe it was Alex Robinson.

Donne checked it.

Jeanne.

Where are you?

Six times in a row.

He quickly wrote back *working*. Hit send. Tapped his fingers on the table. Ran his hand through his hair. Whistled a tune. Waited for Alex.

Martin's cell phone went off next to him. He checked it, put the phone back in his pocket, and stood up.

"Well, gentlemen, it's been real. But I think I'm going to use some personal time."

Carver laughed. This time Donne knew it was him.

"Oh yeah? Got a date?"

Martin nodded. "Something like that. Don't get too crazy."

He buttoned his jacket, nodded toward Carver. He squeezed Donne's shoulder. And then he was gone.

Donne sniffled. He scratched his nose. Tapped his foot. Wanted to run a lap or two. Something. Do something.

Alex Robinson burst through the door with a bag of coke and two cases of Coors Light in tow.

Donne lost three days.

When he came to, he dragged himself home. He found Jeanne at the kitchen table. When she saw him, she burst into tears, but didn't run to him. He went to her and tried to give her a hug, but she leaned out of the way.

"I thought you were dead. I talked to Bill. I kept calling work. They told me you were fine, just busy. You didn't answer your phone. How many texts did I—"

"It's dead," he said.

Jeanne shook her head. "I thought you were."

"I'm sorry."

"No," she said. "That doesn't cut it anymore."

"What do you mean?"

"I'm leaving. Until you get your shit figured out, I'm gone."

For the first time, Donne noticed a bag at her feet.

"I was working."

"Like hell. You told me you had three days off coming up."

"I couldn't help it. Duty called.'

Jeanne laughed. "Partying called. Figure your shit out. Get cleaned up and get out of there."

Donne fumbled for words. Jeanne got up, picked up the bag, and stepped past him.

"Don't go," he said. "Please. I need you."

Jeanne opened the door. "Then where the hell were you the past three days? Where have you been?"

"I love you."

The door closed, and she was gone. Donne sat down at the table and stared at the clock on the wall. The second hand snapped forward in rhythm. Donne listened to it click and, for the first time in months, felt time pass.

After six minutes and twenty-three seconds, he went and found his landline phone. He dialed IAD. He told them he needed to talk.

It all moved very quickly after that.

CHAPTER 40

"THAT SUIT LOOKS big on you."

The Internal Affairs guy leaned against the table. Donne sat back and spread his hands.

"It's what I got."

"How much weight have you lost?"

Donne rubbed his face and didn't say anything. The room they sat in smelled like old cigarettes and burnt brownies. The walls were bare and wood sided. The floor was slick tile. A vending machine for soda and one for candy stood against the far wall.

"You should eat something."

And puke all over the place?

"What's the temperature in the courtroom?" Donne tapped a quick ditty on the table while he asked.

"The air conditioner is on. It's comfortable."

"Not too cold?"

IAD spread his hands. "I don't know. Why?"

"It's going to look really weird if I start sweating on the stand and it's fifty degrees in there."

IAD took a deep breath. His name was Duggan, but Donne didn't want to think of him by name. He just wanted to get this over with and get back to his life.

"We talked about this. We had this conversation already," IAD said.

Donne tapped more beats on the table. His foot bounced in sync with the rhythm.

"You're doing the right thing. Those five guys out there? Complete assholes."

"They were my team."

The door opened and a guy wearing a uniform held up five fingers. Three hundred seconds until Donne's life changed. The guy let the door swing closed.

IAD said, "They *were* your team. You woke up; you're saving your own ass. Judging by the amount of blow we found? You're saving your own life."

He needed to get back to Jeanne, that's all there was to this. Fix things with her. Doing this, making life right again, would help.

"I know what I'm doing," Donne said.

"So then go over it with me. When the lawyer asks who was behind all this you say...?" IAD rubbed his neck.

"Leo Carver." Donne sighed. "What did Chief say about him? He's been here forever."

"Carver came over from New York City," IAD said.

Donne shook his head. "Came *back* from New York to run the New Brunswick Narc squad. He and Bill Martin came up together, walked the beat together. Carver got another opportunity to go to the city, Martin worked homicide for a while. Then after the mob stuff, Carver came back. To help his city, he said."

"I don't need the history lesson," IAD said. "I need you to finger Carver as the ringleader. Martin's turn is next week. The rest? Fuck them, they can get off lightly. But you can put the top guy away, and you'll get your promotion. Your honorable discharge as it were."

Donne shrugged his shoulders and felt the jacket sag

against them. How much weight had he lost? It'd been one meal a day, maybe. Nights awake waiting for them to come for him. Waiting for the end. But he was still here. His stomach never growled anymore. Forcing food down felt like he was swimming upstream.

IAD leaned over. His breath smelled rancid. He put a hand on Donne's shoulder, but Donne shifted and let it slide off.

"You have to take care of yourself, Jackson. You were a good cop once. This will help you be one again. We can't have this department running like that. You know the saying, the one from the Academy: 'Imagine the headline.'"

Donne said, "We actually made the headline."

"And now you can make a better one."

The door opened again, and the same guy came back.

"It's time," he said.

IAD put his hand out to help Donne stand, but he ignored it. IAD was giving directions or last-minute advice, but it was all white noise. Donne turned toward the door and started walking. Everything in him felt light and full of electricity. His brain flashed through the last three years: raids, coke, beers.

He walked through the door into a long white hall. A man wearing corduroy pants and a shirt with a hole in the elbow sat on a bench and stared at him. Donne stared straight ahead, walking toward the double doors at the end of the stretch.

Thirty-four paces.

That's how long it took him to get to those doors. The bailiff held the door. Donne walked through it into the courtroom. The judge stared at him. Thirteen jurors stared at him. The DA. The defense attorney.

Leo Carver didn't. He stared straight ahead toward the empty witness stand. Donne caught a glimpse of a stoic Bill Martin in the audience. He was bouncing his knees. Donne wondered if he was thinking about when his trial would come.

The room was frigid, and sent a shiver through his body. As far as he could tell, he wasn't sweating. Air was coming into his lungs evenly. The static in his ears settled down.

Donne swore to tell the whole truth, and then strode to the stand.

CHAPTER 41

||||||||||||||||||||||||||||||||||||||||||||||||||||||||||||||||||||||||||||||||||||||||||||||||||||||||||||||||||||||||||||||||||

THE CHAIR WAS leather and creaked when Donne shifted his weight. There was enough whispering in the room to cover the sound when he leaned back and took a deep breath. He folded his hands on his lap to keep from wiping his face or giving off any other kind of poker tells.

The lawyer — Lester Russell — from the prosecution stood up, tugged at his lapels, and sniffled. Donne rolled his shoulders and cracked his neck. The judge tapped his fingers. Bill Martin got up and left the room.

Russell looked over the jury, and then turned to Donne.

"Mr. Donne, can you explain your time on the New Brunswick Police Department's Narcotics force?"

As far as Donne knew, he was the last witness. The key to the prosecution's case. Russell was part of the DA office, one of their rising stars. Russell always seemed to have had one coffee too many, bee-bopping and bouncing his legs as he worked. When he first met Donne, his hands never stopped going, *rat-a-tat-tat*ting off the top of his desk

Today, however, he seemed to be the opposite. Dark circles

under his eyes. Hair slightly out of place. Donne wondered if he'd been up all night prepping.

Donne said, "I've been a member of the Narcs for the past three years. We started when Leo Carver came back from New York. It'd been all over the news. The mayor's kid had ODed and died on crack, and then two more Rutgers kids did as well. The mayor wanted the New Brunswick drug problem halted, at any cost. They brought Carver back and paired him with Bill Martin, assembling a team. We worked in pairs. Me and Bill and Carver and Robinson, and Henderson and Moore. We broke up some of the rackets."

Donne kept his eyes trained on Russell, even though he could feel heat from Carver's eyes burning into him. He didn't want to shift his glance away, and tried not to fidget.

"When you signed up for the Narc Division, what were your goals?"

Donne broke the glare and looked down at his hands. Back up again. "I wanted to do the right thing. Put away criminals. Clean up the streets."

"And were those goals achieved?"

Here was the tricky part. For the most part, the Narc Division did their part—achieved their publicly stated goal. They just skimmed off the top at the same time. He needed to sell the jury on that. These guys—the underlings—weren't bad. They just got greedy. Basically, he had to keep his own neck as clean as possible.

"We did," he said. "We put the bad guys away, just like we were asked. We cleaned up the streets."

"Was that all you did?"

"Objection!" The defense attorney stood up.

The judge frowned at him and said, "Overruled."

"No," Donne said, after the judge asked him to answer the question. "That's not all we did. We also had a lot of fun."

There was a murmur from the jury box.

"Care to explain?" Russell prompted.

"We partied. We drank beer. Well, Bill liked Scotch. We did coke, a *lot* of coke, smoked weed."

Russell nodded. "The Narc Division—the one tasked to clean up the New Brunswick drug problem—partied and did drugs? That's ironic."

"Objection!"

"Sustained. This is not the place to opine, Mr. Russell." The judge stared Russell down. "A question perhaps?"

"Where did you get the drugs that you partied with?"

"The evidence locker," Donne said.

"Is that legal?"

"No."

"So, why do it?"

"We wanted to party. Most of us were young."

"How did it start? Just because you were young doesn't mean you don't know what is right and what is wrong."

Donne took a deep breath. Now they were getting to the meat of the issue.

"We were told it was okay. We watched our boss do it. In fact, we were pushed to do it."

"Pushed? How?"

Donne remembered sitting in the undercover car he and Martin used, under the lone streetlight in an alley. They'd just busted up one of the local bit dealers, called the beat guys to bring him in. It wasn't the biggest case, but it was something, so Martin told him they were going to celebrate. He passed Donne a joint, one he'd taken off the dealer.

"It was a right of passage. It proved you were a part of the team. Blood brothers. If you all did it, none of you would turn on your brothers."

"Were your bosses the ones who forced this upon you?"

The question was meant to set up Martin's trial later, as well as take care of Carver.

Donne nodded. "My boss did. Yes."

Russell didn't catch the phrasing.

"Can you say who they were? And if they're in the courtroom, point them out to us?"

Donne's stomach did a back flip. He turned to see Leo Carver shooting daggers his way. Carver barely moved.

It felt like time was ticking by at the speed of a sloth.

Donne pointed at Leo Carver. "Leo Carver made me do it."

Carver barely shifted in his chair. Russell put his hands behind his back.

"Only Leo Carver?"

"Yes," Donne said. "Only Leo Carver."

He and Martin were partners. Partners for a long time. They were still brothers. Tied together.

"Are you sure?" Russell asked. "No one else was involved."

"We all did bad things," Donne said. "But only at the command of Leo Carver."

Russell stalked back to the prosecution table. He shuffled through his papers, reading something back to himself.

"And what about Bill Martin? How was he involved? Did he force you into smoking weed or sampling cocaine?"

"Objection! This trial only has to do with my client."

"Sustained."

Russell tried one more time. "Do you remember being deposed, Mr. Donne? In that deposition, you explicitly state Bill Martin made you try weed, told you that only then were you part of a team."

"Objection!"

"Sus —"

"I must have been mistaken." It felt like all the muscles in Donne's back released their tension at the same time, sending a spasm through him.

Russell sighed. "No further questions."

CHAPTER 42

"**W**HAT THE HELL was that?"

Lester Russell wiped at his nose with a handkerchief as he paced back and forth in front of Donne. They were in the same room with the vending machines. Donne sipped on an overly sweet iced tea. The judge had adjourned for a short break before closing statements.

"I told the truth," Donne said after swallowing.

Russell nodded and then slammed about thirty pages of typed deposition in front of Donne.

"So you lied three months ago?"

Donne shrugged. Drank more iced tea.

"How the hell am I going to spin this next week?" Russell asked.

Donne didn't answer, but wasn't expected to. The defense had cross-examined him and tried to throw some dirt on everything, but Donne held up. Steadfast that Carver was the one who orchestrated the evidence. They tried to question Donne's drug use, but Russell cleared that up on cross-examination. He was forced to do it. He wasn't addicted.

Donne tried to control the shakes that threatened to wrack his entire body. The aluminum can gave way a bit underneath his fingers.

IAD burst through the door, pulled out the chair opposite Donne and dropped down into it. He put his hands flat on the table and leaned in. Donne drank more iced tea.

"What the hell was that?" IAD got spittle all over his side of the table.

Donne nodded toward Russell. "He already asked that."

IAD looked up at Russell, who blew his nose again.

"How long have we been working on this, Jackson?"

It *had* moved quickly. Just six months ago, Donne sat in a room just like the one in the courthouse, big, white, and smelly. He laid it all out for IAD. Told them about Leo Carver and Bill Martin. Told them it was time to get out and do the right thing. That it wasn't enough to put away drug dealers, if you were just going to steal evidence. That was part of the truth; the other part was saving his own skin.

IAD and his partner were like wedding planners that day. They moved quickly, asking if they could get Donne anything. Refilling his coffee. Jotting notes and offering short suggestions. He was in good hands, they told him, just do what he was doing now and everything would be okay.

But Donne didn't follow their advice. Bill Martin was off the table.

"I don't understand why this is such a big deal," Donne said. "You have Carver dead to rights. He was the ringleader. He was the boss-man. You got him. All Lester has to do is nail the closing argument and you have your man."

"We want both of them. We should put away the whole team. But we won't. Those other guys—like you—will get laid off or fired or some shit we'll come up with. But Martin is an asshole. To take him down would have been gold. You're going to testify against him next week."

"No."

"Then your dismissal will be dishonorable."

Donne said, "I gave you what you wanted. Put the bastard

away. Leave Bill alone."

IAD slammed his palms on the table. "Maybe I was wrong. It wasn't Martin. You're the asshole here."

Donne finished his iced tea while IAD stormed out of the room. Russell waited for the click of the door and then used his fingers to count to ten. He put a business card down in front of Donne.

"You screwed me, Jackson."

Donne picked up the card and looked at it. It advertised Lester Russell as having his own business, doing defense. The card had an established date on it. The current year.

He looked up at Russell.

"I'm going private. Working defense instead of state prosecution could be lucrative for me. But I was supposed to go out on top, a superstar for the prosecution. I was gonna put away two corrupt cops. Headlines are the best billboards, Jackson. Remember that." He put his handkerchief into his pocket.

"You can still put away Carver."

Russell shook his head. "I can and I will. And that'll be nice. But two cops? Aw, man. The crooks would have loved me. I'd be gold. Puts away two cops and then goes to work for the other side? Hoo boy. Cha-ching." He rubbed his forefinger and thumb together. "Now, with your testimony, it'll look like I lost."

"You didn't."

"You're a terrible liar. They all saw it on the stand."

Donne smiled. "I didn't lie."

Russell sighed. "All right, Jackson. If I know you, you're going to need a defense attorney a time or two for the rest of your life. If you do, keep that card. I like you. Something about you. You're a good guy. You just make terrible decisions."

"Don't need to be smart to be a cop, I guess."

Russell laughed. He brushed off his suit jacket, tugged at his tie, and said, "I have to go give a closing argument. Be good, sir."

Russell disappeared. Donne got another iced tea. He sat in

the room, nursing it for an hour. He told himself he could hear the verdict on the news or in the paper. He finished his iced tea and stood up. He pushed the doors open and walked down the long hallway toward the courtroom.

He had to be there for the verdict. Had to know how it ended.

This time the courtroom didn't hush over in silence for him. No one even knew he entered the room. They were all focused on Russell, who was waving his arms and doing what looked to be some weird interpretive dance while he spoke. Donne took a seat in the back and waited.

Forty-five minutes later, after the defense gave their statement, the jurors were given the rules on how to come to a verdict.

Twenty minutes after that, they came back in. Leo Carver guilty.

Donne rubbed his face and watched them take Carver from the room. He watched Bill Martin shake hands with his attorney. Someone else was giving Lester Russell a hug. Donne lost track of Bill Martin in the crowd.

And then, Martin was standing in front of Donne. Hands in his pockets, leaning against the bench.

"That was my best friend," he growled.

Donne didn't respond.

"Leo Carver was my best friend," Martin said again. "I *will* destroy you one day."

The following week, the charges against Bill Martin were dropped. He never was told exactly why.

CHAPTER 43

DONNE SLUMPED ON the couch. A Molson was popped on the coffee table in front of him. He watched the sweat drip off the bottle and form in a pool around it. The TV was on, some sitcom that he was having trouble following. Didn't matter, it was just white noise. It felt like his brain wasn't working correctly, like a psychic electrician was up there crawling around, pulling wires and plugging them back in to see what happened.

The clock on the cable box flipped ahead another minute. He wondered briefly how long he'd sat there and then realized it didn't matter. All that mattered was when she got home. When he could tell her it was over, he was out. That was what Jeanne had wanted for the last six months, for life to get back to normal.

Another drop of sweat dribbled off the glass. Donne had only taken two sips in the past hour. The beer was probably warm by now. He wrapped his hand around it, picked the bottle up, and took a swig. Nope. It was fine. He took another sip and then placed it back on the puddle.

The door downstairs creaked open, and the ADT security monitor beeped. Electricity ran through Donne's chest and he sat up and wiped his mouth. He pulled the loosened tie around his neck completely off and tossed it on to the chair next to him. Jeanne's footsteps were gentle, like always, and he counted each stair. Living on the second floor of a two-family house brought familiarity he'd never expected. Counting the stairs until he could see his fiancée was one of them.

She pushed the door open, looked him over, and slumped against the door jamb.

"Is it finished?" she asked.

Donne nodded. His head felt like it was full of stones.

"How'd it go?"

He took a long drink of beer before answering. Finished the bottle off. Jeanne didn't move.

"Guilty."

As if someone had squeezed her tight, all the air went out of Jeanne. She laughed, and then came over and sat next to Donne, putting a hand on his shoulder. She rubbed his back and gave him a kiss on the cheek.

"I'm proud of you," she said.

"Thanks."

"Tell me about it."

He went through it slowly, recounting each question. He told her how he felt, how he didn't even want to look at them. She nodded and kept rubbing his back.

"Lester asked, and I told them," he said. "Leo Carver was in charge of it all."

"And Bill Martin?"

Donne exhaled. "He had nothing to do with it."

She stopped rubbing his back. Her hand jumped off his shirt like it'd been stuck in an electrical outlet.

"What do you mean?"

"I mean—" Donne shook his head. "He was my partner. We'd been through so much together. I just felt like..."

"You're *not* going to testify against him?"

Donne put his face into his palms and rubbed. Jeanne had

moved a few inches away from him.

"Leo Carver started it all. He was the man behind it. He deserves to go to jail. Twenty years they got him for. No parole."

Jeanne sat with her arms crossed in front of her. She leaned back against the cushions.

"What's going to happen to you now?"

Donne shrugged. "I'm out of a job. They're finished with me."

"Unemployment?"

Donne shook his head. "A nice severance, so I have some time."

"And what's going to happen to Bill Martin?"

After running a hand through his hair, Donne said, "I think they're going to demote him. He's been in the department for so long, they're hesitant to get rid of him."

"That's bullshit."

Donne nodded. "Probably. But it's politics."

"You should have—"

He turned to her and saw the tears in her eyes. Reaching over, he put his hands on her thighs. For an instant, it seemed like she flinched, but Donne was sure that was his imagination.

"What's wrong?" he said.

"You." The word was like a sharp dagger. "You're too rash. You make stupid choices."

"We're going to be fine," he said. "Everything is going to be okay."

"You have no idea what's going on. You're too blind."

The laugh track from the sitcom chimed in inappropriately. Donne grabbed the remote and turned the set off. The air in the apartment was very still, and seemed to hang there waiting for one of them to make the next move. Donne noticed another minute pass on the set top box.

"I don't understand."

Jeanne stood up and walked over to the door. Slammed it shut.

"You have to clean up, Jackson. Go to rehab."

"It's just a beer."

"You think I don't know you've been sneaking blow the past few weeks? Not every day, but once or twice? You think I can't tell. Your nerves are rattled. You're missing stuff."

"What am I missing?"

Static was whooshing through Donne's brain and he was having trouble focusing. He was clean. Today he was clean. No coke. Just a beer. That's all. They were supposed to be celebrating.

"Maybe when you clean up, you'll figure it out. I've basically been broadcasting it to you. Should hire a skywriter."

"I don't understand."

"Get clean, Jackson. Get clean or it's over between us."

Jeanne took the ring off her finger, dropped it on the coffee table, and stormed out of the room. Seconds later, the bedroom door slammed. Still, he could hear muffled sobs through the wood paneling. He put the TV on to cancel it out, but it didn't work. He couldn't keep it quiet. Couldn't shut the noise in his head off either.

Not twelve hours later, Jackson Donne found himself in rehab. A year later he opened his own private detective agency.

Five years after that, he was on the run.

And today — in Vermont, of all places — it all caught up with him.

PART III

IT'S HARD TO BE A SAINT IN THE CITY

CHAPTER 44

MATT HERRICK NEEDED time, but didn't have any. By his count, there were maybe eight hours left to convince Donne to get into a car with him and head back to New Jersey before people started dying. But doing that while having a gun pointed at your head wasn't exactly a walk in the park.

Or, for that matter, a dark alley.

"Listen, Jackson," Herrick said, "I have two options, either I can take that gun off you right now or we can be men about this."

"You're a peon. You can't take this gun from me."

"You're not who you used to be, you seem like you've had a couple beers and I'm a former Marine. Come on. Think about it."

Donne flared his nostrils. "I don't want to go back."

"You want more blood on your hands? Like what's on your sleeve?"

Donne flinched and Herrick had his opening. He snapped his body across the room, reached out, and grabbed Donne's wrist. He twisted the gun away from his body, down at the floor. With this free hand, he snatched the weapon away. He brought it back up and cleared the chamber. He dropped the gun on to the couch, letting it out of his grip like it was on fire.

Donne nodded. "Nice."

Herrick said, "Let's go back."

"The minute I set foot in New Jersey, I'm locked up. Put away for something I didn't do." Donne stared off to his right; his voice got smaller. "It was all Bill Martin."

Herrick had followed the news last summer, who hadn't? Donne had been the logical suspect, but the cops kept saying they wanted him for questioning. Never overtly said he was the state senator's killer. And, like smoke in the air, Donne faded from the airwaves. Forgotten.

"You're smart. You know that's not true. I haven't heard your name in the media in almost a year. You've been forgotten about. You think they didn't clear your name with ballistics or DNA or some CSI craziness? I talked to a cop about you, they just want to question you."

Donne shook his head.

"Listen," Herrick said, "I'm going to level with you. If we don't get back to New Jersey in the next seven hours, a man is going to kill someone very important to me."

Outside something squeaked. An odd bit of wildlife, Herrick guessed. Donne didn't seem to notice it. Probably like that fridge in the apartment that hummed. Herrick never heard it unless he had a guest who pointed it out.

"Who is trying to kill—You're bullshitting." Donne paused. "What are you talking about?"

Herrick laid it on the line. "One of your former cop buddies hired me to find you. He thought you were trying to kill him. Two of your other colleagues are dead and Alex Robinson is scared. He hired me to find you before you got to him."

Donne shook his head. He put a hand on his easy chair to steady himself. "That *definitely* wasn't me."

"A man named Lucas Mosley has been messing with my life ever since."

Holding up a hand, Donne said, "Like Steve Mosley?"

"Yes, why? What?"

"Steve was here. Steve was—" Donne tugged on the sleeve to his shirt, and Herrick felt his stomach crawl into the soles of his shoes.

"Do you know Alex Robinson well?" Donne asked, his eyes lighting up.

"We're both PIs," Herrick said. "We've crossed paths." He didn't add anything else. Nothing about their past.

"In a good way?"

Before Herrick could answer, the squeak came again, louder this time. Donne straightened.

"That's not an animal," Herrick said, realization washing over him.

"Brakes," Donne said.

Before either could say anything else, the glass shattered and the room was filled with the sound of gunfire.

CHAPTER 45

THE GLASS WAS the first thing to hit Donne. Like sharp pieces of ice. They sprayed over him as he dove to the floor. He rolled until he was up against the couch, and then brushed some of the glass off. It sliced the side of his left hand and the pain wrapped its way up his arm like a snake. Bullets thudded into the walls.

He scanned the room for his gun, and for Herrick. He found the person first, on the other side of the room, crouching on the floor. The nightstick of his was out, full length, like it would be useful in this hail of bullets. Donne couldn't find where Herrick dropped the gun, though. The bullets kept flying, each round sounding like a cannon in the cold night.

For the first time in over a year, Donne hoped someone had heard and called the cops.

He got on to his stomach and military-crawled in toward the kitchen, away from the incoming fire. As he moved, he felt along the carpet for the gun. He caught a few more shards of glass in his hand instead.

"God damn it," he yelled. "Where did you put the gun?"

No answer. For an instant, Donne though maybe Herrick had one in the chest and was bleeding out, but he turned to see Herrick still crouched. His lips were moving too. The roar of the gunfire was too much.

Didn't this asshole have to reload soon? What did he have? A minigun?

A bullet caught his table lamp, and with a crash everything went dark. He'd never find the gun now. The only light came from the kitchen, and Donne continued to crawl that way. With luck, he could curl up in the fetal position until the assailant got bored.

And, just like that, the gunfire stopped. Donne listened to the remaining glass fall from the windows. Listened to the leaves blow in the wind. Felt the cold air on his skin, along with the pinprick pain from the cuts on his hand. His breath was ragged and his chest felt tight.

An iPhone went off, signaling a text message.

"What the hell?" Donne said.

He rolled onto his back and tried to catch his breath. At any moment there could be another volley of bullets, or someone could burst through that front door. His muscles were on high alert, fast-twitch and ready to go, like a ballplayer waiting for a hundred-mile-an-hour heater.

Then: "Son of a bitch. Son of a bitch."

Donne snapped up with a quick sit-up, and looked toward Herrick. He cursed himself for putting his body back in the line of fire, but Herrick shook his head.

A car engine started and then pulled away, the sound of the engine fading into the night.

"It's over," Herrick said, holding up his phone. He stood up and brushed glass off his pants. Then he tossed Donne the phone.

After catching it, Donne had to flip it around to read the text. It was from a blocked number.

It read: ANY TIME I WANT. YOU HAVE SIX HOURS.

Donne put the phone on his lap and looked at the walls. There had to be a hundred bullets embedded into the drywall.

Instinct told him to grab a shell and save it. Bring it to ballistics.

Yeah, because that's how his life worked now.

"What does this mean?" he asked, tossing Herrick his phone back.

"It means if we're not back in New Jersey in six hours, people I care about die."

"Why didn't he finish the job now? We were dead to rights."

"This guy is fucked up. He doesn't just want to kill me. He wants to mess with me."

Donne closed his eyes. Both brothers were psychopaths.

"And what about me?"

Herrick said, "Did you kill his brother?"

Donne didn't answer. The image of Steve Mosley's crushed head ran through his mind, a bloody piece of meat. His stomach turned, and his breath caught hard in his throat.

"I need a beer."

Donne pushed himself to his feet.

"You?"

Herrick said, "I think I'm due a bourbon after this."

He went into the kitchen and saw the refrigerator riddled with bullets. He grabbed the handle and pulled. One or two of the bullets had made it inside. The shelves were covered in splattered ketchup and spilled Heady Topper.

Donne shook his head at the carnage.

"You're right. It's time to go back," he said.

Herrick came into the kitchen, while compressing his nightstick. He looked over Donne's shoulder but didn't say anything.

"We're going to find out everything about this Mosley guy, what makes him tick, and why he's after you and me. What it has to do with Alex Robinson. And then we're going to take him down."

He slammed the fridge door shut, and said, "You know how hard it is to find that stuff?"

Herrick nodded, but didn't speak.

"Damn it," Donne said. "I was happy here."

It may not have been exactly true. Not after what he saw a

year ago, when he finally decided to look at the news, when he saw Kate was gone. He'd just gotten Jeanne back, just cleared that from his soul, when he lost another one. It didn't matter though; it was ages ago. He was as happy as he could be here. Chopping wood, drinking beer, and reading pulpy thrillers.

That time was over.

"Six hours?"

"Yeah."

"Can you get us back in four?"

"Yeah."

"Let's move."

Donne packed a duffel bag in less than five minutes, and then they went outside. They took it slow, moving to Herrick's car, keeping an eye out for their stalker. They looked for the glint of a gun barrel in the moonlight. The sound of squeaking brakes. They heard nothing. Saw nothing.

Ten minutes later they were on the interstate. Donne's heart pounded, and his palms were sweaty.

He focused on the horizon ahead of him.

CHAPTER 46

WHEN DONNE WAS a kid, after his father had left, his mother used to take his sister and him on road trips to Florida. A two-day drive that started at five in the morning the first day, stopped overnight somewhere in South Carolina, and ended in Orlando. They'd hit the parks, maybe take another long ride to the beach one day, and then come back a week and a half later.

What always stuck out to Donne when he was a kid was how things changed during the time they were away. The local billboard near their home off the parkway always seemed to change. The city would put a new speed limit sign in. Minor changes, but to an eight-year-old, it felt like life had changed. The world went on even when he wasn't there.

As Herrick gassed the car across the NJ border and onto the parkway, Donne was struck with the same feeling. The rest stop where the Starbucks had been was now a Burger King and a Dunkin' Donuts. They'd added digital signs every ten miles or so. Today, they advertised a silver alert, looking for a blue Toyota Solara. They crossed over Route 17 and the car dealerships he could see were still the same. Cars still hummed at a breakneck pace, passing on the right and refusing to get out of the way of people entering the highway. And there were still the left lane slowpokes that policed the speed limit on their own accord; slothlike vigilantes keeping everyone from getting to their destination.

The familiarity caused Donne's heart to race. It felt like a small lizard was crawling up and down under the skin of his arms. He shifted in his seat and tugged on his seatbelt. He told himself to focus on his breathing. Which, of course, was when Herrick decided to speak.

"He's going to call me as soon as we get to Hoboken," he said.

Herrick had filled Donne in on the ride down. It was amazing; this guy with his fresh-shaved face and his close-cropped military hair cut just kept talking for the first hour of the trip. Spilling everything like they were best buds that hadn't seen each other in a few years. Basketball, Alex Robinson, a mugging. Donne wouldn't have told this guy anything.

"We may have an hour on him, the way you pushed the tempo."

Herrick shrugged while keeping both hands on the wheel. "I don't know what to tell him."

"You tell him the truth. That I'm there."

"He's going to want to come and get you."

Donne nodded. "Seems like a good trap to set."

"We don't even know why this is happening."

"If we can catch Lucas, it might be an easy way to find out." Donne rubbed his hands together. "You wouldn't see it, would you?"

Herrick glanced away from the road. "See what?"

"This is all about me."

"That part I got."

Donne rubbed his face. That damned insect had replaced the adrenaline that had been coursing through his veins, and now all he wanted was to shut his eyes and make it all go away.

"Why now?"

Herrick said, "You were in the news?"

"I've been in the news before. They've left me alone for years, and now Alex Robinson comes back making up stuff about me. Someone's sent a hit man on my tail." Donne rubbed his mouth.

Herrick said, "You were on the run. You were vulnerable."

"Not good enough. I was hurt and I was down. That should have been enough. That should have been the revenge. It was Bill's plan."

"Except Bill Martin died. You killed him. You took out another one of their own."

Donne nodded. "Bill was Leo's best friend and vice versa. It's why Bill was always over me."

Herrick didn't speak. Donne was grateful for a moment of quiet. He let the situation play out over itself. Herrick talked to Leo Carver. That's the only reason Donne listened to him. He said he talked to Carver.

"You got into the prison?" Donne said. "They'd kept him locked up pretty good, even though it was general pop. It was hard to talk to him."

"So, you kept track of him?"

"Early on."

"He's not in prison anymore. He's been declared insane. He's in an institution."

Donne blinked. Opened his mouth. Closed it.

Herrick told him about Sandy, about the legal case. Then the move, and how hard it still was to talk to him.

"Damn," Donne said. "He waited that long to make a move, get out into the open."

"I had to bullshit my way in there."

Donne nodded. "And if it was that easy for you, how do you think it went for others? I'm sure he's finally been in contact with the outside world. He heard about Bill. He's pissed."

"So why kill the other two?"

Donne shrugged. "You're the detective."

Donne looked out the window and watched the streetlights pass above them. Herrick hit his left blinker and took the exit onto Route 3. They were going to Herrick's apartment. Donne wasn't home yet.

"We need to buy ourselves some time," Donne said. "Need space to figure out exactly what's going on. Who Mosley is. How Carver is pulling the strings here."

"*If* he's pulling the strings."

"And why Robinson brought you in on this in the first place. Why he put you in danger. Alex Robinson isn't an idiot. He knew what he was doing."

"And how do we get ourselves that time?"

Donne sighed. Counted to five. Rolled it over in his brain.

"Two hours until your deadline. That's how long we have to come up with a plan."

"Totally doable," Herrick said.

"Well," Donne said. "At least you're confident."

He put his head back on the seat as Herrick slammed down on the gas. The cars they passed were metallic blurs. At this time of night, there weren't many on the road anyway.

Lived in Vermont for over a year, nary a problem. Back in New Jersey for forty minutes and there was a target on his back.

"This state sucks," Donne said out loud.

CHAPTER 47

ERRICK'S APARTMENT SMELLED like nutmeg. It felt like Thanksgiving and Christmas all rolled into one, which, Donne guessed, was appropriate. Christmas was coming after all. The coffee table was spotless and empty except for a book on basketball strategies. The carpet had been vacuumed recently. There were two filing cabinets in the corner, each labeled, though Donne couldn't read what they said. The TV, a big flat-screen, was the center of attention.

Donne wanted to pass out. His temples were throbbing, and his eyelids felt heavy. No time for that, though. The clock was ticking. Herrick said they had maybe an hour and fifty-five minutes to figure this out. To buy themselves more time.

"Why didn't he kill us up there?" Donne asked, while plopping down on the couch. It was leather, but felt soft enough that it could envelop him. "He had us."

Herrick dropped the ASP on the coffee table.

Donne said, "He could have walked in, shot us both in the head, and gone home to collect his reward. There's clearly more here."

"He thinks it's a game. We're being toyed with."

Donne shook his head. "There's more. You toy with someone too long, you give them the chance to fight back."

"Let's fight back, then," Herrick said.

For the first time, Donne noticed Herrick rubbing his ribs. He opened his mouth to ask, but thought better of it. It was something he might be able to use later.

Herrick went into the kitchen and came out with a beer and a bottle of bourbon.

"I don't drink beer much," Herrick said. "But this is a good one."

It was called Carton Boat Beer. He accepted it and took a sip. It was low on alcohol but had a ton of flavor. He took another sip, the watery hops cascading down his throat. For once, he didn't miss Heady Topper. He put the bottle on the table, without a coaster, next to the ASP.

Donne watched Herrick, trying to figure him out. He got the gun off Donne quick, up in Vermont. He was faster than he looked, but Donne was pretty sure he didn't have a gun of his own. When he put Donne's gun down, he'd dropped it like it was burning his hands.

Herrick caught him staring.

"You don't trust me yet, do you?" Herrick asked.

"Why should I? The only reason I'm here is because someone shot up my house. You show up and someone shoots at me. Not something that happens too often." He picked up the beer and took another slug. "Anymore."

"I could have killed you in the car, if that was my goal. I could have made sure you got shot in the house. My job was to find you and bring you back."

"Except you could have left me there. You know Robinson is wrong. There's something off on him."

"If I hadn't brought you back, people were going to die."

Donne shrugged. "Still might."

"I need your help."

"I don't do that anymore." Donne sighed. "Any time I'm around people die. Just the way it goes."

"You can trust me."

"I'm working on believing that."

Herrick hadn't taken a sip of his bourbon yet. He was tapping his thigh. The nightstick was still on the table. Donne played through possibilities. Herrick shifted on his seat, inching his right hand closer to the table.

"How are we going to do this? I am devoid of ideas."

"Devoid?" Donne counted the distance. Herrick was farther from the ASP than Donne was. He could get to it first.

Herrick said, "It was the long drive. My vocabulary improves when I'm exhausted. It's a curse."

"Here's my thought." Donne polished off the beer. Herrick still hadn't taken a sip.

"Thank God."

"I think you brought me here, and now you're killing time until Mosley gets here. I think you're going to hand me over, and you're letting me talk this out to buy yourself whatever time you need."

Herrick tilted his head at him. "I'm a basketball coach. I'm not a hired killer. Investigating is my side gig. Do you think I'm going to ruin that by working with murderers?"

"I think, if this threat on your friends is true — and you won't even mention them by name — then you'll do anything to save them. Human nature. What do I mean to you?"

"You're the job."

"What's the matter with your ribs?"

The tangent caught Herrick off guard, and he looked down toward his hands. Donne leapt forward, stepped over the table, and swung a right fist hard into Herrick's ribs, right where he'd been rubbing. Herrick screamed out and fell backwards, into the table next to the couch.

Donne gave him another kick to the ribs, and Herrick went down to the carpet hard. He reached up to try to get to his feet, but Donne didn't wait on him. He sprinted to the front door, out into the hallway, and hit the staircase. He took the steps two at a time, and was out on the street.

The road was quiet, the bars closed, and most of the world

sleeping. Donne took the first corner hard and ran into an alley. He leaned against the wall, letting the cold night air wash over his face.

Maybe Herrick wasn't going to just hand him over, but Donne couldn't take that risk. And, at the very best, he'd bought Herrick the time he wanted and they could both work to end this.

At the worst, Donne was on the run again, and a target was on his back—and he'd lost his only ally.

He checked his watch. Three hours to kill before the first train to New Brunswick left the station. Best to keep moving until then. He pulled his jacket tight around his chest and started off into the night. The sound of faraway sirens faded away from him.

Donne walked aimlessly. He wanted to leave this all in someone else's lap, but he knew better. Twelve hours earlier, he'd killed a man and buried two bodies in the dirt.

This was all about him, and everyone else was collateral damage.

Violence always found him.

CHAPTER 48

"I WANT TO TALK to him," Lucas said.

Herrick had the phone on speaker, an ice pack pressed to his ribs, and a can of beer pressed against his forehead. Screw being on the clock.

"He's not here."

A beat. Herrick took a sip.

"Then someone dies."

Herrick took a breath. The image of the boy in Afghanistan danced in front of him, like a flicker movie on an old TV. His arms akimbo. Yelling. Herrick could feel his hand going for his gun. Realizing the gunshot he'd heard only seconds earlier was the boy killing a guard to get through security.

"Someone always dies," he said. His ribs throbbed against the ice.

"You disappoint me, Matt. You're giving up? Willing to go through more personal pain?"

The boy was still screaming. The jacket flopped open and Herrick saw the straps and the wires. He pulled his gun, wrapped his finger around the trigger in one swift move.

The boy shouted louder, and Herrick squeezed the trigger. A thunderclap.

Herrick tried to blink it away. The boy falling backward. The cloud of dust surrounding him as he hit the ground. Herrick dropped his own gun. Soldiers ran toward the body.

"Why are you afraid of me?" Herrick asked.

Lucas laughed.

"I'm serious," Herrick said. "You're scared. You had me in your sights, and you missed. You had Donne in your sights and you missed. Instead, you're playing this game, threatening others. Come at me."

"You don't want that," Lucas said.

"No," Herrick said. "I do. You already took a shot at me, and I'm still standing. How about you? How's your ankle?"

He saw the gun on the ground. His gun still hot, outlined in Afghan sand. He swore he'd never fire it again. He'd never need to fire a gun again. There were other ways to fight. He'd been trained in them. But killing a boy—him or me—no matter what the stakes? No more shooting.

"Where is Jackson Donne?"

Herrick said, "He's gone."

After another sip, Herrick put the ice pack down, picked up the phone, and took it off speaker. He pressed it to his ear.

"I had him here, just like you said. But apparently, he's tougher than you are. He just beat the crap out of me and ran. I'd imagine he's wandering the streets of Hoboken now, if you want to find him. Or maybe he caught a cab. I don't know how much money he has. We kind of rushed out of Vermont, you know?"

"Find him."

"No."

The movie screen in his head continued to flicker. Generals questioning him. Some congratulating him. The boy's body was still warm. The security guard—his good friend—was dead at the front gate. The bomb squad investigating. It didn't matter.

Herrick wanted out. He just wanted out. To go home, find a way to make things right. They gave him a medal and sent him to a shrink. The shrink told him he could go home. The military officials tried to bring him back, though, until he broke down shaking when they handed him a rifle. That's when they stamped his file, or closed his computer program, or whatever it was they did. That's when the tension left his shoulders.

"You're going to tell me someone will die again, aren't you?" The force behind Herrick's voice surprised him.

Lucas didn't say anything.

"I'm flipping the tables now. I'm going to find you. I'm coming for you." Herrick took another swig of beer.

"You're making a big mistake."

Herrick shook his head, even though he knew Lucas couldn't see him. "I don't think so. I think you're off your game. Your brother is dead, but he was gutsier than you. At least he showed his face to Jackson Donne. Is that why I had to go up there and bring Donne back? Because you're scared to show your face? And you're scared he would take you out just like Steve?"

Something crashed on the other end of the line.

"Don't you say his name!"

Herrick took another sip of beer.   —

"You don't know the mistake you've made."

"That's twice you've said that, but somehow I don't believe it. You had your chance to take us both out, but you fired warning shots. I think you need us alive."

Lucas cleared his throat. "I'm surprised you're willing to risk your friends."

"I think I can get to you before you can get to them." Herrick thought his words over. "You need me for something. That's why you made sure I only got wounded the other day. And it's why you're only threatening my team and my friends. What is it?"

"Oh, you're going to die, and soon." Lucas tried to growl the words, but they came out squeaky.

"But why am I so important to your search for Donne? I was hired by a client, that's all."

Lucas sniffled. "You don't know, do you? You're very

important. But not to me."

The line went dead. Herrick put the phone down and finished his beer. He looked at the clock and saw it flip to 3 a.m. He'd been on the phone a long time. He leaned back on the couch and closed his eyes, expecting to dream of that day in the desert again. It came to him a lot, but he was used to it. Like an old newsreel. The boy's name was Amer. It translated to "One Who Builds." Herrick always wanted to know why Amer came to destroy things.

He'd never get an answer.

Sleep came easily and, for once, Amer didn't visit. It felt like he barely closed his eyes. The ASP was at his side. The tumbler next to it, empty. Herrick didn't dream at all. Not even of the plays he wanted to run during the first game. The team he was forgetting about didn't haunt him either.

It felt like only five minutes passed. In reality it was three hours. The sun was up when Herrick's eyes snapped open. Someone was knocking at the door, slamming on it with a fist. He grabbed the ASP off the table and went to the peephole.

Sarah Cullen was banging on the door.

And she was screaming his name.

CHAPTER 49

ONNE GOT OFF the train and hoped things hadn't changed in the past year. And, at first, outside the train station, things felt right. New Brunswick was still a sleepy college town at 7 a.m. A few people in suits drank lattes and hurried up the hill toward Johnson & Johnson. Donne took the hill too, past the new strip of stores along Easton, and a barbecue joint he wanted to try. He crossed Somerset and continued on into the world of college bars.

A block away, he saw a cop car headed in his direction. Donne ducked his head and made a left. He took the long way, up past Papa Grande, a couple of liquor stores, and several houses that were falling apart. Students tried to keep them in good shape, but who knew how to take care of a house at age twenty-one? He pushed on and turned right, heading back to Easton. The cop car had passed.

Two guys outside a truck munched on breakfast burritos. Donne wanted coffee and his stomach grumbled, but he had other things to take care of first. He got a quick forty-five-minute nap on the train, which left him energized and not groggy.

Some snow flurries wafted down as he walked, and Donne was reminded that winter wasn't just for Vermont. The flakes melted as they hit the last vestiges of fallen leaves on the sidewalks. He could see the Olde Towne two blocks ahead, but with a new neon sign that was already broadcasting itself this morning. Maybe Artie would be around this morning. On slow weekdays, Artie would normally come in at seven to do the bookkeeping and catch up on loose ends. Sometimes Donne would meet him for an early cup of coffee and to shoot the shit. It was one of the few things he'd missed when he went north.

Donne stopped in front of the bar. The name was still the same, but it had gotten a new paint job and had a deck added on to it, for summer outdoor seating. It was clean, and the usual smell of old grease and last night's beer was gone. Donne hesitated at the door for a moment, and then knocked.

When no one answered, he tried the door and found it locked. Perhaps Artie wasn't around, and Donne had gotten the scheduling wrong in his head. Maybe things had changed. He stroked his beard for a moment, and then knocked again—so hard pain traveled up his wrist like an electrical current.

Now he heard movement from inside, a shuffling sound and a muffled voice. The electricity he felt in his wrist now traveled through his entire body.

"We're closed, it's seven in the morning," Artie said as he pulled the door open. His mouth went slack when he saw Donne. After a moment, he said, "Jesus Christ."

"Can I get a cup of coffee?" Donne asked.

"What the hell are you doing here?"

Donne looked up into the sky and squinted at the flakes. "It's snowing. Let me in."

Artie stuck his head out into the world and looked around. After a second, he stepped out of the way and let Donne in. The bar was different now, new tile floors and black plastic barstools. The old wooden bar had been painted black. On the walls were Rutgers memorabilia and Gaslight Anthem album covers. There were pictures of famous locals like Paul Robeson and Joyce Kilmer. James Gandolfini lit a cigar on Easton Avenue in one of them. All were in stark black and white. Flat-screen TVs tuned to SportsCenter and the Big Ten Network were attached to any piece of free wall space. Gone was the dive bar feel, replaced with a hometown sports bar vibe.

"What the hell happened to this place?" Donne asked as he sat on a plastic-cushioned barstool.

Artie went behind the bar and flicked on the coffee maker. He said, "You did."

Donne tapped on the bar for a second, trying to process the words. Finally, he said, "I don't get it."

"For a few weeks you were hot shit. Everyone wanted to talk about you. The news was here every day. That guy who trashes the football team in the *Ledger* wanted to talk to me, get my opinion on if you'd be a distraction to the season."

Donne tilted his head. "That guy's a good writer."

"The article actually was pretty fair."

"It's a column, actually." Donne tried to hide a smile. Like old times.

"He should come in here on a Thursday night. I'm sure he'd get some stories."

Donne laughed. A real, honest to God laugh. It'd been a while.

"So finally, I got an offer I couldn't refuse. That guy from *Bar Hero* came around and offered to redo the place, if he could film himself yelling at me for a day or two. How could I say no?"

"Business sucked?"

Artie shook his head. "No. I needed new TVs. They wanted to capitalize on your fifteen minutes of fame. It was a circus here."

Artie reached behind the bar and pulled out a remote control. He aimed it at one of the flat-screens, brought up the DVR menu, found the episode he was looking for, and hit play. A burly man came on and stormed into the Olde Towne Tavern yelling about cleaning up the back of the kitchen.

Donne watched for a few minutes, and then turned back to Artie.

"What are you doing back, Jackson?"

"It seems like the cops have cooled on me. Realized I hadn't done anything. Time to come back."

Artie shook his head. "That's not it. If that were the case, you'd have been back here eight months ago."

Donne nodded. "Did a PI come to talk to you about me? Maybe a week ago?"

"Yep." Artie nodded. "Maybe a little less than that."

"What did you tell him?"

"That I didn't know where you were."

The coffee maker stopped making coffee, so Artie pulled off the hot plate and poured two cups. Donne fixed his with a little bit of sugar and a lot of cream. He took a sip and the warmth filled him, chasing away the rest of the electricity.

"Did you mention Leo Carver to him?"

Artie took a sip of coffee. It was a short sip. Then he put the cup back down and wiped his lip.

"I don't remember."

"It's important."

Donne looked up at the TV screen again. The host of the show pulled a cockroach out of one of the stoves. He screamed at Artie a bit.

"That really happen?" Donne asked.

Artie shook head. "No, it was a plant. Fun, though." He took another swig of coffee. "I may have mentioned Leo. The guy asked a lot of questions about you. I know I sent him to Franklin and Susan. Do you know if he ever talked to them?"

Donne shook his head. "He said he talked to Franklin. I don't want to bother them or bring them into this if I don't have to."

"Into what, Jackson? What's going on?"

Donne watched the steam rise from his mug and dissipate into the air.

"They did a nice job here."

"Cut the crap."

After a deep breath, Donne said, "Someone's trying to kill me."

Slapping the bar top, Artie said, "Jesus Christ. Again? And you come here? I finally got this place up and going to the point where it's exciting again, and you bring that shit back in here."

Donne looked around. "Do you see anyone here trying to shoot me?"

"Tell me what the deal is with the PI."

Matt Herrick. The Lucas brothers. Leo Carver. Donne filled Artie in on all of the events of the past week. Almost all, anyway. He left Mario out of it. He left the burying of two dead bodies out of it. That didn't seem to be something Artie needed to know.

"I may have mentioned Carver," Artie finally said. "That guy was a big part of your past. And with everything that went on with Bill Martin—I don't know. The PI, he asked a lot of good questions. Lured me into it."

Donne nodded. "It seems like he's okay at his job."

"But you told me you didn't trust him."

"I don't. He's trying to protect those people close to him and none of this is his fault. He's going to do what's best for him, not me."

"By being here, you're not doing what's best for me."

Donne looked around again. "You said this place happened because of me. Because of some terrible stuff I went through. Am still going through. I think I am owed this."

Artie opened his mouth and then shut it. He reached across the bar and squeezed Donne's forearm.

"I'm so sorry about Kate," he said.

Donne felt the electricity wash over him again. He shrugged Artie off and went for the coffee. He didn't saw a word, just guzzled the rest of the hot liquid down. The burning of his esophagus felt like penance.

"It's just like Jeanne," Artie said. "God, have you heard from Jeanne?"

Donne simply said, "No."

As if a light bulb went on, Artie said, "I'm so sorry. I'm so stupid. Jesus Christ. I spent the last year profiting because people around you died. You were gone, I didn't know what else to do. The bar and I thought — "

Donne shook his head. "It's fine."

"I don't know what else to say, Jackson. You were gone. For all I knew you ended up like — " Artie stopped himself. "How can I help you?"

"Did anyone else come in here looking for me?"

"No."

Donne pushed the coffee away from him and stood up. "Good luck with the place, Artie."

"Where are you going?"

Donne shrugged.

"You can stay here. Upstairs. Until you find out what's going on. I won't tell anyone you're here. It's safe. Too many witnesses."

Donne said, "Thanks. One more request."

"Name it."

"Can I use your computer?"

"That's it?" Artie asked through a chuckle.

"That's it." Donne didn't laugh.

Ten minutes and another cup of coffee later, results of a search on Leo Carver were popping up on Google.

CHAPTER 50

SARAH STORMED INTO the apartment, threw her purse on the couch, spun back toward Herrick, and crossed her arms. Herrick hadn't even closed the door yet.

"Are you okay?" he asked while shutting it.

She was flushed red, and some of her makeup was streaked. His palms got immediately damp, and the tempo in his chest went straight to punk rock.

"Do I look okay?" She didn't look injured.

"You're mad about something," he said as the locked clicked in.

"Ya think?"

Herrick ran a hand through his hair and waited. Sarah looked around the apartment, stopping on the two beer bottles, then coming back to his eyes.

"Where have you been?"

"Working."

"I've been calling you."

"My phone's been out of range. And then dead."

Sarah swallowed and plopped down on the couch. She put

her face in her hands, rubbing her eyes. Herrick leaned against the wall. The thumping in his chest slowed to reasonable levels. Back to Nickleback territory now.

"I thought—" she said. She shook her head.

"It's okay," he said.

"We had a good time the other night. Then you left that message and fell off the face of the earth."

Herrick felt his heartbeat picking up the pace again

"I was scared," she said. "I came here to make sure you were alive."

After cleaning up the two empty beer bottles, Herrick took a seat next to her, leaving just enough room between them for the Holy Spirit. He wanted to put a hand on her back, but he didn't.

"I'm doing all right," he said. "I found him."

Sarah sat up and turned toward him, laying her hands on her thighs. "Donne?"

Herrick nodded. "After talking to you at the bar, it became clear." She didn't need to know a homicidal bounty hunter handed the information over to him.

"Where was he?"

"A small town in Vermont."

"You left him up there?"

Herrick rubbed his side. "No. He came back with me."

"Wait. Where is he now?" She turned her head toward the bathroom.

Shrugging, Herrick said, "He, uh, got away."

Sarah shook her head.

"You're not at work," he said.

"I took a sick day."

"Because of me?"

Sarah nodded this time, and her weight shifted on the couch in his direction. The air in the room was cold, an early morning chill, perfect for being under blankets. The heat hadn't kicked in yet, and wouldn't for another twenty minutes. Sun streamed in through the window, just now bursting over the New York skyline. Herrick kept his hands at his side.

"I ," she said. She looked at the ceiling, as if collecting her thoughts. "For you to leave the kids with the assistants last minute, it was weird. Felt wrong. Whenever you've done that before, you gave more notice. This time is so different than your other cases. You were so tense the other night." She coughed. "And then you didn't answer your phone."

"Vermont reception sucks. And then I had a wanted criminal in my car. Didn't really have time to check my voice mail or answer texts."

She punched him in the shoulder. It didn't sting.

"You couldn't spare thirty seconds?"

"Most wanted man in New Jersey in my car. He takes precedence."

"And you let him get away."

"I told you I shouldn't have looked at my phone."

She laughed, and suddenly the room felt warmer. He felt the couch sag as she inched closer to him. Herrick made fists.

Outside, brakes squealed and gas hissed. The buses were moving up and down Washington, picking up commuters. They were getting started with their day. Sarah put her head on his shoulder, and he didn't want to go anywhere.

"You have to find him."

"I know," he said.

Sarah exhaled. "I'm glad you're okay."

They sat that way for a few minutes. Herrick put his arm around her shoulders. The hum of traffic was their background noise. A jolt of electricity went through him. He struggled to find words.

"This is nice," he said.

"Shut up, Matt. Don't be awkward."

Before he could move, she blinked and said, "I forgot to tell you. Something weird happened this morning."

The electricity coursing through his body molded together into a lead ball which settled in his stomach.

"There was this Halloween gift outside my front door. A little plastic skull with a top hat on. It was very weird. It's a little late for Halloween gifts. It's Christmas season."

Herrick sat back on the couch and took his arm off of her.

"What?" she asked. "I just thought it was funny. We're allowed to laugh a little. Weird things happen in New Jersey, right? When I was a kid..."

"Was there a note? Something else?"

"No, just that."

The jingle of Taylor Swift emanated into the room. Muffled. Sarah's ring tone. She jumped up off the couch and went to it.

She grabbed her purse and said, "It's still too early to be work."

Herrick's phone started to ring too. Sweat formed behind his ears, and his breath was ragged. Sarah found her phone and answered before Herrick could get to his.

He saw the unknown number.

Sarah said, "Oh my God. Oh my God! Is everyone else all right?"

Herrick didn't answer his phone yet, turning to her. He could see tears welling up in her eyes.

"My apartment has been broken into. One of the doormen got beat up," she said. "I have to go home. I have to go. The ambulance is there."

She stood up and stuffed her phone back in her purse. Herrick held up a hand and told her to wait, he was going to come with her.

Then he answered his phone.

The voice was clipped. "You think I'm fucking around? You're lucky she wasn't home."

The line disconnected, but Herrick didn't need to hear any more.

They grabbed their jackets and rushed to Sarah's car.

CHAPTER 51

ALEX ROBINSON STARED at his phone.

He willed it to ring, but it rested on his desk, silent. Both Mosley and Carver had promised to get in touch with him. Carver needed to give him the keys to his trust fund; otherwise, he was in deep trouble.

The tea kettle whistled—he couldn't even afford Starbucks Earl Grey or Johnny and Hanges today. And if he didn't get a case soon, he'd be living out of his office. That didn't matter, though. All that mattered was Herrick and Donne and finishing this.

Trusting the Mosleys was smart; they knew the terrain—based in DC, but came up here often. And they were efficient. But Robinson hadn't foreseen Steve Mosley being killed—he hadn't expected rage to play a factor. He got up and fetched himself a cup of tea.

But, he thought, when revenge is in play, rage is always a factor.

Outside, buses honked and brakes squealed. No collision, just a normal day in Kearny.

The phone rang and Robinson nearly spilled his coffee trying to get back to it. Caller ID scrolled across the screen of the cordless.

Mosley.

He picked up.

"They're back," Mosley growled.

"What do you mean?"

"I mean what I said. Jackson Donne and Matt Herrick are back in New Jersey."

Robinson switched ears. "Are they dead?"

Mosley huffed. "Have you ever spoken on the phone before? Someone could be listening."

"No one is listening." His stomach burned. No one trusted him. Carver was sure he was followed and now Mosley thought his phone was tapped.

"They're around," Mosley said.

He had time to find the money to pay Mosley still. With a dead brother, the guy would probably ask for double. He needed to spread this out.

"Don't kill them yet."

"You're an idiot. A mega-fucking-idiot."

The fire in Robinson's stomach exploded.

"Don't talk to me that way! I am your boss. I'm paying your salary."

"I should have been paid already."

Robinson stalked over to his window and looked outside, scanning the sidewalks for Mosley. No sign of him.

"Where are you?"

Mosley didn't answer.

"It's not that I don't want them dead," Robinson said. "It's that I want Herrick to hurt."

"What do you have against him? Haven't I hurt him enough already?"

"Herrick destroyed my life. I want him to have to live with the same sort of destruction."

Mosley said, "You want him to live?"

"Temporarily."

Robinson laid it over the phone, the plan that had come to him the night before. They all thought he was stupid? This would change that.

When he was done talking, Mosley said, "And you wanted me to play a psychopath. You're a sick man, Alex."

"You have to make sure the two of them are together."

"I already have an idea for that."

They hung up. Robinson stared out the window for a long time. Carver never called. Another bus pulled up and three people got off, including a bearded man. The gait was familiar to Robinson, but he pushed it away.

There was too much else on his mind.

CHAPTER 52

DETECTIVE WORK VIA the train in New Jersey wasn't easy. There wasn't a constantly running train that Donne could catch at any time—like a subway. To try and map out a full bus route could take half the afternoon away. Donne found himself on the 1:15 to Lyndhurst, however. From there he hoped to catch the 2:07 bus to Kearny, and then he planned to knock on Alex Robinson's door.

The plan worked, and Donne found himself on the sidewalk just outside Robinson's office. The snow flurries had stopped, but the wind was still kicking, and the dark clouds sat overhead like unwanted visitors. Donne rolled his neck and felt it crack like a knuckle, releasing some tension he'd built on his trip across northern New Jersey. Then he pulled the glass door open, went inside, and climbed the steps to Robinson's office. The building smelled like mold and fried chicken.

Donne hit the intercom buzzer on the outside of Robinson's office door. As he waited for a response, his body wavered as if it'd been recovering from an aftershock. It had been years since he'd seen Alex Robinson. Years since he sat on the stand and pointed out Leo Carver. He hoped to never see them again.

That hope had slipped away very quickly over the past forty-eight hours.

He heard the voice he hadn't heard in years crackle through the speaker. It sounded far away and raspy.

"Can I help you?"

"I need to hire you for a very important case."

The door buzzed and Donne walked into the one-room office. There was a water cooler, a hot plate with a tea kettle on it, two filing cabinets, a desk covered in scattered papers, and Alex Robinson leaning back in his chair behind it. Donne waved. It took Robinson a second. Maybe it was the beard.

Then he got it.

"Oh no way!"

He nearly toppled out of his chair.

"Hi, Alex."

"Jackson, you gotta get out of here, man. I didn't do anything to you."

Donne pulled out the chair across from the desk and sat in it. He watched Robinson's hands.

"How about we sit right, Alex? And keep the hands where I can see 'em."

"That a threat?"

"No. I'm not going to hurt you, Alex. But I don't particularly want you hurting me either."

Robinson straightened up and put his fingers on the edge of the desk. He'd put on some weight since Donne had last seen him. His fingers looked like hot dogs, and a gullet hung underneath his chin.

"Uh-huh. So why are you here?"

"I want to talk about the last ten years."

Robinson nodded. "Sure. Old times. Old times. Some of 'em were pretty good. But who says I want to just sit here and reminisce?"

"Doesn't look like you have much more else on your plate."

Because you probably ate it.

Robinson lifted his hand and Donne tensed. He didn't have

a gun on him, no weapons at all. But Robinson didn't know that. Donne exhaled when Robinson pointed at his landline.

"I call the cops, whaddya gonna do?"

Donne spread his hands. "Talk until they get here and lock me up?"

"That doesn't sound like you. Thought you were a runner." Robinson held the phone, but didn't dial.

"I got older. Knees hurt."

"Haven't we all?"

Donne nodded toward Robinson's hand. "I think it's time you converted to wireless."

Robinson put the phone back in the cradle. "I hate dropped calls."

"Explains the amount of business you seem to do. Most of this shit is online and you don't even have a computer."

"You gonna kill me or what?"

Robinson's left fingers were still on the desk, but his right hand was just out of sight. Donne swallowed and tried to think of a way to get the hand back where it should be. Words like that weren't coming, however. Because Donne was caught up on what Robinson had just said.

"I'm not going to kill you. That's not what's going on here. You hired a guy to find me."

Robinson blinked. "Because I wanted to find you before you found me and took me out."

Donne leaned forward. "That doesn't make any sense. I've been minding my own business for the past year. And now all of a sudden, I'm gonna pop up and take you out? You're not hard to find. I could have done it years ago."

Robinson didn't answer immediately, and Donne's muscles tensed even more. He really wanted Robinson to put his hand back on the desk.

"You killed Bill Martin." Robinson's tongue tripped him up around the word *killed* and he needed to stop for a moment before saying Martin's name.

Donne shook his head. "You know better. You wouldn't hire someone to find me, and hire someone else to kill me.

That's just bad business, man."

For an instant, Donne thought he'd played it wrong and said too much. Robinson rolled his eyes and took a deep breath, gathering himself.

"Man, fuck you."

The whole room felt wrong. Robinson's left hand had beads of sweat on it. Full beds. Donne didn't think he'd ever seen that before.

"You didn't think I was going to kill you," Donne said. "You wanted to flush me out."

Robinson's nostrils flared. "That's the cops' job."

"And when they gave up?"

Donne saw Robinson's right shoulder twitch, and he moved quickly. Instead of backing away, he leaped across the desk and grabbed Robinson's shirt. He yanked hard and pulled Robinson against the wood. He slapped Robinson with his left hand.

Robinson said, "Ow."

"We need to take a ride," Donne said. "That's why I'm really here. Let's make this reunion complete."

Robinson exhaled. Realization flashed across his eyes. "You really don't want to do this."

"Take me to see Leo," Donne said. "I miss him."

CHAPTER 53

HERRICK WADED INTO the muck.

Flashing lights, people talking, someone crying, the crackle of a police radio, and the click of an iPhone taking photos lined the sidewalk outside of Sarah's building. She was at his side, clutching his elbow as he pushed through the crowd trying to get to the front door.

At the front of the crowd, two cops were taping off the stairway leading to the front doors. Herrick could see the dark stain of blood — a shade of red so deep it looked almost brown — on the top step. Next to it was a plastic skull with a top hat. That was drenched in red.

Sarah saw it too and whispered, "Oh my God."

The grip at his elbow became a vise, pressing down on his nerves and muscle. He didn't dare shake her loose, however.

A cop approached them, holding up a hand.

"Can't go in there," he said.

"I live here," Sarah said.

"Sorry, ma'am, it's a crime scene."

Herrick said, "I'm a private investigator. I think this may

have something to do with a case I'm working on."

The cop froze, and then pulled the receiver attached to his uniform close to his mouth. He uttered something Herrick couldn't quite make out due the rumble of the crowd.

"Wait here," he said.

TEN MINUTES LATER, someone had brought both Herrick and Sarah coffee. They were sitting in the back of the police cruiser waiting to talk to the detective in charge of the case. In Hudson County, towns didn't have their own homicide detectives; they used county cops who worked out of Jersey City.

Sarah sipped her coffee and didn't speak. The steam from the cup fogged the windows. Herrick drank some coffee and checked his email on his phone. Nothing but spam. He deleted it and went back to the bitter coffee. Someone had gotten a Box O' Joe from Dunkin' Donuts and it'd been sitting out. The things cops suffered through for the love of their jobs.

The front passenger door to the cruiser opened and a hefty man in a light gray raincoat slid in. The seat groaned underneath him. He had thinning black hair and compensated for it with a thick mustache. He wiped at it, coughed, and then smiled at them.

"I'm Chaz Martinez," the detective said. "This is my case."

Herrick nodded at him.

"So, lemme get this straight." He pointed at Sarah. "You live here." He pointed at Herrick. "And you're working a case that might tie into this attack."

Herrick said, "Yes."

At the same time, Sarah said, "Is Lionel okay?"

"I don't know," Martinez said. "The ambulance took him to Clara Maass fifteen minutes ago. I haven't gotten an update yet."

Sarah nodded. "If you hear anything, please."

Martinez uttered something sounding like an affirmative, and then turned his attention to Herrick.

"What's your case?"

Herrick told him.

"The guy who killed the senator?"

Herrick shrugged. "He was involved."

"I thought they cleared him."

Herrick shrugged. "I think he's officially wanted for questioning. They don't brief you on this stuff?"

"Not really my jurisdiction. And you can't trust the news." Martinez coughed into his fist. "So is he the guy who attacked — what was his name? Lionel? Was it Donne?"

The crowd was off to Herrick's right. He could still see them loitering, watching cops take pictures and do whatever it was cops did at a crime scene. He took another sip of coffee, the steam filling his nose with the sweet smell.

After swallowing, he said, "I don't think so. At this point, almost a week ago, a man attacked me. I have reason to believe his name is Lucas Mosley. He's a bounty hunter."

Martinez typed something into his phone. "I've heard of the Mosleys. They haven't been around in a while though. They're efficient guys who run up and down the coast. We think they took out a couple of Bloods downtown last year."

"Steve is dead. Up in Vermont."

Martinez said, "How do you know that?"

Herrick shrugged again.

Sarah stared at him. He could feel the heat from her eyes on his neck. He tried to ignore it. Talking to the cops wasn't going to help end this case any more quickly, and it didn't appear Martinez was going to give up much information voluntarily, so Herrick had to hand something over.

"I was there last night. And Lucas Mosley told me." Sounded true enough. "He's been calling me, threatening my friends. Threatening me. My basketball team."

Martinez let the comment go, but Sarah didn't.

"The team?" Sarah gripped his arm tight. "The kids?"

"I told the cops in Jersey City, there's plenty of extra protection. We're not in any danger."

"My doorman just got beat up. Someone left a skull outside

my door. If I hadn't come to see you this morning..."

"I know, I know." Herrick had been trying not to think about that aspect since he got the phone call.

"You should have called us," Martinez said.

"I just said I told the Jersey City police."

Martinez shook his head.

"What happened to Lionel?" Herrick asked.

"Not exactly sure. Someone was trying to get into the building. When he was found, they said Lionel was mumbling that he just tried to stop them. Or him. Witness couldn't tell exactly what he was saying. The responding officer said Lionel's face was pretty messed up. Surprised he could talk at all."

Sarah put her hands in her face and let out a long sigh. She'd held it together longer than Herrick expected.

Martinez opened his mouth to ask another question. The words were drowned out, however. All the sounds, the static from the police radio. Ambient crowd noise. It all faded away.

Herrick felt the shock wave first, as the back windshield shattered. Then the heat rushed over him, licking his face. The smell of smoke rushed into his nose and thunder filled his ears. Everything was hot and loud. His muscles went tight and his mouth was open. He could have been screaming for all he knew.

The car rocked up off its left wheels and then back down again.

He pulled Sarah into him close and went toward the seat to protect both of them. Her nails dug into his chest.

The apartment building went up in a ball of flame.

CHAPTER 54

ARAH'S MOUTH WAS wide, her eyes were closed, and her hands were balled into fists. But no sound came out of her mouth, at least as far as Herrick could tell. Then again, the entire world had gone silent, save for an intense ringing in his ears. He brought his hands up to his ears. Everything was wet and sticky. He pushed himself back away from Sarah.

He tried to say "Are you okay" and felt the vibrations in his throat. But Sarah didn't respond.

Looking down at the back of his hands, he could see they were covered in blood and glass shards. The rear windshield had blown out and scattered all over them. If he hadn't fallen on Sarah, it might have been much worse.

He turned toward the front seat and saw it was much worse for Martinez. The front windshield had blown as well, in much larger shards. One had embedded itself in Martinez's head. He was shuddering and shaking like he was having a seizure.

Herrick reached forward, but couldn't get through the metal mesh that separated them. Sarah followed his movements and must have seen Martinez for the first time. She screamed. Now the hearing started to come back to Herrick, her wail pouring into his ears. He wrapped her in his arms tight, and tried to tell her it was okay. Then he released her and tried the door. It was child locked.

But the windows had blown out of the doors as well. Herrick reached up and pulled himself through. He landed on his feet, and his vision clouded momentarily. His hands burned, and his ears ached, but he seemed otherwise okay.

Then he surveyed the world around him. A goddamn war zone. Even the muted sirens, muffled with dust and rock, brought back memories of snatch-and-grab missions. Quick bursts of fire, or a grenade. He'd been there time and again. When he went back and put his gun down, he thought he was done with this.

It all came rushing back today.

People were scattered on the ground, covered in ash and dirt. One man was trying to force himself to his feet, but kept tumbling back to the ground. Herrick saw a right limb halfway across the street. Afghanistan all over again.

Martinez was gone. He had to be. The two cops by the front door were gone, torn to shreds by fire and shrapnel. The air smelled of burned flesh—kind of like overcooking a chicken— and brimstone. As Herrick's hearing came back, the howls for help filled his ears.

He stood, arms at his sides, and tried to catch his breath. Blood dripped down to the ground from his fingers.

THE AMBULANCE CAME first.

By the time it got there, Herrick had fished Sarah out of the car. They worked while they waited for the paramedics. Finding survivors and trying to stop the bleeding with towels, shirts, whatever they could find.

The EMS took over, and Herrick pulled Sarah away from the crowd. He held her tight against him and felt her weep. He blinked a few times, trying to hold his own tears back.

Two more ambulances pulled up. Each advertised a different

town on its doors. The paramedics hustled out and started searching for people they could help. One of them mouthed "Oh my God." Herrick pulled Sarah tighter. She reciprocated.

A news helicopter hovered above. Several more police cars rolled in. News vans were setting up live shots. The mayor lingered a block away, surrounded by people in black suits.

Herrick felt his phone vibrate in his pocket. He knew who it was. Gently, he pulled away from Sarah and told her to go to the car. The police would want to talk to her, he said, and he would send them to the car. It was safe in the car. She wiped her face and nodded.

Once she was out of range, Herrick grabbed his phone.

"I will kill you," he said.

Lucas Mosley laughed, and Herrick felt the muscles in his back tighten. He was a rubber band pulled tight, and all he wanted was to snap.

"Do I have your attention?" Lucas asked.

"You've had it for a while."

"No more fooling around. You will bring me Jackson Donne."

"Find him yourself. You better hope you find him before I find you."

"Where is he? If you won't tell me, maybe one of his old friends will."

Herrick spoke through gritted teeth. "All this for a paycheck?"

"This isn't about payment anymore. It's about revenge. I won't be stopped."

Herrick wanted to scream.

"I wanted you to know what would have happened if you didn't shoot that boy."

Herrick looked at the paramedics scrambling, screaming for help for more equipment. Someone was doing chest compressions. The world went out of focus and he could see his brothers on the ground — their limbs scattered. His superior officer shouting commands, losing control.

"Bodies everywhere. And it would have been your fault.

Because you could have stopped it."

Herrick said, "I did stop it."

"Now you know you can't stop everything." Mosely took a deep breath. "You can't stop me."

Herrick had been coming at this all wrong. He'd been on his heels for the past week, letting Robinson and now Mosley push him around. Even Donne had dictated pace. That was not what he wanted his team to do, and that was not what he was going to do. Time to flip the tables and push the tempo.

"I'm coming for you starting now."

Mosely said, "Bring it."

CHAPTER 55

"**L**IKE HELL," ROBINSON said. "What makes you so sure I can even get in to see him?"

"Herrick."

Robinson sat back in his chair and folded his hands across his chest. His cheek was red from the slap, and the other side was flushed as well. Donne was impressed he didn't rub it.

"What about him?" Robinson shrugged his shoulders.

"Come on, Alex, I'm not an idiot. Last I heard Carver is in lock-up, taken away from society. Then Herrick tells me this story of Sandy and the prison. Now he's in a mental home? Sounds just like Leo. Finding ways out of everything."

Robinson said, "Almost everything."

Donne licked his lips. "Anyway, let's put the timeline together."

Robinson said, "Go ahead."

"Sandy hits, Leo fights the system. Bill Martin—Leo's best friend—tries to screw me over again and kills himself in the process. But to the rest of the world, it looks like I did it. At least at first."

Robinson said, "Now there was someone who got to see Leo a lot."

Donne nodded. "I'm glad you're helping me out here."

"I don't want to get slapped again." He cut the words off with his teeth.

Donne nodded again. "So Martin dies, and I disappear. How did Leo feel about all of that?"

Robinson didn't say anything. He twiddled his thumbs. The red in his cheeks was starting to fade. He chewed the bottom of his lip. Drops of saliva formed at the corner of his mouth. Donne decided to look out the window at the clouds.

"I still have questions though. Why kill the other two?"

No hesitation from Robinson. "Because this has nothing to do with Leo. Someone is coming after us, Jackson. I thought for sure it was you."

"If it was me, you would have been dead ten minutes ago. The slap would have been nothing, right?"

Now Robinson's hand went to his cheek.

"Basically, I think you're lying to me," Donne said.

"Get out of here, Jackson."

Donne spread his hands. "Why? I'm here now. You guys want me dead, don't you? Isn't that what this is about? You hired two men to kill me."

Robinson slammed a fist on the desk. The papers on his desk bounced. "I have nothing to do with this."

"Then take me to see Leo."

No answer from Robinson. He sat and rubbed the bottom of his fist.

"I know you went to see Leo within the last two days," Donne said. "Herrick followed you there after you guys talked. Might have been yesterday. I don't know, when you don't sleep much, the hours kind of blend together."

"He's a liar and always has been!"

Donne pressed his lips together. The smell in the air was bitter and stale.

"In this case, I don't think he is." Donne paused. "If you

don't trust him, why did you hire him?"

Robinson went flush again, and Donne felt something tickle the back of his brain. There were connections, but it felt like he'd only found the edges. The big picture wasn't there yet.

"You know the Mosleys?" Donne tried.

Robinson nodded. "I've heard of them."

"See? I haven't. I find that really interesting. I've only been gone a year. It takes a while to build up that kind of reputation. And I've been involved in enough stuff the past ten years, I think I would have heard of them."

Robinson rubbed his nose. "You thought you were helping us out by only fingering Leo. We loved him. Always have. He was our meal ticket. Now look at me. I'm struggling to get by with old coffee and taking cases no one else will take. And Martin was one of the lowest on the totem pole in the department after you were finished with us."

"And the other guys?"

"The dregs of society. Drugs. Alcoholics. Their deaths — it probably put them out of their misery."

The words hung in the air for a minute. Donne finished his coffee.

"You screwed everything up, Jackson. The last eight years of my life have sucked because of you. I'm out hustling every day to make a case, but I don't have the reputation. Others get my gigs. And now I'm scared you're coming here to kill me."

Donne shook his head. "I'm not and you know that. You've known that from the start."

"Get out of my office."

"Fine," Donne said. "Let's go see Leo."

"No."

Robinson's phone rang. The landline. Donne watched his hand move gracefully as he went for it. Half of Donne expected him to ignore the call and pop up with a gun. But there was more going on here. Donne couldn't put the pieces of the puzzle together yet, but he could feel it.

Robinson answered and said, "Hold on a minute." He

passed the receiver across. "It's for you."

Donne froze. Who would be calling him? The only one who knew he was coming here was Artie.

"I'm not here," Donne said.

Robinson shrugged and hung up the phone.

CHAPTER 56

ROBINSON HAD MOVED from his thumb to his index finger, yanking hangnails away with his teeth. He didn't speak, waiting for Donne to start.

"Let's go," he said.

Robinson laughed. "Like hell."

"Now." He tried to add a knife edge to his voice.

Robinson reached forward toward his desk and came back out with a gun. Donne didn't hesitate, and leaped forward, just as he'd done earlier. He cleared the top of the desk and caught Robinson straight in the chest linebacker style. They toppled backward into the chair. The gun clattered away without going off — a lucky break.

Robinson swung an elbow up at Donne's temple, but Donne was able to dodge and catch Robinson with a left jab. He swung again, connecting with a right hook. Robinson's head snapped back and thudded into the floor. He raised his knee and hit Donne in the stomach, sending the air from his lungs. Donne gasped and rolled off Robinson.

Shaking it off, Donne tried to get to his feet, but lost balance.

Robinson was scrambling along the ground, groping for the gun. But Donne saw it first, leaning against the wall in the corner of the room. Donne got to his feet steadily this time, ran over to Robinson on the opposite side of the office, and hit him twice with two rabbit punches. The second one brought a stream of blood from Robinson's lip. It splattered all over the wall. Robinson went down to one knee, cursing. Donne hit him again, and he went flat like a dead fish.

Donne raced to the other side of the room and snatched the gun. He checked the safety and saw it was off. They were both really lucky the gun hadn't gone off in the fight. He raised it and aimed it at Robinson, who was struggling to get into a sitting position. His eyes were red and teary. He was trying to stop the bleeding in his lip with the back of his hand, causing the cuff of his shirt to stain red.

Donne said, "I'm not negotiating and I'm not playing games."

Robinson held his hands up in a way that said *I surrender.*

"Let's go see Carver. Now." How many times did Donne have to repeat himself before Robinson got it?

"This is the wrong play, Jackson."

At least one more time.

Donne shrugged, still keeping the gun leveled on Robinson. "At this point, it's the only play I got."

"You're only going to piss him off even more."

Donne nearly laughed, but kept it together. After all this time, the last thing Donne was afraid of was pissing anyone off. It seemed for the past ten years that was all he did. But it didn't matter, and Donne was still here.

"It's a really dumb decision," Robinson said.

The second time in forty-eight hours someone told him that. And Donne agreed. But that was his life. Pissing people off and making dumb decisions.

"Every time I've made a dumb choice," Donne said, "I've figured out what I've needed to. Let's go."

This time it was Robinson's turn to shrug. He pushed himself to his feet and rattled his keys out of his pocket. For an instant, Donne thought he was going to pull another weapon. Instead, he heard a car on the street beep its alarm unlocked. Robinson was on the up and up this time. Things change when you have a gun pointed at your face.

"Your funeral," he said.

CHAPTER 57

‖‖‖

THE HOMELESS GUY had new Jordans and a fresh bottle of Old Grand-Dad. That tipped Herrick off.

He'd dropped Sarah off at the school and called his cop friend McKinny and updated him. There would be a cruiser on campus all day, and they'd find someone to keep an eye on her at a local hotel at night.

When Sarah got out of the car she said, "Some sick day." She touched his arm and kissed him on the cheek. Her fingers trembled as they made contact with him. She still had soot on her cheek.

For the next four hours, Herrick walked Jersey City. He wanted to find the men Mosley had hired to limp in front of the school. Jersey City was an area where people were always hanging out on stoops or in front of coffee shops. Even in the cold, people were out in the open. Herrick needed a lucky break. And when he saw the new Jordans and nearly full bottle, he figured his gamble had paid off.

Sitting against the wall of a small liquor store, the homeless guy tipped his newsie-style hat back on his head and squinted up at Herrick. He had a leathery face covered with what appeared to be a couple-of-days-old beard.

"Where'd you get those shoes?"

"Man, forget you." He yanked the hat back over his eyes. The liquor in the Old Grand-Dad bottle sloshed around as he sat back against the wall.

Herrick sat down next to him. The scent of onions and uncooked hot dogs wafted his way. And it didn't come from a street vendor's stash.

"How the booze?" Herrick asked.

The homeless guy offered him the bottle. "It does the job, but it kind of sucks," he said.

"Well, in that case, I don't really want to drink it."

The homeless guy unscrewed the cap and took a long swig. Two gulps' worth. When he pulled the bottle away from his lips he didn't grimace, he just wiped the residue away with the back of his hand.

"So the new Jordans."

"You try to take them and I'll stab you."

Herrick held up his hands, surrendering. "I don't want them. I don't think they'd fit. I'm just curious where you got them."

"Foot Locker on JFK, but they're all sold out. You get these things at midnight or you don't get 'em at all."

"Like an iPhone?"

"Bigger."

"They're expensive, aren't they?"

Herrick knew the answer to that. In fact, he knew all about the shoes. It's all his team talked about on release day. They would plan on lining up. Or sending two freshmen to line up outside the store with a ton of money. First time they did that, the principal had the seniors who orchestrated it in his office. Reamed them out. But with AAU coaches lingering around, the kids—the really talented ones—could get whatever pair they wanted whenever they wanted. It was easy for them.

But not for guys with their hands out, just looking for more booze and a warm place to sleep.

"They pricey." He laughed. "But I had a good day on the PATH train. My singing, you know. People gave me cash."

"What do you sing?" Herrick asked.

"Motown."

"Ten bucks to hear some."

The homeless guy grinned. His right incisor was missing. He broke out into an a cappella rendition of "Ain't Too Proud to Beg." It was all right. It wasn't five hundred dollars good. Herrick slid him a ten after the first verse.

"That's good."

"Thank you."

"What's your name, for when you make it big?"

Homeless laughed and said, "Sheldon."

"No way you made four hundred dollars in a day though."

"I did."

"Singing?"

Sheldon opened his mouth. Closed it. Coughed into his free hand. Then said, "Some."

"The rest some guy gave you, didn't he? Asked you to walk in front of St. Paul's with a limp?"

Sheldon sat up straight. The bottle clattered against the sidewalk but didn't shatter. The bottle cap held as well.

"I wasn't supposed to tell nobody that."

"My guess is you were supposed to spend some money on food too."

"My feet were cold."

"Tell me about the guy who sold them to you."

"No way, man."

Herrick held up his wallet. "I got another five hundred bucks, plus I'll go inside and get you the bottle of your choice." His gut winced as he said those words.

Sheldon licked his lips. "He was tall and thin, like me. He had a limp."

C'mon, Herrick thought. *Tell me something I don't know.*

"He has a big car, a black Tahoe. It was cool. He called me up to it. When I looked through, he'd just reset his odometer. I know because I asked mileage. I love seeing those big things trying to rumble down these tiny streets."

"How was it?"

Sheldon rubbed his chin. "He said it was shit in the city. But he'd just driven like forty miles on the parkway. No traffic, and he got some good-ass mileage."

"You were by yourself?"

"No, I was with my boys. He paid all three of us." Sheldon coughed again. Picked up the bottle of Old Grand-Dad, unscrewed the top, and drank some more. "We were just supposed to limp down the street like assholes. Scare some dude."

Herrick nodded. "I was that dude."

"Oh yeah? Did it work?"

Herrick laughed. "At the time."

"Glad I earned my cash."

"Anything else stick out to you?"

Sheldon shook his head. "He had one of those interlocking BF magnets on the back of his car."

"Ben Franklin U?"

The newly private university had long been a basketball school, but just started investing in big-time football.

Sheldon nodded. Drank some more.

"Anything else? Those BFs are on like half the cars in New Jersey."

"He had season tickets or worked at Ben Franklin or something."

"How do you know?"

"Like I told you, when I looked through the window I saw something crumpled up on the front seat. Like a parking tag. It said Blue Lot on it."

Herrick stood up and opened his wallet. He counted out the money and handed it over.

"They aren't going to let me in there," Sheldon said. "You gotta go in for me."

"Get yourself something to eat."

"Not hungry."

Herrick turned around and walked away. The knot in his

stomach eased as he did so. Money was one thing, but he wasn't going to up this guy's blood alcohol level even more.

"Hey, you promised!" Sheldon yelled at him.

Herrick didn't answer. Instead, he picked up the pace. The next stop was down the shore. Forty miles on the parkway was a little low, mileage wise, but the BF magnet was corroboration.

And he was going to have to call in a major favor once he got there.

CHAPTER 58

ERRICK PULLED INTO the Mauve Lot. It was adjacent to the Emory Green Athletic Center, affectionately known as the GAP, a trapezoid-shaped building where the team played basketball. He made his way through the parking lot to the front door and pulled it open. Practice was going on, the sound of dribbled basketballs echoing in the rafters.

The hallway and smell of old popcorn brought him back years. His father used to bring him here when he was a kid, instilled the love of basketball in him. It was a father-son journey—they'd go once a year, sit in the rafters, and do the dumb cheers with the students. Until his dad went away.

Ambling up to the glass divider, Herrick leaned over it and watched lay-up drills. Coach was yelling at them to go faster, but the speed didn't increase much. One of the assistants looked up toward Herrick and gave a little wave. Herrick counted two seconds before the coach realized who he waved at, stopped what he was doing, and jogged up the stairs in his direction.

Herrick was a top high school basketball coach, AKA hoops royalty. Craig "Boots" Marrone hit the lobby and headed toward him, big smile plastered on his face. He held out his hand and Herrick shook it.

"What are you doing here, Coach?" Boots said.

The nickname came ten years ago when he was a rising assistant coach at UCLA pounding the pavement trying to bring in the best recruits in the country. Any time he entered a high school gym, coaches would say "Boots on the ground!" It stuck. Last year, Ben Franklin had hired him to fill out the assistant staff for the new coaching regime. So far, they'd made a dent with AAU coaches on the recruiting trail. Mostly due to Boots.

Herrick shrugged. "You asked me to come check out a practice."

Boots frowned. "You're supposed to call first."

"I actually need a favor."

"Name it."

Herrick held out his private investigator's license. "It's about a case."

Boots laughed. "Really? How did I not know this about you?"

Herrick shrugged.

"Can you get me out of a parking ticket?"

Herrick shook his head. "Suspect of mine had a Ben Frankline U magnet on his car."

"You can get those anywhere."

Herrick shook his head. "They're sent from the ticket office here, mostly."

"Yeah, and…?"

Herrick put his hands in his pockets. "He also had a Blue Lot tag. I want to look through your mailing addresses."

"C'mon, man. I can't do that."

A whistle blew from the court below. Shoes squeaked on the floor, and then the noise stopped. The head coach addressed the team. Herrick couldn't hear exactly what he was saying.

Herrick took a breath. "If I can look through those addresses, you get an in-home with Chandler."

Boots paused. "You serious?"

"I can probably get him here on an official too." College

recruits got five official visits. Jersey kids *never* took official visits to schools like Rutgers or Ben Franklin, because they could just show up whenever they wanted. Having an official on-campus visit would create a buzz in the recruiting circles.

"You're a hard-ass, you know that?"

"You know it. But can you afford to say no? Your boss face to face with Chandler. You know he'll have a shot."

"Let me see what I can do."

Fifteen minutes later, Herrick was sitting in front of a computer scrolling through the names of every football and basketball season ticket holder for the university. One of the ticket guys told Boots to be careful, that if something like this leaked out, Ben Franklin would be screwed in the papers and legally, of course.

Herrick said, "You've been through worse."

Boots lightly punched Herrick in the shoulder. "Don't tell anybody."

Scrolling in alphabetical order, Herrick slowed when he hit the M's. No Mosleys. He pulled his phone and dialed Alex Robinson. It rang and went to voice mail. He put the phone down. Boots was tapping his foot.

"Shouldn't you be running the second team?" Herrick asked.

"Think I'll stay here."

Herrick ran it back in his head. He knew he was here on a whim and a long shot. He scrolled backwards to the C's. No Carvers. Not that there would be a Leo anyway. No reason for a locked up dude to hold on to seasons. He went back up through the R's, and that's when a name caught his eye.

"Couldn't be," he said.

He took out his phone and did a quick search in Google. The results surprised him. An address that'd been plastered all over the news for six weeks in the summer.

He waved Boots over and pointed at the name on the screen. Boots leaned over his shoulder and squinted. A few seconds later he said, "Yeah, and?"

"That's not his address. It's the address of a dead guy."

Boots said, "People buy tickets and die mid-season. Sometimes their family keeps the names on the list so they don't lose the points. Kind of morbid, if you ask me. If you transfer them over, the points go with them."

"Yeah, this guy's been dead for over a year. It was a big news story."

"I'm new to the state."

Herrick stood up, turned to the ticket broker, and thanked him. The guy shrugged and asked him not to say anything. Herrick told him not to worry.

He went back out to the lobby. Down on the floor the team was stretching or getting up some extra shots. Herrick watched for a moment, trying to process what he'd read on the computer screen. He couldn't make the connection, but it was such a big coincidence he couldn't let it go.

"So," Boots said, "Chandler?"

"I'll be in touch."

Herrick shook Boots' hand again, but his mind was elsewhere. He gave a wave down to the court and Coach waved back. Probably didn't even know who he was waving at, but a good college coach was a good networker.

Herrick walked out of the GAP into the parking lot. The sun had dipped behind the buildings, and the wind picked up. Class was letting out, and traffic was backing up on Ambulance Road. It would take Herrick forty minutes to get to the address, according to the Google Maps. Didn't matter. He had to check it out.

The tickets were under a name that had to have been hanging over Donne's head for the past year.

Herrick wanted to see why Alex Robinson had football season tickets labeled with Bill Martin's home address.

CHAPTER 59

THE DRIVE TO Bethlehem Institution was a quiet one. Robinson fiddled with the radio occasionally, sometimes settling on sports talk, other times on Top Forty. Every time he reached for the knob, Donne cleared his throat to make sure Robinson knew the gun was there. Donne's palm sweat made his grip a little slippery.

They pulled into the institution and Robinson found a parking spot. After putting the car into park, he turned to Donne and exhaled.

"Two things. One: I can't even guarantee we'll see him."

Donne wiggled the gun. "This will make sure you get us in."

Robinson held up his hands. "And two, you bring that thing in, you're going to bring a shitload of cops down on you. You know that, right?"

Donne pursed his lips. He knew. He could keep it tucked in his jeans and hidden under his jacket, but that wouldn't keep Robinson quiet. He'd sell Donne out the minute they came near a security guard.

Beyond that, he could leave the gun in the car, but that left too many variables. Best bet was the jean tuck.

"Let's go," Donne said. "You say a word, draw any attention to me or the gun, and when everything goes to hell, you'll have a hole in your chest."

"I thought you didn't want to kill me." Robinson smiled. "Well played."

They got out of the car, Donne tucked the gun, and they made the long walk through the cold air toward the building. There was a small covering of snow on the ground. The air was raw and crisp. The last of the leaves from an oak tree floated to the ground. They crunched underneath Donne's steps.

The lobby smelled like a funeral parlor. Lilacs and death hung in the air like meat at a butcher's. Someone was singing a song from *West Side Story* out of tune. Robinson eyed the receptionist, who nodded at him. He walked toward the doors that led to the main area of the building. Donne followed. With each step his insides knitted tighter together.

"Wait."

They both turned. The receptionist pointed at Donne. "Who's he?"

"Part of the deal," Robinson said.

The receptionist nodded again. As Donne started to turn back, he watched her pick up the phone and say, "He's going to be in for testing."

THE CROSSWORD PUZZLES.

One of the details that had fled from Donne's memory in the haze of booze and coke. Carver sat on his bed in white pajamas, working out of a crossword puzzle book. Still in pen. He always worked on the puzzles in pen.

When Carver looked up from the book, Donne felt like he was twenty-two all over again. He wanted to stand at attention and salute. It was because of Carver's eyes. The stone-like stare saying you weren't doing what you were supposed to.

"What is he doing here?" Carver directed his question

toward Robinson. His voice was even, acting like a confused party host. Maybe the E-vite went to the wrong person.

"We need to talk," Donne said.

"He has a gun," Robinson said. "My gun."

Carver didn't say anything.

Donne gave Robinson a glare, but didn't go for the gun. He'd come too far.

"Might as well get it over with," Carver said. He held his hands up in the air. "You killed Bill. Finish the job."

"I didn't kill Bill Martin."

"Must be a coincidence then. You were there with him. On top of a building. With a gun. A rifle. After you shot a state senator. He was a cop. I'm sure he tried to stop you."

"You know that's not true."

Carver looked at Robinson. "You disappoint me."

"Stop," Robinson said.

"Expected more of you, friend. I can't believe you brought him here."

Carver threw the crossword book against the wall. It bounced off and landed on the desk with a thud. He turned to Donne.

"You want to shoot me? Go ahead. It seems to be the way you solve problems. But I made my peace with you."

Donne said, "I should go."

"You always run, don't you. Remember? Last in?" Carver shook his head. "No, you probably don't. You don't remember anything from back then."

Shaking his head, Donne said, "You said you made your peace."

"God," Carver said. "You were more screwed up than I thought. You were a sweaty nervous mess."

Robinson was leaning back on the chair, and it was up on two legs. Donne glanced at him, and he nodded.

"Way I remember it," he said. His voice wasn't as steady as before.

Carver nodded. "I kept tabs on you. Don't you get it yet? You're an unreliable fuck-up with a trail of dead bodies in your wake. I was going to be nice. I promised myself. But now you're here."

He looked out the window on the closed door. Patients and nurses walked by not bothering to peek into the room. In fact, it seemed that the employees' walking speed picked up once they came into view. Carver was a special case. He ran this place. Donne had no idea how. Sweat formed at his brow.

Carver noticed it.

"There's nothing you can do to me that won't be a blessing. Or, at the very worst, destroy your life even more." Carver shrugged. "Win-win for me, I'd say."

Donne threw a curveball, turning to Robinson. "What about Herrick? What's his deal?"

The chair dropped to the ground. The sound of it echoed in the room. "It's time to go," Robinson said.

"You hired him to find me and protect you. But I don't think that's the real reason. It doesn't make any sense."

Robinson stood up. "Let's go."

Donne said, "I thought we were just getting comfortable."

Carver said, "You might as well tell him. You've messed up enough today."

Robinson screwed up his face, twisting his lips into a scowl. "Ask him about his team. Ask him about the one time he finally put his gun down."

Donne paused. Something about the words stuck with him. His mind traveled back to Vermont, and the time he had to ruminate. Violence begets violence.

"It's time to go," Robinson said.

He went to the door and pulled it open. Donne wasn't ready yet. He wanted Carver to open up more, tell him how he was getting the word out. What connections he made. He stood up and grabbed Robinson's arm. Robinson whirled and caught him in the jaw with a right cross. A rocket of pain traveled up into Donne's brain as he toppled backward. His vision clouded.

Carver apologized. The door swung shut and Robinson was gone. Donne grabbed his jaw. He could feel a lump beginning to form already.

Donne stood up, but lost balance and went down to one knee. Robinson was probably gone already, in the parking lot, rushing toward his car. He took a deep breath and steadied himself.

The gun was tight at his hip. Donne reached down for it. He patted it and took a breath.

A trail of bodies.

He walked to the front desk. There, he called a cab. Twenty minutes until pick-up. While he waited, he let everything Carver said stew over and over in his brain.

No chance he was right, Donne told himself.

The muscle spasms in his back and throbbing pain in his jaw said otherwise.

CHAPTER 60

ERRICK PULLED UP behind the black SUV with the Ben Franklin magnet on it. The truck was parked. Herrick took his phone out and took a picture of the license plate. He texted the photo to a cop friend and asked him to run the plate. Hopefully, he'd hear back soon, but if the cop was off-duty, it'd be a while.

Bill Martin's apartment was just upstairs. Herrick recognized the view from all the news reports. He watched the windows for a while, looking for movement or some sense that life was there. He saw nothing. No one peeked through the curtains, nothing fluttered. Before driving over, Herrick had done a quick Internet search of the address. It appeared no one had rented it out since Martin died. For a while, it was considered a crime scene. Then the cops held on to it. Perhaps it was one of those local budget things, the state or city kept paying the rent and no one knew why.

But the fact that the SUV Sheldon had described was sitting outside it made Herrick think otherwise.

A text message came in. It was simple, but the words made Herrick's blood go cold. BILL MARTIN. And the address was exactly where he sat now. Martin had been dead nearly a year and a half. Even if he had no family to deal with, his registration would have expired by now.

Herrick pulled the ASP from the console and attached the case to his belt. His heart was thudding harder than he expected. Whatever was going on in that SUV or in that apartment wasn't what he'd expected.

And Herrick didn't like when things went against expectations.

But, as Herrick had told his team so many times, "You can't control what happens to you, you can only control how you react." He dropped that phrase often, something he once heard a college coach say during a clinic. Any time he uttered it, he thought of the boy and the bomb. Today was no different.

He got out of the car and approached the SUV. Better to check that first, make sure it was empty. Last thing he needed was to head to the apartment only to be attacked from behind because the driver was just getting out of the car. He made his way around to the passenger's side, cold wind searing his face as he went. The driver would be able to see him in the rearview, but would still have to crawl across the seats to get to him.

Hand on the ASP holster, he crept up to the passenger's side window. He paused, counting to three. Nothing happened. He leaned forward and looked in the window. The car was empty. He tried the door, but it was locked. No one was ever that lucky.

He snapped the ASP open and swung it at the passenger window. It shattered, and the alarm went blaring. Herrick ignored it, reached inside and unlocked the door. He opened the door and then the glove compartment. He started to dig through paperwork. Everything belonged to Bill Martin. All the expected paperwork. Herrick's heart pounded harder.

If Donne was here, Herrick wondered how he'd react. How had no one noticed this? The police had to have been all over that place, they had to have seen Martin's body, they had investigated everything. Bill Martin couldn't have faked his death.

The alarm stopped with a squeak. Herrick wrapped his

hand around the ASP tight.

"Excuse me," a familiar voice said.

Herrick turned around. A tall, thin man stood on the doorstep of the apartment.

"What are you doing to my car?" The voice was unmistakably Lucas Mosley's. The build of his body as well.

Herrick said, "I thought Bill Martin owned this car."

Mosley took a breath. His keys were in one hand. His other one was free. Herrick had expected a gun. "Don't you have a game to coach?"

"Maybe we should end this, Lucas."

Mosley nodded. "The police are on their way."

"It'll be fun to explain who you are."

"Yeah, they're going to listen to the guy covered in broken glass, holding an ASP."

"We should talk."

"You have a game to coach."

"My assistants will take care of it."

Mosley laughed. "Yeah. If it happens. Haven't you lost enough?"

"Why are you torturing me?"

Mosley shook his head. "If you loved your team, you'd get there."

"They can win without me."

"Not if the game doesn't happen."

And that's when the light bulb went on in Herrick's brain.

"What did you do?"

Mosley shrugged.

Herrick didn't ask again. The sirens were coming closer, howling in the distance. But he didn't wait. He dashed to his car. He'd lost too much already.

He wasn't going to lose his team. Behind him, Mosley laughed.

Herrick didn't care. He'd get another chance.

CHAPTER 61

ERRICK PULLED AROUND the corner and saw the smoke hovering in the air over Easton Avenue. His sense of direction set off alarm bells in his head, and he pulled over for a second to process it. He'd been in that area only days earlier, and the smoke in the air was probably not a coincidence.

Sarah's apartment had been blown sky high, and now a place where Donne had spent a lot of time. Life does not often offer up coincidences that big. He put the car back into drive and headed toward the smoke.

Three minutes later, he was searching for a place to park amongst media, cops, and firemen. The bar was a husk, dark clouds billowing out of the windows. The flames licked the siding and reached into the sky. A stream of water arced into the sky and crashed into the walls. Herrick threw on his hazards and double-parked the car.

He got out and started searching the faces, looking for anyone familiar. Looking for Donne. Over near an ambulance, he saw the bartender. He was standing by himself, blanket over his shoulders and a mug of something hot in his hands. Herrick moved in that direction, searching his brain for the guy's name. It came to him when he was within three feet of Artie.

Artie saw Herrick coming and said, "Jesus Christ."

"Are you okay?" Herrick asked.

"Is this your fault?"

Herrick couldn't smell the drink wafting from the cup. He could only sense the cinders.

"The same thing happened to my—friend's—house this afternoon," he said.

"I don't want to be involved in any of this."

"Is Jackson here?"

Artie took a sip of coffee and swallowed it like he was downing the strongest whiskey. He crushed his teeth together and steam inched its way out between them.

"He was. But not when this happened. They threw a bomb into my bar. It was all I had." His eyes were red. He drank more.

Artie told him everything. Herrick listened, but the details were vague. Artie was in the back. He heard a crash, then a boom, and then there were flames. He called 911 and then ran out.

"Where is Jackson?" Herrick asked.

"Hell if I know. He said—" Artie drank. "He said something about Carver. I've tried to get in touch with him, but nothing."

"Did you talk to the police?"

Artie laughed. "How could I not?"

"Artie!" The voice came from behind them. Herrick turned around. It was Donne, clearly not afraid of being spotted by the cops.

"'Bout fucking time," Artie said.

"I'm sorry," Donne said. "I'm so sorry."

Artie just shook his head. He turned and walked away, around the corner of the ambulance. Donne stood next to Herrick, arms at his sides.

"We have to talk," Herrick said.

"He could be going to find a cop," Donne said. "I'm ... I'm ..."

"My car is over there," Herrick said. "Let's go."

Once settled, Herrick pulled a U-turn and went back toward Bill Martin's apartment. He filled Donne in.

"You let him go?"

"He had a gun, and leverage. The cops were on their way."

"Why was he taking Bill Martin's identity?" Donne rubbed his hands together. His voice was softer than earlier. "Let's go back there. He could be there."

Herrick obeyed, but the SUV was gone, like he suspected. Donne stared out the window, looking upward. Herrick wondered what he was thinking.

"I'm sorry about this morning."

"You can trust me," Herrick said.

Donne shook his head.

"You're coming with me. I have a game to coach. We can talk on the way, and figure things out."

"Just what I want to do. Watch high school basketball."

"Better than moping." He sounded like a grandmother.

Herrick accelerated on the open road. He caught the turnpike and pushed the car to seventy. The road was wide open.

"You ever lose someone important?" Donne asked.

"The reason I went into the military at age eighteen. My parents went away."

Donne nodded. "They're alive?"

Herrick didn't look at Donne. Shrugged. Traffic slowed as they neared the Newark Airport.

"Every time I get close to someone," Donne said. "Every time. People die or get hurt because of me. I can't do this anymore."

Herrick kept driving.

IT WAS DARK by the time they reached St. Paul's. Donne filled Herrick in on the trip to see Carver.

"What about Robinson?" Herrick asked.

Donne told him what Robinson said—to think about the team. And when he put the gun down for good. Herrick's gut burned trying to figure out what Robinson meant when he told

Donne that. He didn't have time to consider it more. He got out of the car and heard the bounce of basketballs. In the gym, the team was shooting around, already in uniform. The stands were just starting to fill.

Herrick nodded for Donne to follow him into the locker room. Herrick had to change into a suit. It was the head coach way. No sweatpants tonight. He always kept his suit locked in one of the lockers the AD let him use. Too often he was out on a case working before a game, and never had time to go and change. So at the beginning of each game week, he brought a suit to the gym and kept it there. At the end of the week, he took it to the dry cleaners.

"You're just going to stash me back here?" Donne asked.

"For now."

Herrick's phone rang. He looked at it and saw the unknown number. "It's him," he said.

"Answer it."

Herrick did.

"I'm surprised you ran away," Lucas said.

"Live to fight another day."

"Today is the endgame," Lucas said. "In fact, I think it's right now. Jackson's there right now, isn't he?"

Herrick's heart rate picked up and he took a look at Donne, who mouthed the word *what*.

"You'll like this," Lucas grunted. "Alex came up with this one. I was just talking to him. He came to check out my handiwork and saw you two together again."

Herrick waited. Donne tapped his foot.

"Look in your locker," Lucas said.

"You're close to us."

"You have no idea. Look."

Herrick turned toward the locker. He opened it. His suit was hanging there, neatly pressed and still in plastic. Below it, resting on the bottom of the locker, was a pistol. The room got cold.

"Put me on speakerphone," Lucas said.

Herrick did as he was told. "You're on."

"Here's how it's going to go." Lucas laughed. "It's going to be fun. If you don't do what I say, I'm going to take out the school like the apartment and the bar. Don't believe me? That wouldn't be smart.."

Herrick said, "Tell me what you want."

"How long has it been since you used a gun?"

"I think you already know."

"Pick it up and shoot Donne. You don't, the place goes up in smoke." Lucas laughed. "You have three minutes. I'll let you talk it over. Leave the phone on. I want to hear this."

CHAPTER 62

ROBINSON TAPPED HIS fingers on the desk and stared at his landline. Too much of that these days. Too much waiting. Too much praying.

It took a lot to convince Mosley to let Herrick live. Hell, it took a lot to convince himself. He promised Mosley extra money on top of the original agreement. Money he didn't have and money he couldn't get.

Robinson pulled the top drawer open on his desk. The gun wasn't there, taken by Donne. But the switchblade was. It was the only option Robinson had anymore.

Once Mosley completed the job, he was going to have to come and get his cash. His unmarked bills.

And Robinson was going to have to kill him.

Herrick, meanwhile — man, he was going to suffer. Lose his job, his girl, and he would have shot a gun again. What choice would he have had?

The phone didn't ring.

Robinson stood up and walked over to the window. The sun had set, but the New York crowd was just arriving via New

Jersey Transit. Men in suits and women in dresses hurried off the local and tried to find their cars. A few of them waved at family members who were picking them up.

A family that cared.

A family that existed.

He couldn't bring himself to think of the good times, when he and his sister were little. Not for a long time. But suddenly, as he watched the buses pass, it all came swirling back. Sitting in the kitchen as the toaster went off — *ding* — on a Saturday morning. That was the sign to watch your head. First, you'd hear the marble roll down the tube. It would clink into something, and the stovetop would go on. Eggs.

Bernie would cackle, and his mother would yell that they were going to make a mess. And, sometimes they did. A lot of times, these crude contraptions his dad made to make Saturday mornings fun didn't work exactly. If one thing went wrong, the eggs would splatter against the kitchen window and they'd end up at a diner. It always bothered his sister. She wanted things to be perfect.

Complicated perfection.

Just like Leo's crossword puzzles.

Tonight had to go perfectly.

Robinson leaned his forehead against the window. The air outside made the glass cold.

Soon it would be winter.

Even sooner this would be over, and he'd be able to breathe again.

CHAPTER 63

"**D**o it," DONNE said.

Herrick put the phone on the bench next to the gun. He sat down next to it. The flush of adrenaline coursed through his body like a rushing wave. He stared at the gun, resting at an angle. All he had to do was snatch it up, pull the trigger, and watch Jackson Donne crash to the ground.

He looked at Donne, standing against another row of lockers, his hands at his sides. His face was slack, the beard low, eyes droopy. His skin was pale.

"What do you have to lose if you shoot me?" Donne asked. "I have nothing left. If this is what Alex needs, if this is how everything will go away, then do it. Just shoot me."

Donne spread his hands and gave Herrick a fine target. It was just like when the boy spread his hands and called out to Allah. Herrick picked up the gun, hefting it. Just a quick squeeze, a loud bang, and he'd be done with this. Lucas Mosley would be a memory.

Shooting Jackson Donne. Just like the boy — all the problems would go away. No.

They wouldn't. Just like they didn't the last time he shot a gun. The investigation. The tears. The nightmares. The weeks, months—a year?—of therapy.

He took the coaching job to give back. Not make things worse around here.

The silence hung in the locker room like icicles on a gutter. The gray metal of the gun glinted in the pale fluorescent lights above them.

"What are you waiting for?"

"I don't want to do this."

"It's the only way." Donne's voice was calm and soft.

Herrick took a breath and turned the gun on Donne. Muscle memory was kicking in. Instincts and training taking over. Just a few pounds of pressure. Herrick kept his finger on the trigger guard.

The gun was heavy, like a medicine ball. The grip dug into his palm. He put his finger on the trigger. Donne took a step forward. A split second and Donne would be dead, and Herrick could move on from there.

The next step.

Was Donne right? Did this job mean people close to you would get hurt? He pictured Sarah out in the gym hearing the shot go off. He thought of the team—the kids he asked to trust him—confused and then running in terror.

Herrick adjusted the grip of the gun.

"I pull this trigger, and your problems are over, Jackson," Herrick said. Then he shook his head. "But mine would just start."

The phone crackled. "Now you're getting it. Two minutes."

Donne tilted his head. "Shoot me."

Herrick aimed.

"Think about it, Jackson. I pull the trigger—guns aren't quiet. They're going to hear it. Coach shoots man in locker room. Great headline."

Donne said, "You can work your way out of it."

It would be so easy. Just like it was in the sandbox.

"Do you have a death wish or something?"

Herrick lowered the gun.

"I'm just tired."

"There has to be another way."

"Sixty seconds," the phone crackled.

Herrick put the gun down, reached for the phone, and hung up. "Now we can talk."

"You probably just accelerated his plan."

"He seems to play by rules. A sick set of rules, but rules nonetheless," Herrick said. "Take the gun and see if you can find him out there. I'm going to evacuate everyone out the front of the building."

"What if that's where Lucas is?"

Herrick shook his head. "That's not a smart attack point. If he's serious, he'll take out the gym. With all the wood and rubber and open air, it'll go up in flames quick. Take the gun, but don't let anyone see you with it. Go out the door we came in. Find him."

Donne reached over to the bench and picked up the gun. He tucked it into his pants, and then untucked his shirt. "If this were anywhere else, you would have shot me."

Herrick shook his head. "Go get him."

DONNE SPRINTED ACROSS the basketball court, sidestepping a lay-up line on the St. Paul's side. One of the kids told him to watch the fuck out. He ignored the comment and hit the door at full stride. He heard Herrick behind him asking for the crowd's attention.

Donne kept moving, the crunch of asphalt beneath his feet and the weight of the gun in his waistband. The street was quiet. Halfway down the block, Donne could see the whirling blue light of a police car. Donne squinted and could see something next to the cruiser, leaning up against the driver's side door. His stomach clenched.

He approached, his nerves jangling like Christmas bells. Fight-or-flight kicked in—a feeling Donne had experienced too many times in his life. Always so easy to run away. He took a breath and pushed through it, turning up toward the cop car. He kept the gun hidden. That was the last thing he needed. The moment the cops figured out who he was, the tenor of the day would change.

Three feet later, Donne realized what it was he approached. The blue light from the cop car glinted off a small piece of metal on the front of the oblong shape. It was reflecting off a badge. The person wearing that badge wasn't moving.

Donne shot forward and called out. "Hey! Hey, you okay?"

That was when Donne realized the police cruiser was still running. And someone was behind the wheel. The siren wailed first. Then the engine roared. The car leapt from its parking spot and headed directly toward Donne. He dove out of the way, praying the cop was able to keep his head.

The cruiser sped by Donne just as he hit asphalt, shoulder first. Fire ran up his arm into his fingertips. He grunted and rolled on to his back. He pulled the gun, sat up, and aimed. But the cop car turned the corner before he could shoot.

He stood up slowly, letting the pain wind down into a dull throb. He spotted the cop, leaning head first along the curb. His body was twisted awkwardly like a human pretzel. Donne jogged up to him and found the officer, mouth open, no air escaping.

Donne tried to find a pulse, but couldn't. The cop was dead. He turned back toward the school and saw the police cruiser had made a U-turn. It was now sitting at the corner of the T, pointed nose first toward the school. A flame sparked up in the driver's seat.

Time was up.

CHAPTER 64

DONNE HAD SCARS from bullet wounds all over his torso. Any time he showered, he rubbed soap over the grainy bumps, and remembered. He'd remember seeing bullets flying in his direction, his mind usually playing it in slow motion. Bill Martin pulling the trigger, the flash going off and then the impact knocking him back onto the warehouse floor.

Now, as he charged the police cruiser, his stomach wasn't full of butterflies or nerves. What he told Herrick just minutes earlier was correct. He didn't care. All that mattered was saving the people inside the gym, and if that meant he had to take the fall, so be it.

Donne pulled his gun, stopped running, and aimed. The flash of fire in the cruiser grew brighter. Donne squeezed the trigger and fired three bullets in quick succession. He didn't aim at the glass, didn't want to kill Lucas. He wanted to talk to Lucas. All he wanted to do was draw the man away from the school. The bullets embedded themselves into the police car passenger door with three thumps. The flame flashed left; Mosley was looking at him.

Donne jogged forward three more steps and saw the passenger window recede. The ball of light came his way, a bottle of alcohol flying on a low line drive. It wasn't a kill shot, no way it'd even travel enough distance to hit Donne, but it shattered in front of him, a burst of flame and heat spreading along the street. Donne stepped back, a wave of sweat forming at his forehead. He cringed and leveled the gun at the police car again.

He blinked the light out of his eyes and tried to focus his aim. The fire lit the dark sky, giving him a better view. He took a deep breath and prepared to shoot. Then he noticed it; no one was in the cruiser.

Donne exhaled and looked left. The quickest route around the flames would be to the left, if Mosley were coming his way. Nothing. If Mosley was heading toward the school he'd go right. Before Donne could twirl, his back exploded. And then again. He went down hard, the gun clattering away from him toward the last remnants of the fire. Donne thought he heard sirens.

He rolled onto his back, looking up into the eyes of the thin man standing over him. The man wielded the police baton over his head like a sword.

"Mosley," Donne said. "Just kill me."

The words came with such ease it surprised even Donne. Kate appeared before him, reaching out in his direction smiling. He was surprised. He expected to see Jeanne or Bill Martin or any of the other names that had been with him longer. His body relaxed and Kate faded, leaving Lucas Mosley standing there, smiling.

"With pleasure," Mosley said.

The baton cut the through the air heading toward Donne's head. Donne closed his eyes and listened to the wind.

HIGH SCHOOLERS NEVER panic. They'd been through enough fire drills that the alarm to evacuate did not cause screaming or running. It caused some chuckles and some groans of annoyance. The fans in the crowd and the teams picked up their belongings and moved toward the exit of the gym.

Herrick had told them it was just a drill. That the state needed to evacuate events from time to time as practice, and this time they were going to go out the gym doors and to the front of the building. It sounded legit, even if it wasn't. Herrick caught the eye of Sarah and the principal, who made their way toward him as everyone else went out the big wooden doors.

Sarah grabbed the principal's arm and told him to stay with the students and they'd be right out. She'd get to the bottom of this.

The principal turned and said, "This is the sort of thing that can get you fired."

"*If* we win state this year, I can get enough donations to keep the doors open." Herrick kept his voice even, despite feeling his pulse in his ears.

The principal's shoulders slumped and he turned and headed toward the students. Hopefully, he'd also deliver that proclamation to the nuns.

Sarah put a hand on his shoulders. "What's going on?"

Herrick took a deep breath, and then told her about Mosley. Her face went white.

"How is this stuff coming back to us? It never has before."

Herrick shook his head. "I shouldn't have taken this case. It was too big for me. I should have stuck with what I do best. Coaching the team."

"You've come this far," she said. "Might as well see it through." She squeezed his shoulder.

When his player died last year, she didn't react that way. He had thought he had seen the case through and got the kid home safely. But he'd made a mistake: Gangs don't give up, and they get what they want. Especially when it's what the kid thinks he wants too. He didn't think Mosley would either.

"I will," he said. "Can you stick with the crowd? I'm going to go find Donne."

Sarah agreed. She took one step away and that's when they heard the gunshots. And then the explosion.

His ASP was still at his hip. He snatched it out and with a snap of the wrist it was at attack length. Running toward the door, he wished he'd said something to Sarah, something inspiring.

But he wasn't sure it would have mattered. She wouldn't have heard him.

Not over the screaming of the kids.

ONNE OPENED HIS eyes. The blow had never come. Instead, Mosley's arm was stuck mid-swing, Herrick's ASP deflecting the blow.

Mosley swung left and chopped Herrick in the stomach. He gasped and stepped backward.

Mosley said, "You're both here. Nice."

He swung the baton before Herrick could regain his balance. It caught Herrick in the stomach again, and he fell backward. He landed on the ground and didn't move.

Fire burned in Donne's gut. If he let Mosley kill him, Herrick would be next. He couldn't let that happen.

CHAPTER 65

ONNE SWEPT HIS legs, catching Mosley in the ankle. Mosley's knees buckled and he toppled to the ground, the baton clattering off somewhere. Donne jumped up and straddled him, raining three crosses into Mosley's jaw. The bounty hunter's head snapped backwards and caught pavement. He went limp.

Donne leaned back and took a breath. The cold air singed his sweat and cooled his skin. Before he could get to his feet, Mosley snapped up and caught Donne in the stomach. The air went from his body and he toppled backwards. Donne hit the ground and rolled. He took a look at Herrick.

He wasn't dead.

In fact, he was pushing himself off the ground with one hand, up on one knee and wiping blood from his face. Donne nodded at him, but it was a waste of time. Mosley hit him like a wrestler, tying him up with a hold. Donne tried to gasp for air, but it stopped at the back of his throat. Donne put two hands on the arm around his windpipe and pulled. The arm wouldn't budge. He tried to call out for Herrick, but no sound escaped his lips.

Turned out he didn't need to call for Herrick. Mosley went slack when Herrick hit him hard. Donne wasn't able to see where, but he heard the grunt and something crack. Donne fell to his knees and gasped for air. It made its way to his lungs this time. The iciness felt soothing on his insides. Some of the tightness loosened.

Donne didn't know how much time he had to catch his breath. He rubbed his throat, massaging the muscles looser. He turned and faced the fight. Herrick had regained his ASP and returned the favor Mosley had given him by rapping him across the face.

The sounds of sirens filled the air. After the explosion and the gunfire, Donne was surprised it took this long.

Mosley tried to scramble back to his feet, but Herrick wouldn't let him, whacking him with another overhead shot from the ASP. He raised his arm once more, and Donne was afraid this would be a killing blow. He sprinted over to Herrick and grabbed his wrist. The force of Herrick's swing pulled Donne forward, but he was able to stop the blow from landing.

Herrick turned toward him. His teeth were gritted, and the muscles in his arms were taut, like a rope pulled tight. His breath was ragged.

"Don't," Donne said. "Cops."

"Like that would stop you." He forced the words out in gasps.

Donne shrugged, trying to stay calm. He could do a body count, and it would take more than all ten fingers. His stomach lurched. Calmness fled.

"Maybe not," he said. "But to you —" Donne pointed at the school. "You have a lot to lose."

Herrick paused, and then relaxed his arms. He closed the ASP and replaced it in his holster. Mosley staggered onto his elbows. Herrick pushed him back down with his foot. Mosley did not put up a fight.

"Another day," the bounty hunter said.

"Doubt it," Herrick said.

Down the long street, the flashing blue lights appeared. The sirens weren't far behind, echoing in their direction. Donne figured they had thirty seconds. He looked at Herrick, who already had his wallet and ID out.

"You really want to be around when they get here?" Herrick asked.

"They'll see me running if I bail now. That won't help your story." Donne pointed over his shoulder. "There's a dead cop over there you can't explain. They only want me for questioning, right?"

Herrick gestured to Mosley. "He can explain the cop."

"I can corroborate." Donne rubbed his wrist.

The first car squealed to a stop and two more followed. Doors flew open, guns were drawn, and people were screaming. Herrick's hands went into the air. He shouted his name and job over and over. Donne kept his own hands up as well.

Two cops approached them, and shined a flashlight in Herrick's face.

A cop, whose name tag said Sanderson, said, "Matt, what the hell?"

"This guy. He's trouble. He took out one of yours." Herrick pointed down the street toward the crumpled body.

"Jesus," Sanderson said. "You guys, go check him out."

Two cops sprinted over toward the body. One of them was calling for an ambulance into the radio receiver pinned to his shirt. Donne couldn't hear what the dispatcher responded with, but the words were fast and high-pitched.

Two more cops approached, and Herrick got off of Mosley. The cops snapped cuffs on Mosley. "Only reason we aren't doing it to you, Matt, is 'cause we know you. But that thing—"

"Understood." He passed his ASP over to one of the cops.

Sanderson turned the flashlight on Donne's face.

"Who the hell are you?"

He felt Herrick's eyes on him as he said, "Jackson Donne."

"No shit." Sanderson stepped closer. "Wow. Big day here, guys."

Donne didn't move.

"He's with me," Herrick tried.

Sanderson laughed. "I can't help you with that one, Matt."

Suddenly, Donne's hands weren't over his head anymore. They were behind his back. The cold metal of handcuffs wrapped around his wrists and bit at his circulation. He was pushed, hard, and started walking toward one of the cop cars. Donne didn't resist. One of the cops recited Miranda rights.

Sanderson said, "They found three bodies in Vermont. One of them was a cop, and this guy's prints were everywhere."

Sanderson kept talking to Herrick, but the words faded. He could feel the sharp edge in tone, however.

Three cop cars, and two suspects. They slammed the door on Donne. He looked out the window back toward the scene. An ambulance appeared at the corner, turning slowly toward the situation. The two cops who checked on the dead one were running. Sanderson's arms were out in a placating way.

And then they handcuffed Herrick as well.

CHAPTER 66

THEY PUSHED HERRICK away from the other two, into an interrogation room, not a holding cell. They didn't pull his arm gently, they tugged and pushed him through the crowd of onlooking cops just getting on duty or filling out paperwork in their cubicles. Somewhere a TV played the opening quarter of the Knicks game. The Garden was almost as quiet as the police station.

His entire body throbbed.

The interrogation room was just like every other one in police stations across the nation. The only difference was, instead of plain white walls, they'd painted this one blue. The Jersey City police station had to be rebuilt a few years back after some psychopath tried to blow it up. Since then, that at least gave this room a soothing look.

Two detectives — Patrick McKinny and someone Herrick didn't recognize — stood against the far wall. McKinny had a duffel bag over his shoulder. The door slammed shut behind him, and the nameless one walked over and unlocked the cuffs. Herrick rubbed his wrists. The nameless one pulled out a chair for Herrick and asked if he wanted a coffee. Herrick said that sounded great. But maybe an icepack as well.

The cop left. Herrick sat. McKinny put his hands on the chair on the opposite side of the table and leaned over it.

"What the hell, Matt?"

Herrick sat back in the chair, crossed his fingers like he was praying, and didn't say anything.

"Jackson Donne?" McKinny's voice cracked.

Herrick stayed silent.

"I'm not charging you with anything," McKinny said. "You can leave if you want. The other two ..."

The nameless cop came in with the coffee and ice pack. He put them down on the table. He left. Herrick watched the steam swirl into the air and dissipate. The paper cup was thin, so he didn't touch it yet. He wasn't in the mood to burn his fingers too. His stomach hurt like hell.. He was stunned, but he didn't think anything was broken.

He reached over for the icepack, and then pressed it against his ribs. Pain throbbed against the cold. The pain from the knife wound in his side had come back too, like an old friend he hadn't seen in a while, but hadn't missed.

"Those batons of yours, they hurt," he said. The words sounded dull, as if he were drugged. Might be because his mind wasn't moving as fast as it should have.

"Are you okay?"

"Who was he?" Herrick didn't like talking all that much, but he really wanted to know.

McKinny rubbed his face and took a long breath. "John Higgins. He was twenty-eight. Has a baby girl and a wife at home. He was a good cop. Goddamn good police officer."

"I'm sorry." A tremor ran through Herrick. "It's my fault. I could have handled this."

McKinny shook his head. "You got police protection. You did what you were supposed to. And John was doing his job. It's just ..."

"You wish I never brought this rain of shit down on you."

"Was it Donne who did this, Matt?"

Herrick shook his head. "He's the good guy."

"He's a murderer according to the APB we got. Another dead cop up there? Plus two others they're trying to identify."

Herrick closed his eyes. The ice pack started to warm. He adjusted the pack to find another section of cold.

"You need a doctor?" McKinny said.

Herrick didn't respond. He opened his eyes. The coffee had stopped steaming in front of him. After picking up the cup, he took a sip. The liquid burned the inside of his mouth anyway. He put the cup down and pressed the pack harder against himself.

"No," he said. "I need to get out of here."

"Tell me about the other guy."

"Lucas Mosley," Herrick said. "That's the guy you want. Bounty hunter. Worked with his brother. They were bounty hunters for criminals. You should talk to him. Look him up."

McKinny nodded. "What is this all about?"

Herrick leaned back. The blood shifted and now a different part of his torso throbbed. The back of his head hurt too. Not enough ice packs to ease his pain. He wondered if he should even try to sleep tonight. The haze had started to clear in his mind, but he still felt groggy and sleepy.

"At this point," he said, "hell if I know. Revenge? Can I go home now?"

McKinny shrugged. "You're going to help us out with this, aren't you? I'm trusting you here. One of ours died."

"Yeah. I got you." Herrick exhaled. Even breathing hurt. "Mosley wanted me dead. I'm not sure why. There was a contract out for me and for Donne. Apparently we're connected somehow, even though before yesterday the most I knew about Donne came from NJ dot com and stories people told in bars. But there was enough of a connection that the Mosleys were after us."

"There is more than one of them?"

Herrick thought about correcting McKinny and letting him know what happened to the other Mosley. Decided not to.

"I need to rest. I'll figure things out and call you in the

morning."

"Probably shouldn't drive tonight. I'll call a cab."

"No," Herrick said. He gave McKinny Sarah's number. He needed to make some more amends. He needed to know if the team was okay. He needed to know if the electricity that was there this morning still ran between them.

Reaching into his duffel bag, McKinny took out Herrick's ASP. It was closed. The cop placed it on his desk, and took a deep breath.

"You are good guy, Matt. I trust you."

McKinny left the room. He was gone for a long time. Herrick stared at the drop ceiling. He wished he had a pencil to toss at it.

Instead, he forced more coffee into his mouth and tried to ignore the pain. He focused on keeping everything in focus.

There was still too much to do.

Like getting Donne out of here. In a way that didn't get the both of them into more trouble. And then dealing with Leo Carver.

It was time to end of all this bullshit once and for all.

The ice pack had lost its chill.

CHAPTER 67

THE PUNCH SENT Donne reeling smack into the iron bars. He gasped for air and grabbed his chin. The bars, however, caused pain to shoot from back to front of his torso like a race car down a straightaway. A race car with a knife attached to its front fender.

The cop's right came flying in and Donne couldn't get his arms up quickly enough to block. The fist smashed into his nose and caused his vision to blur. He grunted and went down to his knees. Tears formed in his eyes. He caught a foot to the ribs and rolled onto his back and then into the fetal position. He worked hard not to make a sound as more blows came raining down.

"That's for John!" one cop yelled.

"Cop killer!" another said.

"In prison, no one can hear you scream." That brought laughter. And more kicks to the ribs. Donne didn't respond.

When everything throbbed, it became not a series of bruises and cracked ribs, but just one wound. Donne was one giant sore. He'd come back to help and instead, was getting his "comeuppance," as one of the cops put it.

For doing nothing wrong.

But the cops didn't know that. He didn't know how long he lay there. Consciousness faded in and out. The blows didn't. He kept his eyes closed and fought to keep breathing. He was lucky this was the Jersey City precinct, not the New Brunswick one.

"Hey! Okay!" It was a different voice. Donne thought it sounded hazy. "That's enough."

Someone spit on him.

"I said enough! Get back to work. We got him. It's over."

Donne stayed frozen in the position. A drumbeat played throughout his body, his nerves trying to figure out what pain he should focus on first. The room got hot. Then cold. He wondered if he was going into shock.

"I can't believe you idiots. Nobody took video, did they? Delete that shit. Someone gets fired because of a Vine video ..."

Donne rolled onto his back and sprawled out. He dared to open his eyes. The light dangling above him obscured his vision at first, but after blinking a few times, the world came back into focus. Cops surrounded him like in a football huddle. Two of them were on their phones. He exhaled and the air wheezed out of him.

One cop crouched down next to him. He whistled. "The famous Jackson Donne."

The pain had fallen to a dull roar, the kind you feel after your first ever workout. The cops knew what they were doing, and minus the first two punches, they avoided his head.

"You need a doctor or a hospital?"

Donne shook his head. The huddle dispersed, except for the crouched cop.

"Good. What the hell are you doing back here? You the reason shit is blowing up everywhere today?" The cop reached out a hand. Donne ignored it. He liked the cold, concrete prison floor. It was like ice on his bruises.

"I didn't bomb anything," he said.

Shut up. Shut up! You know better. Keep your mouth shut and get your lawyer on the phone. His brain was running a mile a minute.

Jesus, would Lester even take your calls anymore?

"I didn't do anything wrong," he found himself saying. Couldn't even listen to his own advice.

The cop pressed his lips together and shook his head.

"Did you think the beard would fool anyone? I mean, you do look like a lumberjack. But once you waltz back into this state and start fighting with people... One of our contacts down in New Brunswick was at a fire today. He said the owner of the place said to look out for you. He told them to call us. So our ears perked up. And then you walk into the middle of a fistfight outside of a school."

"Trying to help."

The cop shook his head. "Not what the guy next door said. He said he was trying to stop you. That you killed our friend."

"That guy is insane. A murderer." Donne swallowed and a burst of light exploded in front of his eyes. "He killed the cop."

"You shot a senator."

Donne shook his head. His mouth was dry and talking hurt his throat. That was on the bottom of the list of injuries to worry about, but at least it was something he could control. He worked on breathing steadily instead.

"You have a lawyer?" the cop asked.

"I didn't do anything."

The cop laughed. "Really? After all the times you've been in the news, you think we can't get you on *something*? I'll ask again. Lawyer?"

Donne nodded and hoped Lester Russell was still in business. The images of the dead danced in his mind and formed figures in the light above his head. Ghosts in a jail cell.

"Better get him on the phone," the cop said.

"What about Mosley?"

"We're dealing with that. Not your problem." The cop laughed. "Well, judging by the stories he's telling about you, he is your problem."

"Herrick."

The cop stood up, brushed off his pants. "Not your problem either. You going to get up or are you going to lay there for a while?"

Donne didn't answer.

"Let me know when you want the phone."

"Water," Donne said.

"Yeah, we'll take care of that. Jesus Christ, what a night."

Donne rested his hands on his chest and stared up at the light. It wobbled a bit, swaying after the jail cell door slammed shut. It was hypnotic and for an instant Donne thought he could fall asleep right there. Just five minutes. He would need it.

He had the feeling there wouldn't be many more restful sleeps coming. He felt like everything had finally caught up with him.

He didn't need to go to hell when he died. He was already there.

Stuck in a Jersey City prison cell with the ghosts of the past floating around him, about to reap their vengeance.

CHAPTER 68

THEY DIDN'T SPEAK on the drive home.

But Sarah got out of the car with Herrick and helped him up to his apartment. She'd gotten lucky and found a parking space only half a block away. Hoboken was notorious for double parking and police tickets, so this was a minor miracle. The first, and only, one of the night.

She sat Herrick down on the couch, fetched him Advil and water, and then sat next to him. The earth didn't crackle at their closeness. Herrick downed the Advil and the glass of water. He wished the liquid was stronger.

"You hit your head on the asphalt," Sarah said.

Herrick chuckled. Just this morning, that probably would have meant something else. Now? He rested his head back on the couch and looked at her.

"I'm okay," he said. "Love tap."

"This is bad, Matt. I'm not kidding."

The couch was soft and his eyes were heavy. Maybe he could just close them for a few minutes. A charge of electricity jolted him awake. Sarah had pinched him.

"I'm talking to you." Her voice was stiff.

"Did anybody get hurt?" Herrick exhaled. "The kids?"
Sarah patted him on the thigh. "No. Everyone is okay."

"I'm gonna win state with them this year."

"Well, you better be able to explain how you happened to
have a fire drill as a maniac and a fugitive were out behind the
school trying to blow the place up."

He thought about Donne, wondering how he was holding
up. Herrick needed a plan to get him out of there. A hotshot
lawyer maybe or a piece of evidence that would pin everything
on Mosley would work. But not tonight, his brain was working
fine, his mind wasn't cloudy. Maybe self-diagnosing wasn't
the smartest move he ever made, but they did it all the time in
Afghanistan. Avoid the medic and just keep pushing.

He just needed some sleep. Herrick needed to get his mind
just a few moments of rest. Needed to stop playing things over
in his head. He blinked. When he opened his eyes, the boy was
there, arms akimbo, mouth moving just like it had years ago
when Herrick pulled the trigger.

And then the words came spilling out of his mouth.

"I don't know what to do." His throat got tight and his eyes
burned.

He started to gulp for air and his chest was tight. His hands
were shaking. Sarah sat up straight and said his name. It came
to him as if it were cutting through static. Herrick tried to catch
his breath, but it wouldn't come. His heart was hammering.

Sarah wrapped her arms around his shoulders and pulled
him in close. He put his head on her shoulder and returned the
embrace. The world started to come back into focus. He held
Sarah tight.

"You're okay, Matt." She caressed his hair. His heart rate
started to slow. It'd been years since his last attack. Not since
the army psychiatrist's office, when she made him play out the
worst moment of his life over and over again. Describe in detail,
as if she was going to get the guilt out of him through words
only. Instead it sent him into fits and gasps.

Now, he pulled Sarah tight into him. The pain went away,

replaced with the fire of the adrenaline in his veins, and his body trying to settle itself down. Sarah pulled into him just as tightly. Herrick blinked away the heat in his eyes.

Sarah pulled back away from him.

He looked in her eyes and took a deep breath. It went down into his lungs like it was supposed to.

"I'm getting there. I'm sorry. I—"

She smiled, brushed some hair off his forehead. "Don't apologize. I get it."

He opened his mouth one more time, but stopped before he could say anything dumb. Instead he leaned in and kissed her. Sarah returned it, her lips pressing against his. They did that for a while.

When they broke the kiss, Sarah also broke the embrace. Herrick's face was warm. Sarah's cheeks were flushed. She laughed. Herrick started to talk.

"Don't you dare apologize," she said.

"Happy hour?" he asked.

"Any time." Sarah straightened her shirt and ran a hand through her hair. "You need to fix stuff with the boss."

"I need to fix a lot of things." The pain in his jaw started to throb its way back to the forefront. "I have to get Jackson Donne out of prison. He doesn't deserve to be there. We got the guy. The cops got the right guy too."

"Let them figure it out." Sarah got up and picked up the empty glass of water. "They're cops. It's their job. They'll get it right."

Herrick shook his head. Bad idea. "I need to help them out. I need to finish this."

"You just told me you didn't know what to do."

Herrick waved her off. His breathing was normal now. On the street outside, a couple of drunk kids were singing Katy Perry at the top of their lungs.

"It all comes down to Alex Robinson," Herrick said.

Sarah went into the kitchen. He heard her moving dishes and glasses around. A few minutes later, she came back with a glass of red wine. Probably one of the bottles he'd gotten from clients that he'd never decided to open.

"I'm going to stay here tonight."

Herrick felt his face heat up again.

"Just to make sure you're okay. I'll sleep on the couch. Check on you during the night." Sarah took a sip. "They closed the school for tomorrow. Too much press. Too much police presence."

Herrick nodded.

"Go try to sleep," she said.

She didn't have to tell him twice. He got up, gave her a kiss on the cheek, and went into his bedroom and lay down. In the other room, Sarah turned on the TV. Herrick closed his eyes and was out before he heard the end of the first commercial break.

CHAPTER 69

ONNE WAS STILL on his back.

They'd given him a cell phone to call Lester Russell, who promised he'd be in in the morning. Then Donne made it up to one of the benches in the cell, and even that took effort. Once he got on it, he needed time to catch his breath. Time passed, but he wasn't sure how much. Occasionally, someone would scream or puke or sing an Irish shanty, but most of the beats of time were passed with silence. His back made it feel like he was lying on the edges of rocks.

The door to his cell swung open and Donne fought through the agony to sit up. He expected to see more cops, maybe with nightsticks this time. And there was one cop, in uniform, frowning in his direction. But what worried Donne more was what the cop was escorting.

Lucas Mosley.

He walked normally, and didn't seem slowed or stiff. His face was clear of bruises and marks. Except for the smile plastered across it.

"Hmph," the cops said. "Seems like we're all filled up

tonight. Gotta put you two together."

"What a coincidence," Donne said. The vibration of his vocal cords felt like nails on a chalkboard to the rest of his body.

The cop closed the cell door, and the lock *thunked* into place. He said, "You going to be all right?"

Mosley said, "I got this."

Donne's stomach turned to mush as the cop disappeared from view. Mosley took the area on the bench where Donne's back once was. There wasn't much room on the bench, and his thigh was pressed against Donne's. Mosley patted the thigh, gently. He touched one of Donne's bruises and fire erupted up to his stomach. Donne clenched his teeth and tried to keep the pain inside.

"This isn't how I usually do things," Mosley said. "I don't like being front and center. But those cops, they offered me a sweet deal."

Donne folded his arms in front of him. Waited.

"They call me a bounty hunter. My brother too, you know. But that's not really what we are. Hit men is probably better, but you don't get much business advertising that way. I kept having to correct Alex. He was messing with my brand.I mean sometimes we'd track people down and talk them into turning themselves in, but you know what I really like?"

Donne still didn't answer. The Irish shanty picked up again, echoing down the hallway.

Mosley leaned in closer, his arm digging into Donne's. More fireworks for his nerves.

"I like when people off themselves because of me. Or come to me and beg me to kill them," Mosley whispered. "I really don't like getting my hands dirty."

Donne tried to flex his muscles and wake them up. The beating had brought an exhaustion and stiffness to them. He wasn't loose, and Mosley leaning against him wasn't helping.

"But here's the thing," Mosley said. "I have lot at stake here. Payment is due. Cops don't like you, don't even want to play with a trial. Your lawyer is good, they said. But there's one more thing ..."

Mosley brought a quick, flat left hand up and tried to crush Donne's windpipe. Donne got his right arm up to deflect, but he was a hair too slow. Mosley adjusted his blow and only glanced Donne's throat, but it was still enough to close off Donne's breathing. He gasped and fell forward flat into the floor.

"You killed my brother, didn't you?" Mosley's voice still wasn't above a whisper.

Donne opened and closed his mouth, fighting for air, but only able to slightly wheeze.

"Damn it," Mosley said. "They said they softened you up. Well, at least you can't scream."

Donne got to his knees and kept his left hand on the ground for support. With his right he massaged his throat. Air was starting to flow in again, but it was in fits and starts. Mosley grabbed a handful of shirt and picked him back up, so he was just on his knees.

Donne swung his left arm wildly and connected with Mosley's ankle. Mosley grunted and went down to his own knees. They must have looked ridiculous, like two drunk frat boys trying to have a game of wrestling, but barely able to stand on their own.

Mosley swung an elbow into Donne's gut. The contents of it almost came up. His vision clouded and he was almost out. Donne couldn't take much more of a pounding, if any at all. The cops had done the dirty work. Mosley was just here to clean up the mess.

Donne coughed. He was nearly blinded by lightheadedness. He was sure Mosley was winding up for the end.

Donne fell backwards, letting his legs kick out in front of him. He landed on the hard floor, just like hours before. The light above him was blotted out by the frame of Lucas Mosley, who'd gotten to his feet. He lifted his left leg up and brought it down on Donne's crotch. Donne screamed, a wheezy, almost airless scream. Tears flooded from his eyes.

This was how he was going to die, in a prison cell, covered in phlegm, bruises, and tears.

Mosley brought his leg up again and Donne rolled toward

the one he'd planted into the floor as fast as he could. He caught the leg with his own and pushed harder. He felt the leg give from the floor and saw Mosley falling backward.

The crunch came. Donne curled up and waited for Mosley to rebound. He coughed hard and tried to catch his breath. The guy who sang the Irish Shanty was screaming now, asking what the hell was happening.

Mosley didn't attack. Donne counted to ten. Breathing normally was an option again. He opened his eyes.

Mosley sat on the floor across from him. The sharp, metal corner of the bench they'd both sat on was embedded in his skull. His eyes were wide and lifeless. A long gurgle came from his mouth, then nothing.

Two cops rushed into the hall and unlocked the cell door.

One of them said, "What happened?"

"He fell," Donne said.

Then he passed out.

CHAPTER 70

HERRICK WOKE THE next morning and inspected the bruise on his stomach. It was black, blue, and a tinge yellowish. It ran from the corner of his pelvis bone up to the bottom of his ribs. And it throbbed like a marching band drum section in double time.

He tried to blink away the pain and force it out of his nerves, as if it was just temporary. But that didn't work. Chewing anything more solid than oatmeal was going to be hard for the next few weeks. He took a shower, pulled on some chinos and a black knit sweater, and went out into the living room. Sarah was still there, sitting on the couch, holding a cup of coffee with two hands.

"You remember me waking you up last night?" Sarah's cheeks were red.

Herrick nodded. "Twice."

"First time, you barely moved. I thought you were dead."

"I was tired."

"Well, if you have a concussion—"

"I don't have a concussion. I got hit in the stomach."

Sarah sipped coffee. The redness of her cheeks deepened. "There's a full pot in the kitchen."

Herrick said, "Thank you for taking care of me."

Sarah nodded. "Someone has to make sure you survive your decisions."

The sun streamed through the blinds, and onto her hair. Flecks of blond that he'd never noticed before shined and added more volume to it.

"Did you get any sleep last night?" he asked.

"Some. I only got up to check on you. Set the alarm on my iPhone."

He sat next to her on the couch, leaned in, ignored all the throbbing pain, and kissed her on the cheek. She turned her head and smiled at him, their eyes locking, cutting through the steam from the coffee. Herrick wanted to say something smart or classy. Nothing came to mind.

Sarah's fingers brushed his ribs. The not-bruised side, thank God.

"How long do you think before you heal?"

"I'm lucky my ribs aren't cracked," he said. "A couple of weeks, I'm sure."

Sarah nodded.

Herrick got off the couch and went into the kitchen and fixed himself a cup of coffee. Cream and sugar, just enough to cut the bitterness. Someone once told him he just needed to learn to make coffee better. That skill was never in his wheelhouse. What he made was just fine after the swill he drank in Afghanistan.

An image crossed through his mind; pouring coffee in the desert, talking to Angie. It was the morning of the boy. When Angie had security duty at the gate. Herrick's desire to drink the brew faded.

"What are your plans for today? Just resting, right?" Sarah asked. "I'm here at your beck and call. Get some rest. I can make you lunch, run to CVS to get you Advil. Maybe some cans of soup."

Herrick came back into the living room.

"Awkward first date," he said.

Sarah laughed. "I don't think last night counted."

He took a deep breath. Warmth rushed through him, counteracting the fire in his jaw.

"Today I finish it," he said. "Then I can rest."

Sarah frowned. "What do you mean?"

Herrick sat next to her. This time there was space between them, and Herrick didn't expect leaning in to be taken so well. Sarah kept the cup of coffee glued to her lips. She was sipping slowly, looking at him over the rim of the mug.

"Jackson Donne was trying to help me," he said. "And now he's in jail. There is a man out there who deserves to be put away and it's not Jackson. If I can get him to talk, I can save Jackson and this will all be over with."

"You shouldn't do that, Matt. Your job was to find him, and you did. What about the stuff with the assassination? The police need to look into that. Not you."

His stomach grumbled, and that didn't hurt. Baby steps. Some food would help get things going. All he had in the house were fiber bars.

"But," he said, trying to measure the right words, "we got one of them. We got Mosley, but Jackson said something to me last night. About the guy who hired me. About the day I put my gun down. I wasn't able to process it at the time."

Sarah knew the story. And she knew enough not to start talking about it. She put her cup down and waited.

"Alex Robinson. I knew his sister. When Robinson hired me, he told me I owed him."

Sarah blinked. "What are you saying?"

"That this wasn't just about Donne. The whole time, Alex saw it as an opportunity to take me down as well."

Sarah said, "It's not over for you."

"Not yet. Alex hung his sister's legacy over me, forced me to take the case."

"What are you going to do?" Sarah put the coffee cup on the table. It was empty, but he could see the rim stained tan.

"I'm going to go talk to him. Get him to confess and then get Donne home."

"Just take care of yourself. You don't owe Donne anything."

"He saved my life last night."

"You've saved people before."

Herrick shook his head. "There was someone I didn't save once. And it's why all this is happening."

Sarah got up from the couch and walked over to him. She wrapped her arms around his back and pulled him in tight. Herrick's heart pounded faster than the throb in his jaw line.

"You're a good man," she said. "You take way too many risks, but you're a good man."

"Taking a risk is one of my redeeming qualities," he said.

"Shut up."

Herrick did. He enveloped Sarah in the hug, pulling her as close as he could—despite the punishment in his gut. They stood there for a while, holding each other, not speaking. The only sounds were the morning traffic. People going about their days, just trying to pass the time and then get home to dinner or happy hour or reality TV.

At that moment, Herrick only wanted time to stop.

CHAPTER 71

ᴌ ᴇsᴛᴇʀ Rᴜssᴇʟʟ ᴍᴀʀᴄʜᴇᴅ into the interrogation room, slammed his briefcase on the table, and then jammed his hands in his pockets.

"What the hell do you want me to do, Jackson?"

Donne folded his hands on the table and resisted the urge to put his head down. He looked up at Russell, now more gray than black, his hooknose seemingly widened over the past few years. The wrinkles in his face were deeper, and the bags under his eyes heavier. He had a gray suit on, with a white shirt and a black tie. His attire was the only thing about him that was crisp.

"Help me," Donne said. "I didn't—just please help. You've done it before."

Russell pulled the chair opposite Donne out and sat down. He opened his briefcase and, while Donne couldn't see what was in there, he heard papers being shuffled.

"You killed a man," Russell said.

"I didn't do it," Donne said. "It was Bill Martin."

"Last night." Russell slammed the briefcase shut. "You killed a man last night."

"He fell."

"They have it on videotape. Jackson, this is bad. Really, really bad."

The noise outside the room was dulled, but still Donne could hear clicking, someone walking on tile floor. The footsteps got louder, then faded away.

"Is this being taped?" Donne asked.

"No."

"You sure?"

Russell frowned. "You've been gone a long time."

"I had no choice."

"Running made you look bad. They only wanted to ask you some questions. Now there's rumors that you were in Vermont?"

"It was nice there."

"They found two bodies buried in the forest near where Mosley told these guys you were hiding out. And a dead cop. And your fingerprints."

The air went from Donne and he slumped back in his chair. The bruises all over his body cried out in agony as he did so, but Donne willed himself not to grunt or even grit his teeth.

"Sit up," Russell said.

Donne did. The bruises didn't like that either. He coughed.

"You sit back like that and you look guilty."

"You said we weren't being taped."

"Like that matters."

Russell leaned forward, elbows on the table, and put his chin in his hands. He looked like an enraptured two-year-old. As if *Thomas the Tank Engine* was on TV. Or he was daydreaming.

"Are you guilty?" Russell asked.

"You once said you'd never ask me that."

Russell nodded. "Yeah, I know. I'm asking you now, though. Are you guilty?"

"Of what?"

Russell nodded again. "That's what I thought. Listen, we aren't winning a case here. Evidence from Vermont may be circumstantial, but it's damning. Too much is out in the public.

Then they have video of whatever happened in your cell last night. You're going to prison."

Donne closed his eyes. He could see Bill Martin laughing. It's what he always wanted, the tables turned.

"Can we cut a deal?" Donne asked.

"You'll probably still go to prison."

"And if I plead not guilty?"

"They have four bodies, one of which you killed on film. Everyone remembers the Senator Stern incident. You'll still go to prison, just for a longer period of time."

Donne fought against his body giving way, but it didn't help. He'd only gotten maybe fifteen minutes of sleep the previous night. After they dragged Mosley out of the cell, they questioned Donne for nearly two hours. He no commented everything as if he were a politician talking to a room of reporters. Once they put him back in the cell, he was able to get comfortable on the cot, but every twenty minutes or so, someone would bang on the jail door. Now he ached, his eyes were heavy, and his thoughts were traveling through his mind like a cow through mud.

Either way, Russell's news wasn't good news.

"So, what are our options?"

As Russell spoke, he held up a finger to tick off each part of the list. "One: plead guilty, lesser jail time. Two: go to trial and try to win. Three: Go to trial and hope for a mistrial."

"How likely is a mistrial?"

Russell blew air out through his nose. "I say we try for a plea deal."

Donne rubbed his face, his dry palms ruffling his beard.

"It's time to shave that thing."

Donne agreed.

"So," Russell said, "what do you want to do?"

Donne stood up and limped around the interrogation room. There was a scratch on the far wall where some of the paint had peeled away. Donne wondered what other deals had been cut in this room. Who had fought with the cops and tried to get out. Who had come in innocent and left a prisoner. He flicked at the scratch with his index finger, while regulating his breath.

He thought of Kate, deep in the ground because of him. Jeanne was on the run somewhere. Bill Martin was dead too. Mario. They were all gone, and he'd had his hand in it. Years ago, he left two bodies decomposing somewhere near Atlantic City. Jackson Donne was a good man—he always tried to tell himself that, but anytime he left the Olde Towne Tavern to work, the world went to hell. He couldn't even keep himself in college and get his degree. He was cursed.

He was a curse.

Every decision he'd made since he turned on the Narcs was the wrong one. Everything had consequences, and he'd suffered the wrath. And, even worse, as he tried to save people, those people ended up suffering as well. Donne didn't belong here. He didn't belong out on the streets trying to put people away. Everything always went to hell.

Donne turned around and walked back to his seat. Some of the paint he'd flicked at on the wall had stuck to his finger. He brushed it off and took a long, deep breath. Russell sat across from him, waiting, hands folded like he was praying.

Donne said, "I want to plead guilty."

Lester Russell nodded. "That's probably your best choice."

Donne's eyes stung. But for the first time in a long time, he felt that maybe the demons of his past could be purged.

Violence begat violence. But, it seemed, this was the best way to end that cycle. No family. No children.

Only Jackson Donne behind bars.

CHAPTER 72

I T DIDN'T TAKE much for Herrick to find Robinson. After all, he wasn't hiding. Herrick parked in Kearny, got out of the car, crossed the street, and approached the office. As he did, he took out his iPhone and opened up the memo app. Just before opening the door to the office, he hit record. New Jersey was a one-party consent state. He didn't have to let Robinson know anything. When he walked in, Robinson was pouring a cup of tea. There were donuts next to the teapot.

Robinson turned, saw Herrick, and nearly spilled his tea. He regained his composure without losing a drop, though.

"Now you?" Robinson rolled his eyes. "You want me to rearrange your face?"

Tough guy.

Herrick walked over to the table and picked up a donut. Took a bite. The sugary goodness went down his esophagus and into his stomach. The knife wound and the nightstick wound didn't complain. Progress.

Robinson was back around his desk and about to sit. Herrick shook his head.

"We're going for a ride."

"Couldn't you two have come at the same time? It's a hassle of a drive."

Again with the eyeroll.

"We're going to talk to Leo and we're going to get Donne out of prison."

Robinson drank some tea.

"You made a mistake dragging me into this," Herrick said.

Robinson put the cup down. He said, "No kidding. You're not dead."

"You took advantage of all of this as a way to take care of me too?" Herrick put his hands in his pockets. The case for the ASP bounced against his leg with the beat of his movement.

"We needed an investigator. And then to clear the path," he said.

"This is stupid," Herrick said. "So, so stupid."

"You let my sister die," Robinson said. "You saved everyone else, but you let her die."

Herrick took a breath. "Alex, we talked about this. We cleared the air."

"Cleared the air? Try telling that to my parents. The ones who look at the picture of their daughter in her uniform every day. The one who made them proud. That she died and everyone—*everyone*—else lived that day. And me? What do they see of me? A man who should have done a good job, and now I'm just a disgraced motel snoop. It's not fair, and you could have saved her."

Herrick balled his left hand into a fist. "No. No I couldn't. Do you understand, Alex? She saved us. If she didn't get shot-" He hated saying the word and Robinson flinched at its sound. "If she didn't, we would have never known about the boy with the bomb. Your sister—Angie—she was the first line of defense, Alex. She was a security guard. They shot her so they could get past the gate and get to us."

Robinson shook his head. "She should still be alive."

"We'd all be dead. There was no other way."

"You saved everyone else but her!"

Herrick still held the donut in his hand. He wanted to take another bite just to break the tension but his stomach was starting to get upset..

"Well, after all of this, we should be even," Robinson said. Steam still swirled from his cup. And then it didn't; something dissipated it quickly.

It was Robinson's hand. It dove out of Herrick's field of vision, and then came back up with a knife. Herrick did the first thing he could think of. He threw the donut.

Robinson flinched, surprised to see it coming at him. It gave Herrick enough time to dive to the ground and unsheathe the ASP at the same time.

"Motherfucker," Robinson said.

He came around the desk, knife in hand. Herrick was too quick, however, and swung the ASP. It caught Robinson in the knee, which buckled. He went down to one good knee. The knife went flying and thunked into the ceiling. Someone screamed.

Herrick rolled left and popped up, swinging the ASP as hard as he could. It connected with Robinson's jaw. Robinson grunted, and Herrick swung the ASP back and connected with the other side of his face. Matching bruises. Robinson fell backward.

Robinson bounced back up and swung wildly at Herrick. He only connected with the teapot. It clanked and felt off the table, spilling hot liquid into the carpet. Herrick got to his feet and took a step backward. Robinson tumbled toward him, screaming. Herrick hit him again with the ASP, this time on the back of his skull. When it connected, there was a sickening *crack*.

Robinson yelled, "I hate you! I hate you!"

The words were slow and garbled, but Herrick could make them out. As if lost in darkness, Robinson kept moving forward, each step threatening to take him down. Herrick didn't understand how he could still even be on his feet. Adrenaline? Fear? He took another swing of the ASP, but Robinson stumbled at the last minute, and the blow missed. It connected with desk, splintering some of the wood.

But, like a tennis player, Herrick took one more swing—a backhand. It caught him in the temple, and Robinson went down hard.

His breathing came in fits and starts, but his eyes were closed and he wasn't moving.

The sirens were loud. Someone in the building had called the cops. Herrick's gut said to run. There was too much to be finished. But that was the mistake Donne had made too many times, and Herrick wasn't about to start getting a bad rap. He had connections, and he could talk his way out of this, he was sure of it.

Just explain the truth. He'd play them the tape. He switched the recorder app off.

The ASP would get Herrick in trouble. The Jersey City or Hoboken cops would overlook it because he knew them, but Kearny cops? No chance. Herrick stepped out into the hall and slid the ASP behind a radiator. Hopefully, it would blend in and he could come back and grab it later. The cops would be incessant in pulling evidence inside the office, but—Herrick hoped—maybe they wouldn't check the hallway all that much.

Plus, once they heard the voice memo on his iPhone, they'd have all the evidence they needed. That wouldn't get Jackson Donne out of jail, but at least it would clear his own name.

Two cops rushed up the stairs and burst into the room. Herrick already had his hands up in the air. They cuffed him before they asked any questions.

Second time in less than twenty-four hours he was in handcuffs. He'd come a long way from suicide sprints on the hardwood.

CHAPTER 73

THE KEARNY POLICE Station was a building that took up a whole block. Two-toned gray and two stories high, it reminded Herrick of the Jersey City Police Station more than he wanted it to. Herrick expected a small outpost connected to City Hall. Instead, he got the big time.

The cops brought him in through the garage, and no one was there to watch. That was more professional than the Jersey City cops. It wasn't a Lee Harvey Oswald–style parade. No one watched him come in. The worst part was the piercing smell of engine oil.

They took him to a holding cell and uncuffed him. They'd taken his phone, wallet, belt, shoelaces, and watch. Herrick just wanted them to play the memo. The cell was the color of wet concrete and smelled like an unclean gym locker room. Just one cell, empty, and the size of a closet.

Two hours later, a cop came by and asked if he wanted a lawyer.

"No," Herrick said. "I want to go home."

The cop nodded. "You put a man in the hospital."

"Is he dead?"

"No."

The cop leaned against the wall, arms crossed. He wasn't angry or impatient.

"It was self-defense," Herrick said.

"Can you prove that?"

Herrick nodded.

The cop laughed. "Go for it."

"On my phone, there's a voice memo. I recorded the whole thing. It's probably fifteen minutes long. He came after me with a knife. The one you found embedded in the ceiling." Herrick smiled. "I threw a donut at him."

The cop nodded. "I'll go get the phone."

An hour later, Herrick was back out on the street with orders not to leave the state, and to get a lawyer. They'd be in touch. Easiest experience he'd ever had with the cops. Most painless. Like, at this point, they couldn't be bothered. Or maybe they realized Robinson had been the assailant that brought them to the office.

Good to be savvy, Herrick thought as he walked back to get the ASP—and his car.

HERRICK SAT BEHIND the wheel and pondered his next step. Without Robinson, it was going to be tricky to get Carver to speak. He imagined at this point he'd have no problem getting in to see Carver, but talking—there was no impetus to get him to talk about what happened with Donne.

Unless.

Herrick called McKinny. The phone rang twice and then went to voice mail. That probably wasn't good. Herrick dialed again.

Five rings, then, "What?"

"Did you let Jackson go yet?"

"Let him go? Matt, we got him dead to rights. We aren't going to let him out on the street. So he can run again?"

"He's innocent," Herrick said.

"Of which murder? We got him on at least four bodies, and who knows what else over the past five or six years."

"There were people trying to kill him," Herrick said. His hands were warm as he gripped the steering wheel. Everything Donne had done was on the table now, and Carver might be his only hope.

"There's a guy in Bethlehem Institution, it's Donne's ex-boss."

"The guy I helped you go see?"

"Yeah." Herrick pulled out of his parking spot. "If I can get him to talk ..."

McKinny coughed. "It's not going to work, Matt. I'm sure his lawyer is going to hire people to review our evidence, but Donne killed somebody in our jail cell last night. We got him. It's over."

The words cut through Herrick like an ax through a mushroom. "Who'd he kill?"

"Mosley. Lucas Mosley. Donne says he fell, but we have it on video." McKinny did something that made a tinking sound, like metal hitting metal. "Donne beat the shit out of him."

"Uh-huh. And what did your guys do to Jackson?" Herrick nearly blew a red light as he drove. He slammed on the brakes. "Donne didn't kill your officer. It was Mosley. I was there."

Someone honked the horn behind him. The light had turned green. Herrick accelerated, and the next thing he knew, he was getting on Route 21, heading toward Newark. There he'd connect with Route 78 and go see Carver.

"Someone's got to pay for this, Matt. Might as well be Donne. Can you believe it? Biggest news story around here in years and I catch the last guy involved."

Herrick said, "Bye." He disconnected the call. Then he dialed Sarah. She picked up quicker than McKinny did.

"Matt, are you okay?"

No easy way to answer that one. At least his jaw had stopped throbbing in the past twenty minutes. Maybe, though, that was because of adrenaline. "Are you still at my apartment?"

She was. Sarah told him she'd gone out to get lunch, and to

buy a book. But she came back. She wanted to be there when he got back.

"Please stay, then. I'm going to be home soon. It's almost over."

He pictured her sitting on his couch, reading a paperback. She liked thrillers, people on the run, stakes high. He thought about asking if somewhere inside, she was enjoying hearing him tell this story. He doubted it.

"Tonight, we'll go out and get some dinner." He smiled. "I want to do this right."

"Me too," she said. "How're you feeling? Can you move okay?"

"I'll figure it out."

"Where are you now?" Sarah asked.

"Trying to help Jackson."

"Do you think you can?"

Herrick looked at the stretch of road in front of him. Some brake lights flashed up ahead. The lights of the city skyline were starting to flicker, as the sky got darker. Only half past four, and it was already dark outside.

"Give me two hours," he said. "I'll be home then."

"Matt, I asked and you didn't answer. Makes me wonder if what you're doing is worth it. Can you get him out?"

Herrick took a breath. "No. I don't think I can. Maybe I can find someone to testify for him, though."

CHAPTER 74

"I T DOESN'T TAKE much to know they got ya," Russell said. His voice was quiet now. It had lost some of the power he'd had earlier. Guess that happened after bouncing ideas back and forth for hours.

Donne was still in the chair, with an aching back and cramps in his calves. A McDonald's burger wrapper crumpled on the table, next to half-eaten fries and an empty cup. His stomach gurgled uncomfortably. He'd already been escorted to the bathroom once, and now didn't want to get dragged through the hallway again.

He could wait.

"They're letting me talk to you for this long, which means they don't care what we figure out." Russell gnawed on a French fry. "They got you dead to rights."

"What's the next step?"

Russell shrugged. You never want to see your lawyer shrug.

"You shouldn't have run, Jackson."

Donne stood up, and his back cracked. Kate flashed before his eyes. He thought he'd chased that image away up in

Vermont. The linger of her voice as she told him she had her beer goggles on. A sign that everything was going to be okay. He ran, and it was the wrong move.

A life of wrong decisions.

"Spur of the moment type thing," he said.

Russell nodded now. There wasn't much force behind it. The smell of the fries still hung in the air. The light was starting to bother Donne's eyes. A dull ache hung in his sinuses.

End of the road.

"So, when do we plead?" Donne said. He wondered how many years he'd get. Five? Ten? Life? Maybe it didn't matter anymore.

"We've got some time." Russell ate another fry. They were probably ice cold. "I'm going to double check the cops. My investigators will follow up and see what they really have. We'll get the tape they have, and maybe we can find an out there."

"We should just plead now."

Russell shook his head. "Not how it works. We go through the rigmarole. We'll see if they offer a plea. Maybe we do better than we think."

"And if not?"

Russell ran a finger across his throat. "You'll be away for a long time."

Donne took a deep breath. "Maybe that's how it should be."

Russell stopped chewing his fry.

"All these years, how many times have you gotten me out of trouble?"

Russell smiled. "I have a beach house."

Donne didn't laugh. His eyes felt heavy, and the pain in his head was expanding. He could get some sleep in the cell. His body could heal.

"How many times did you help when you thought ... maybe you shouldn't have?"

Russell didn't answer.

"I thought getting away and going to Vermont was the answer. I thought if I hid and stayed out of everything down here, I'd be okay. After Kate, I felt like I had to hide. Staying there ... no one else would get killed. I could drink my beer, cut some trees down, and maybe find the light." Donne rubbed his face. "And hell still managed to find me. People died again."

"Jackson, you didn't say this to the cops, did you?"

Donne smiled. It hurt to smile. "I make dumb decisions, but I'm not that dumb."

"Good."

"It's time to go away, Lester. Let's take a plea."

Russell wiped his nose. "If they offer it."

"Otherwise, we tell the judge I'm guilty. Whatever happens then happens."

Russell looked over Donne's shoulder. There must have been a camera there. Maybe he was looking for a microphone. Screw it all.

"I'll be in touch," Russell said. "You gonna be okay tonight?"

"I need to sleep."

Russell rubbed his face. He closed his briefcase and clicked the lock shut. Then he grabbed all the wrappers, fry boxes, and cups and threw them into the brown paper bag it all came in. He crumpled the top of the bag closed. He pushed out his chair and stood up.

"I'll talk to them. You're important property," he said. "I imagine the state cops are going to want to talk to you too, but they probably want you to sweat."

Donne shrugged. "I don't have any sweat left."

Russell walked to the door and knocked. "I'll make sure you get your own cell tonight."

Donne shrugged again. "I had it and they still beat the shit out of me."

"They won't do that again. Now that they have you on tape killing a guy, they'll leave you alone."

"I didn't kill that cop. Either cop." Donne coughed. "I would never."

"I know. But they don't care."

"Can you get the tape of them beating me up?" Donne asked. "I think that'd help."

Russell laughed. "I'd imagine there was a malfunction with

their equipment at the exact moment you got your ass kicked. But I'll ask."

"Just not my day."

"Hang tight. I'll be back before they lock you up tonight."

The door opened and Russell left. As the door swung back closed, the cop who let Russell out stared Donne down. The door clicked shut.

Donne took a deep breath. He folded his hands together and rested them on the table. The metal table top was icy cold, and that radiated through his wrists. It sent a shiver through his body. Donne closed his eyes and breathed. His body was humming and he willed it to stop.

He opened his eyes and looked across the room at the white wall. It was empty. He focused in on the paint chip, a small imperfection in an otherwise impeccable piece of nothingness. The gray drywall contrasted with the white, a lone raincloud in a sea of clear sky. He stared and tried to will it larger.

Then he laughed. A long, loud guffaw.

This was how he was going to spend the rest of his life, staring at walls and trying to wish them to fall down. Like he was Obi-Wan Kenobi. But he wasn't. Not a Jedi. Not an escape artist.

He was just a man who tried to do the right thing, and always managed to get it to blow up in his face.

He caught his breath before the laughter could morph into tears.

CHAPTER 75

THE LOBBY WAS quiet.

Herrick had only been here twice and both times, it was in the middle of the day. The bustle of visitors had dimmed, and the waiting room was empty. A man wheeled a tray full of dinners through the room and then into the hall that led to the inmates. He reached into his pocket, took out his iPhone, and started another voice memo. Only the receptionist was in the area with him.

Herrick wasn't about to deal with her.

Instead, he rushed by. Act like you belong and no one will question you. He made it through the doors and into the hallway before he heard the receptionist shouting. Herrick kept moving, not listening to her requests to wait.

Carver's room was up on the right. The door was closed, but Herrick turned the handle and stepped through into the room. He locked the door, turning the little switch on the knob.

Leo Carver was lying on his bed. He turned his head toward Herrick and said, "They have keys, you know."

The desk chair was in arm's reach of Herrick, and he

grabbed it. He dragged it over to the door and jammed it under the doorknob. The glass of water on the desk wobbled as he pulled, but it didn't spill.

With luck, the receptionist didn't see Herrick's face, and they were still scrambling to see who and where the intruder went. Outside, the tempo and volume of voices were starting to pick up.

"We don't have much time," Herrick said.

Carver sat up, putting his feet flat on the floor. He folded his hands in his lap.

"I'm not sure I remember who you are." Carver was very still. "Do I know you? You've been here before."

Carver's name had been so engrained in Herrick's mind the past few days, he barely remembered he'd only talked to Carver once. Over a week ago. Before he'd even found Donne. The second time he'd been stopped.

"I'm Matt Herrick. You hired me to find Jackson Donne."

Carver tilted his head and knitted his eyebrows. "No. I most certainly did not."

"Well, maybe not you specifically, but you had Alex Robinson do it."

"No, I didn't."

Herrick wanted to lead Carver, but not give him all the answers. This was his first misstep. But they had to rush things a little bit, because once the hospital attendants figured out where he was, they'd be working hard to get in here.

The cacophony outside grew louder and more panicked. Herrick was pressed against the wall next to the door, like he'd been instructed during school lockdown practice. They shouldn't be able to see him through the little window in the door.

"Alex Robinson," Carver said. "He used to work for me. Comes to see me from time to time. A good man."

"Listen," Herrick said. "I'm going to get you out of here. Help me get Jackson Donne out of jail."

It was something Herrick had thought of on the drive down. Offer something that Carver would want. Freedom. Sidle up to him and become his confidant. Make him believe in you.

Didn't work.

"I don't even know you," Carver said. His voice was even. "And who says I want to leave. I have my crossword puzzles, good food, and people I can talk to who make sure I'm okay. I don't trust myself always."

Herrick sighed. He reached into his pocket and took out the iPhone and held it up for Carver to see. He face remained stone. Herrick reached over and stopped the recording. The moment Carver said he didn't trust himself, the memo stopped working. It threw everything into doubt.

Someone knocked on the door. Carver gave them a wave. No one tried the doorknob. It didn't jiggle.

Carver exhaled. "He got one phone call. And he called me."

Herrick put his phone away and waited.

"Have you ever lost, Mr. Herrick?" Carver cracked his knuckles.

"I'm a basketball coach," he said. "I lose a lot. But I've also won state championships."

Carver nodded. "How do you deal with those losses with your team?"

Where was he going with this?

"We go back to the film. We practice. We get better for the next game."

Carver nodded. "Well, maybe you'll become a better private investigator."

Herrick didn't respond.

"You're going to lose today, Mr. Herrick."

It amazed Herrick that Carver's voice never wavered. There wasn't emotion behind it. It kept the same tone as an NPR broadcaster, the entire time he was speaking. Maybe, just maybe, Herrick thought, he could detect a little joy in it. But that was tentative.

Herrick's heart, however, was going a mile a minute.

"You're going to help me get Jackson Donne out of prison. You're going to tell everyone what you've done."

Carver spread his hands. "What did I do? Nothing. I've

been here for over a year. Before that I was in Rahway State Penitentiary. Eastern New Jersey State. Whatever they call it now."

Herrick searched for the words. Looked for a comeback. Like when he was a coach and just wanted to stop the opponent's run. He once read a Hall of Fame coach said calling a time-out during the opponent's run was a sign of weakness. That the players needed to find a way out of the situation. Just get a stop on their own.

He wanted nothing more than to call a time-out right now.

"You know," Carver said, "years ago, I wanted Donne to be dead. Not anymore. I forgave him. He did what he thought was the right thing to do. He tried to save his partner and the rest of the crew. But he put me away. Maybe I deserved it.

"And I wasn't lying before. This?" He waved around the room. "This isn't bad. I can do what I like. The employees here look out for me. They protect me. I'm safe here. It's not the empire I once had, but it's my own Elba. I can live my life for now. Maybe one day I'll be 'cured' of my illness and see the world again. But this is okay. But Jackson? He's going to suffer."

Herrick didn't say anything. There was nothing to say. His mouth was dry and his palms were wet.

"You want me to testify on his behalf? All I'd be is a character witness, and there is no way I'll say anything gold about him. He put me here, and some might say that was a good thing. But ultimately it got three good men killed. Three people who worked hard for me."

"Why? Why did they have to die?"

Carver shrugged. "Because Alex Robinson is and always was a baby. He never figured things out—never grew up. The other guys? They figured out their lives. Two of them became very good private investigators. Family men. But Robinson couldn't stand that. He had them killed And he didn't even do it just to start his little plan. If he was going to be miserable, everyone else would be too. He was the imperfect piece to my crossword puzzle. And I let him."

Carver shrugged as if to say *There you have it.*

"Now, it's time for you to go. Tail between your legs, of course." Carver stood up. "Now, we can do this the easy way or I can make sure you're dragged out of here and have to deal with the police again. I'm still Robinson's boss. I'm a better father to him than his was. So I won't let him go away because of my words."

Herrick stood up straight. A lead ball had formed in his stomach.

"Give me your phone, or I will yell for them." Carver held out his hand. "Do what I say and you get to walk out of here without a scratch."

Herrick rolled the situation around in his head, looking for possible outs. The sounds of police sirens and the shouting in the halls gave him no choice. Carver was right. Tail between your legs. He pulled out his iPhone and handed it over. Carver took it and dropped it in the glass of water. Some of the water splashed onto the desk.

Out loud, Carver counted to ten. He reached into the glass, pulled the phone out, and handed it back to Herrick.

"Now, walk over, open the door, and tell them where you are."

"They're going to—"

"Trust me," Carver said. "You're showing good sportsmanship."

Herrick pulled the chair out of the way, unlocked the door, and stuck his head out into the hallway. Two of the employees were standing right there.

"I'm here," Herrick said, and then ducked back into the room.

The two employees rushed in behind him. They were burly men, more like bar bouncers than asylum nurses. But, Herrick guessed, when you're dealing with insane meltdowns, sometimes you might need some toughness. Herrick braced for the beating.

Carver held up a hand again.

"This is my fault," he said. "He came to visit me."

"You don't get visitors," one of them said.

"Exactly," Carver said. "He didn't know he had to check in."

One of the guys looked at Herrick, who shrugged.

"You're an idiot. Do you live in the real world?"

"From time to time," Herrick said.

"Come on," the guy said. "Let's go."

Herrick started to follow, but gave Carver one more look.

"You win some, you lose some. You'll get better." Carver winked. "It does suck to lose, though, doesn't it? Believe me, I know."

"Maybe I'll get another shot at the title."

Carver shrugged.

Herrick's legs and abs burned hot from adrenaline. He followed his escorts back into the lobby. They didn't pound him into meatloaf, but their muscles were tense and their hands were fists. One wrong move and he'd be chopped meat.

They stopped at the front desk.

"Mind if I make a phone call?" Herrick asked.

"You got a cell phone."

Herrick shook his head. "It's waterlogged. Gotta get a new one."

The bouncers didn't respond. They just crossed their arms. The receptionist passed the landline over. Herrick dialed Sarah. He was surprised she answered, since the number was likely unknown.

But she did.

"It's over," he said. The heaviness of those words sat in his chest. "I'm coming home."

CHAPTER 76

TOO MUCH TIME in police stations.

That was Herrick's thinking as he walked through the Jersey City station double doors and felt the *whoosh* of the heaters on his face. Outside, the first hard December snowfall was covering the pavement. Thank God it was Saturday. After school had been closed the day before, St. Paul's couldn't afford this early a snow day. By the afternoon, they could have seven inches—and it wasn't supposed to stop until the next morning.

McKinny was at the front desk waiting. Herrick had called in advance, let him know he was stopping by. When Herrick got to the desk McKinny winced.

"You look worse than the other night," he said.

Herrick didn't mind, it was just a hangover. He'd had them before. The bruise on his stomach was pure yellow now, though. The knife wound had scabbed over. Healing, he told Sarah.

"Nah, life's getting better."

"Let's go to my office," McKinny said.

Herrick knew the way, but didn't take the lead. McKinny took them down a long hallway, away from the cubicles and uniformed cops. They went into his office, a sparse room with a filing cabinet, a picture of his family framed on the wall, and a large window looking out toward the Hudson. Unfortunately, the view was marred by most of the buildings in the way, but if you squinted, you could see the Freedom Tower.

McKinny sat behind the desk and typed something into his computer. Clicked the mouse a few times, then turned back to Herrick. Herrick liked McKinny's guest chair. The padding didn't have an indentation in it. He didn't have many visitors.

"You can't see him," McKinny said.

"I bring recruiting information," Herrick said. "Syracuse, Duke, Notre Dame. They're all coming next week."

McKinny shook his head. "Not my call."

"What's going on?"

McKinny sat back and took a deep breath. The wheels on his chair creaked.

"He killed a guy. The other one we brought in. Mosley."

McKinny pressed his lips together hard. Waited. Herrick didn't speak. He didn't know what to say.

"We have it on tape. Only person we're letting see Donne is his lawyer."

"Jesus Christ," Herrick said.

He'd spent the night before with Sarah, doing things to loosen the tension in his chest, back, and neck. It had worked. Sarah hadn't asked much about what had happened at the institution, and Herrick only told her he'd talk about it after he saw Donne. Now everything came back in one huge lump. He felt like the Tin Man, frozen in place and begging for oil.

"I shouldn't even be telling you that much," McKinny said. "But I think we have him."

"Have you talked to his lawyer?" Herrick asked.

"A little here and there. But even the great Lester Russell looks defeated."

"Jackson Donne is the good guy." Herrick's mouth was starting to go dry. He wiped at his lips. "The guy you should be talking to is Leo Carver about Alex Robinson."

It was his last-ditch effort. Put the right guy away. Make

sure Jackson Donne was cleared of all charges and back on the street.

McKinny shook his head.

"He's in Bethlehem Institution," Herrick told him. "He was the guy who led the Narc squad when Donne was a cop. Donne turned on him when the Narcs were skimming off the top. He went away."

"Didn't Donne work with Bill Martin?"

Herrick shrugged. "Carver was the head of everything. Martin was number two. Donne told me he was supposed to finger them both, but when he got up on the stand, he panicked and only snitched on Carver."

McKinny said, "So he felt guilty years later and killed Martin too?"

Herrick wasn't going to win here either. He talked for twenty minutes, laying everything out for him. Why Donne went on the run, how the Mosleys were hired to kill him, and how Herrick tied into it all. McKinny listened, fingers steepled, stopping to ask a clarifying question here or there, but not judging.

"Call Kearny," Herrick said, finally. "Ask about Alex Robinson. Maybe you can get him to flip."

Herrick wasn't even sure Robinson knew everything. The Mosleys may have been hired by Robinson, but they probably didn't keep him in the loop.

Silence filled the room. McKinny stared Herrick down. He didn't blink, and Herrick's chin started to ache. It was nerves — that's all — not the power of the stare.

McKinny went for the phone, and Herrick breathed again.

"Yeah," McKinny said by way of a greeting. He identified himself and then paused, listening. "Can you give me the cop who dealt with Matt Herrick last night?"

Herrick nodded. Might as well use his name.

"Hi." McKinny identified himself again. "Yeah, I have Matt Herrick sitting here. He is having me call to ask you about a key piece in a case I'm working on involving Jackson Donne. Yeah, that guy. Can you believe I caught him?" McKinny laughed. "The state guys are coming in this afternoon if the snow doesn't keep them home. Everyone wants a piece of him."

There was a long pause. Herrick looked out the window. The snow was intensifying. He couldn't see Manhattan anymore. He could barely see the building across the street. Smart move taking the Light Rail.

"Yeah, I want to ask you about Alex Robinson."

Herrick didn't need to hear anymore. When the color went out of McKinny's face, he knew. Somehow Carver had contacts everywhere. Little minions he could send out to do his business. He was clearing the deck. Donne was in prison, and Herrick was silenced.

McKinny said a few more things that Herrick didn't catch, then hung up the phone.

"Alex Robinson killed himself in prison last night."

"How?"

"They won't say. Sounds like someone on their end screwed up."

Herrick put his head in his hands.

McKinny shrugged. "You're sure about this thing win Donne, huh?"

Herrick nodded.

"I think he's going to plead guilty, Matt."

"Let me talk to him."

McKinny shook his head. "You've known him—what? A week? What does he mean to you?"

"It's the right thing to do."

"Anyone with that amount of death following him around shouldn't be on the street. Even he knows it at this point."

Herrick slumped in his chair.

"Go home, Matt. Let yourself heal. Get your team better." McKinny stood up and held out his hand. "You win some, you lose some. You know that."

Herrick stood and shook hands. Too many people were telling him he lost. Maybe it was time to accept it. The court-long pass to Laettner didn't work this time.

He left the station and walked out into the snow. Flakes settled on his jacket shoulders and in his hair as he walked to the Light Rail.

CHAPTER 77

"**LOST.**"

Herrick got through the doorway and slumped against the wall. His face hurt, his side hurt, the total sum of all his injuries overtook him. It was as if his body had given up the fight. It was just trying to hold on long enough to get through this case and let everything hit at once.

Sarah got off the couch, ran over, and held him tight. He tried to hold his weight up so he wouldn't crush her by falling into her arms. She held on and he put his left arm around her and pulled her in.

"Let's get your coat off," she said.

He took it off and dropped it on the floor, a clump of snow falling with it. Water started to spread across the hardwood. Sarah took his hand and led him over to the couch. They sat and she wrapped an arm around his shoulders and snuggled in with him. She was warm and the heat started to transfer into his body.

"Tell me," she said.

He did. Everything from Donne's arrest, to Mosley and

Carver, and finally to the meetings with all the different police officers. As he was talking, he realized it was all a rambling mess. He wasn't sure if Sarah was following, but McKinny must have. He hoped he hadn't fucked it up even more by trying to speak.

"You did lose," Sarah said.

"It could cost Donne his life."

He pictured Donne sitting in a cell. Did he even know it was snowing out? He was probably just staring at a gray wall, counting time in his head. Maybe the blood from Mosley was still on his hand, crusting up, digging into his fingertips.

He felt Sarah close his eyes against his arm, her eyelashes rubbing against his sleeve.

"New Jersey doesn't have the death penalty," she said.

"Not what I meant. I meant—he's going to jail for a long, long time. Maybe even life."

"You can't save everyone, Matt."

He thought about his father. "It's funny—our parents make decisions and it affects us years later."

"Tell me about it."

"Not today."

Herrick stared at the TV across from him. Sarah had muted it when he came in. Two SportsCenter talking heads were going back and forth about something. An image of the Bulls logo was splayed across the screen behind them. The movement was distracting. He pulled Sarah in closer and kissed her hair. It smelled like Head and Shoulders shampoo. She'd been here three days and hadn't gotten her own shampoo yet.

"I had to try," he said.

He thought about Alex Robinson's sister. He could have been there sooner, gotten a shot off and stopped the boy even earlier. The more people he could have saved, even though it meant a child would die. He'd made peace with that ages ago.

At least, he thought he had.

"Maybe he's not worth it," Sarah said.

"Everyone should have a chance."

"He did. You gave it to him."

"McKinny thinks he might plead guilty."

Sarah sat up and looked at him. She brushed the good side of his face with her hand.

"Then that's his choice and that's his answer." She grinned. "The way I'm looking at it, you won."

"How is that even possible?"

She stood up and walked into the kitchen. He forced himself up and followed him. When he got there, she was standing at the refrigerator. She pulled it open. It was stocked with two six packs of beer, a bottle of wine, and a bunch of pizza toppings and dough. There was a bottle of Angel's Envy bourbon on the counter.

"We're going to be snowed in this weekend. I went out this morning and got beer, wine, and some stuff to make pizza. I even bought you a pizza stone and bourbon. And what blizzard is complete without" — she pointed at the top of the fridge where a bag rested — "a bag of potato chips."

"Thank you," he said. "But you said I won."

"You did," she said. "Think about it. Your team is okay. You didn't lose them. We have this weekend to get you better. Physically and mentally. It sucks. The past two weeks have been hell on you, but by Monday, you have to get back to the team. Like I said, they need you too."

"We have a championship to win," he said. His body still ached, but some clarity was coming back to his thoughts.

"That's right. And I have faith in you. Those kids have faith in you." She put her hands on her hips. "But you're forgetting one other thing."

He smiled. "No, I didn't. There's one other way I've won."

"Go ahead," she said, matching his grin.

"You."

She walked up to him and gave him a kiss on the cheek. "Knew you'd figure it out eventually. Took me a while to figure it out too."

They went back into the living room, and Sarah turned off the TV. They sat together for a while, she leaning on him, he occasionally kissing her hair. Too much kissing hurt but he didn't care. Occasionally one of them would look out the window and comment on the snow. They could barely see three feet away at this point.

"There's one more thing I have to do," he said, sometime later.

"You're not going out in the snow," Sarah said. "I was just about to go get you a beer."

Herrick shook his head. "No, it won't be for a while. I want to see how the trial turns out. If there even is a trial. But there's a way I can help Jackson. One more way. I don't talk about it much."

"Well," Sarah said, "you don't have to think about it now."

"I didn't think I'd have to worry about it ever."

They didn't talk about it again. Instead, they kissed and drank and made pizza and had a good weekend.

Maybe, Herrick thought, even when you lose, you win.

The snow fell through Sunday afternoon. They never left the apartment. Monday came and Sarah went back to work. He went back to coaching. The team was ready to be coached.

Life went on. His wounds healed.

Wins came.

SIX MONTHS LATER
FOR YOU

CHAPTER 78

ERRICK SAT IN Rahway State Penitentiary in the visitors' room. He sat at a table looking around. No one else was there. It was a Monday morning, and — he suspected — most visits happened over the weekend. He waited.

Donne had pled guilty only days before. Ten years. Five for good behavior. His lawyer made a deal to get him in Rahway, close to home. Herrick went to watch on the first day of the case. Donne sat in a suit, sullen and reserved. He didn't make eye contact with the jury or the crowd. The plea deal must have come at the last minute, because even the selections were finished. Donne and Lester Russell stood up in front of everyone and announced their guilty plea. Cameras went off, some people gasped. One guy groaned; on the way out, Herrick heard him complaining about giving up three days of work for a plea deal.

Now Herrick waited. He tapped his fingers on the table and whistled to himself. The security guard had taken his phone and wallet, promising he'd get it back when he left. Herrick had been smart and left the ASP at home.

Time passed, but Herrick wasn't sure how long.

The door opposite the one he came in swung open. Jackson Donne came through it. His right eye was swollen and black. His left arm was in a sling. He walked slowly, but without a limp, over to the table Herrick sat at.

"They don't do the phone and glass thing anymore," Donne said. "We're just on all sorts of cameras."

Herrick nodded. "Heard you had a rough couple of days."

"I put some of my new roommates in here years ago. They missed me," Donne said.

Herrick tried to stifle the laughter, but couldn't. Donne didn't join in.

"Sorry," Herrick said.

"How are things on the outside?"

Herrick thought, but didn't say, good. He and Sarah were going strong. Herrick made cash working divorce cases. Messy, but simple. The team came in second in the Tournament of Champions. Not enough to make everyone happy, but enough to keep St. Paul's open. His two seniors found spots in North Carolina and UCLA. That's all that mattered.

But Donne didn't want to hear that.

"Life goes on," Herrick said.

"What the hell are you doing here?"

"I think I can help you."

Donne nodded. "I don't need help."

Herrick sat back in the chair. The plastic back bent a little bit.

"I thought I could get you out. Those first couple of days after the school stuff. I thought I could clear you."

Donne shook his head. "You didn't have to. I didn't want you to. I think I deserve to be here."

Herrick nodded at the sling. "You don't deserve that."

Donne pursed his lips and breathed audibly through his nose. His eyes rolled up to the ceiling. Herrick waited.

"Maybe I do," Donne said, finally. "Nobody should have to live the life I had without punishment."

Herrick said, "It always seemed like you were trying to do the right thing."

Donne huffed.

"I think I can help you." Herrick forced the issue.

Donne didn't respond. They sat in silence for some time. Herrick thought about the move he was about to make. The thing from his past he was about to make public. He had only told Sarah this last night. He only told her because if he was going to share it with Donne, he had to be fair. She took it well.

Herrick wondered what Donne was thinking about.

"I miss beer," Donne said. "That would help. Did you bring that?"

"That probably would have been a better gift, you're right."

"You could have tracked down some Heady Topper."

"I'm not a miracle worker."

Herrick reached into his pocket and pulled out a folded slip of paper. He put it on the table, keeping his finger on it. He counted to ten before passing it. Needed to make sure it was the right choice. Seemed like it was the best one, anyway.

Donne didn't touch the paper. It sat in front of him, a corner of it starting to unfold against its own tension.

"Are you offering me a job?" Donne looked around the room. "I'm a bit busy at the moment."

"Open it," Herrick said.

Done sighed. With his good hand, he picked up the paper and unfolded it. He read what was on it and then looked at Herrick.

"Who the hell is that?"

Herrick took a breath. "My dad."

Donne shrugged. "And?"

"He's in there." Herrick pointed at the door Donne had entered though. "He's been in there a long time. It's how I ended up in the military. My dad got arrested and my mom... Well, I had no other options."

"What did he do?" Donne asked.

Herrick shrugged. "Doesn't matter. What does matter is you tell him you know me, and he'll help you out. Make sure stuff like that sling doesn't happen anymore."

"You're giving me a buddy."

"A mentor."

Donne grinned. "How come you came to see me and not him?"

"It's a long story."

"Uh-huh." Donne shifted in his chair.

"He's not a bad man. He reminds me of you. He made a mistake and now he's paying for it."

There was a banging at the door. The guard called out three minutes. The words echoed across the empty room.

Donne crumpled up the paper and put it back on the table. It rolled to the left a little bit.

"I didn't make a mistake," Donne said. "I'm here for a reason."

"He'll help you get by."

Donne stood up. The door opened and the guard stepped through. His hand tapped on his hip in rhythm as he waited.

"Thank you," Donne said. "I'll look for him."

He turned and walked toward the guard. Thirty seconds later the door slammed shut and Herrick was alone again. He picked up the paper and uncrumpled it. He looked at his dad's name — Kenneth. He sighed and put the paper back in his pocket.

He hoped Donne would actually take Herrick up on the offer. It would help.

Matt Herrick made his way out of the prison and into the bright summer sunlight.

Though the season had been gone for months, for Herrick it finally felt like winter had broken.

ACKNOWLEDGEMENTS

When I was a kid, and just getting into reading mysteries, my dad, Martin, broke out this manuscript he had stored away in the attic. It was a private investigator novel he'd written years earlier. It featured a detective out of New Jersey named Matt Herrick. I always loved the character's name, so when it was time to introduce a new character into the Jackson Donne universe, I blatantly stole it. Thanks, Dad.

Big thanks to my mom, Carol, as well. Ever since I first started to write, she was there to read first drafts, proofread and offer pointed suggestions. In one draft of an early novel I wrote, she pointed out where the book really took off, and she may not know it, but that one comment got me thinking a lot about pacing. So, if this book moved at the speed I wanted it to, it's her fault.

In fourth grade, I wrote a Sherlock Holmes story and when I was finished I showed it to my teacher, Julie Schmidt. She held on to it for a few days, and when I asked her if she liked it, she smiled at me. "I liked it so much, I passed it on to be published in the school literary magazine." It was my first experience with publishing, and I've had the writing itch ever since. Thank you so much, Mrs. Schmidt.

Jason Pinter saved Jackson Donne off the scrap heap. This book is dedicated to him. Thanks, man. I hope you know how much I appreciate you and all of Polis Books.

To Bryan Hackett, a good friend who regaled me with some great Superstorm Sandy stories. And to a great Rutgers fan, and lawyer, Robyn Veasey, who helped with some of the legal scenes in this book. Anything I got wrong is my fault, not hers.

Thanks to Bryon Quertermous, Sarah Weinman, and Alex Segura for their copious notes and thoughts on the world of Jackson Donne and other pieces of writing.

Thank you to the rest of my family — Tom, Jessica, Eleanore, Thomas, Kristin, Fred, Daniel, and Brandon. They are so supportive, and I really appreciate it — even if I sometimes spell their names wrong.

And, of course, to Erin and Ben. You're my heart and soul. Both of you inspire me each and every single day. You mean everything to me and I love both of you so much.

ABOUT THE AUTHOR

Dave White is the Derringer Award-winning author of five novels: *When One Man Dies, The Evil That Men Do, Not Even Past* and *An Empty Hell* in his *Jackson Donne* series, and the acclaimed thriller *Witness to Death.* His short story "Closure," won the Derringer Award for Best Short Mystery Story. *Publishers Weekly* gave the first two novels in his *Jackson Donne* series starred reviews, calling *When One Man Dies* an "engrossing, evocative debut novel" and writing that *The Evil That Men Do* "fulfills the promise of his debut." He received praise from crime fiction luminaries such as bestselling, Edgar Award-winning Laura Lippman and the legendary James Crumley. His standalone thriller, *Witness to Death,* was an ebook bestseller upon release and named one of the Best Books of the Year by the *Milwaukee Journal-Sentinel.* He lives in Nutley, NJ. Visit him online at www.DaveWhiteBooks.com or @dave_white.